LAW OF FIVE

(A Kate Reid Novel)

By Robin Mahle

D1598469

Published by HARP House Publishing
December, 2014 (1st edition)

Mahle, Robin
Law of Five

ISBN-10: 0692335323 (trade back)
ISBN-13: 978-0692335321 (trade back)

Cover design: Covermint Design

Editor: Hercules Editing and Consulting Services

1

THE CAULEY CORNFIELD maze, the biggest attraction this side of Louisville, was closing down for the year as the autumn skies had grown somber. The season began its surrender to an unforgiving successor. Field hands began making their rounds, removing the litter left behind by too many careless visitors, and dismantling the pumpkin displays. Cleaning up after a long season of surprised teenage lovebirds huddled in dark corners, or no longer having to find little ones who had gotten separated from their parents was a time to which Wade Burrows had looked forward. It meant getting back to normal and no longer acting as some kind of amusement park manager.

He steered his small John Deere tractor through the paths, taking down the scarecrows and stacking the now-rotten pumpkins in the open trailer attached to the back. Others in his crew worked their sections, radioing one another at the completion of each area. Wade headed towards the eastern boundary of the cornfields. It backed up to the highway with a thirty-foot buffer in between the two that was county-owned land, obscured in knee-high wild grass and shrubs.

The twelve-foot bordering wall of the maze towered in front of him now. The section was cleared and he was ready to turn back towards the entrance to dump the overflowing trailer. As he was about to leave, the boisterous squawking of birds captured his attention and he turned his gaze upward at the sound. He'd spent countless hours working to keep the damn birds away from his crops and now here they were, a whole murder of crows. It occurred to him in that moment that he disliked the term and wondered who had decided they should be called a "murder." Wade didn't like it much; it left him feeling unnerved.

The tractor engine whined as it shut down. Wade jumped off, pushing the brim of his beige Stetson hat down to shield his eyes from the glare that poked through the clouds. There must have been ten or fifteen of them, some diving down behind the tall corn stalks, disappearing from sight.

Sizing up the wall ahead of him, Wade knew that pushing his way through wouldn't be easy. The long-sleeved cotton shirt and jeans would help avoid a corn rash, but inevitably, his face would suffer the paper-cut-like marks resulting from contact with the leaves. Still, something wasn't right and the time it would take to drive around the fields to the back side wasn't worth it. He figured it was a dead dog or maybe a bison calf that might have found its way out of the Boyles' land adjacent to his fields. Either way, it was a dead something or other. Crows were scavengers and they'd eat anything.

The stalks soon parted with the force of his gloved hands. The wall was thick; five, maybe six feet. They tried to discourage visitors from cutting through them to find their way out of the maze, and so the thicker, the better. Most of the time, the guests were respectful, but there were always the local thugs that liked to ruin things for the rest.

The noise escalated as he pushed through to the other side. It seemed the birds sensed his approach, complaining to one another that their meal was about to be cut short.

The end was in sight as he stepped through the final few stalks and emerged out the other side. He spotted the highway, raised high above the fields. Wild grasses and flowers covered the steep slope that led to the bottom where he now stood. Drainage for the highway, the ground was soft from the recent rains.

Wade turned his head in the direction of the dark cluster and began walking towards it. His pulse elevated slightly on approach. It was the smell that set his nerves on end. He trudged through the deep grass and finally stopped where it had been flattened. "Shoo, shoo." He began swatting at the birds. They flapped away, cawing at him in a harsh, piercing tone. "Oh my Lord, Jesus." Wade removed his hat and knelt down.

She was not clothed and parts of her body were caked in mud. The crows had already done a number on her flesh. He looked up the hill. She had not rolled down it; instead, it appeared as though someone had walked down, dragging her behind. The trodden grass revealed shoeprints and a trail about a foot wide. It appeared as though the woman had been placed deliberately in this position: face up, arms folded across her chest, holding what he thought looked like weeds, but on closer inspection, saw that they were dandelions; bunched up and held firmly in her hands that were already in a state of rigor.

Beneath her folded arms was a sight that compelled Wade to turn away, abating his gag reflex. He pulled his cell phone from his shirt pocket.

"911. What's your emergency?"

"I—I found a woman. She's dead."

Wade stood roadside, ready to flag the authorities down as they approached. He'd already put a call into the owner, Mr. Cauley, who was on his way in from town.

It didn't take long for him to see the flashing red and blue lights in the distance, speeding towards him. He waved his arms, holding his hat in his left hand, hoping to draw their attention. It appeared that he had been spotted as the cars slowed and moved towards the edge of the road. There was no barrier, although there probably should have been. The slope was fairly steep.

Several law enforcement cars lined up on the empty stretch of highway. This was a small town and the Cauley farm was on its outskirts. Not many people traveled this way unless they were headed out to St. Louis in neighboring Missouri.

A tall man with a round belly stepped out of the first car. Three others were lined up behind him, and then an ambulance. The man placed his uniform hat – brown and a little too large – on his head and began walking towards Wade.

"You Wade Burrows?"

"Yes, sir."

The officer wasted no time. "Deputy Boudreaux. Can you show me the location of our victim?"

The men exchanged a brief handshake.

"Yes, sir; just down here." Wade stepped sideways along the slope, working to keep his balance on the slippery grass, still damp from the rain three days ago. He knew of the deputy, but never had any run-ins with the law and so had no cause to call upon him until now. "Them crows caught my attention. It ain't right for me to see that many hangin' round one spot. Me and my boys was just closin' up shop on the corn maze when I spotted them. Mr. Cauley's on his way down. I rang him right after y'all."

They stopped at the bottom, a few feet away from the body.

"There." He pointed. "She's just there. I ain't never seen nothin' like that, Deputy Boudreaux. Lord have mercy on that poor woman and her family."

The deputy approached the body. A few of the birds were still trying to go in for a bite, but he kept them away as best he could. "Son of a bitch." He placed his hands on his hips and shook his head. "Henry, come on down here and have a look."

Another officer, a young man in top form and appearing gung ho to find out what his boss needed, quickly approached, jogging down the hill. "Yes, sir."

"Henry, take a look at that." Boudreaux pointed to the woman's bare chest.

"What's that she's holding, sir?"

"Flowers, by the looks of 'em. But take a gander at what's on her chest."

"Jesus Christ Almighty. Is that a V carved into her skin?" Henry replied.

The flesh had been cut deep, forcing the skin to fold over itself, but there was no blood from the wound. It was as if she'd been cleaned up, except for the mud on her that was a result of being dragged down the hill.

"That's a damn V, all right. Christ sakes," the deputy began. "You heard about that woman they found last week in Virginia?"

"No, sir."

"Same goddamn thing. Looks like we better call in the big boys, Henry."

◆◆◆

The odor reached Katie's nose as she and Marshall approached the front door of the stately home. It seemed to hang in the air like a cloud, wafting out of the house. Several other officers were already on scene, taping off the immediate area, working to keep any interested neighbors at bay.

The case was starting to grow cold until they got the call this morning. Celia Hernandez had been taking her morning walk, pushing the stroller with her one-year-old past the home two doors down. This suburban San Diego neighborhood near Del Mar was supposed to be safe. Living in obscenely large and extravagant homes, the people who occupied this community were exceedingly affluent. Celia, a stay-at-home mom whose husband worked for a financial firm downtown, was the target demographic.

She had spotted the teenage girl poking her head out of a bathroom window. In that brief moment that their eyes locked, Celia knew something wasn't right. The girl's brown hair appeared dirty, stringy, and matted, as if it hadn't been washed in days, maybe weeks. Her face was pale, gaunt cheeks with circles around her desperate-looking eyes. Then the girl disappeared, but not before she mouthed something to Celia.

The window was small, too small even for this young girl to have been able to slip out. Celia looked around, eager to spot another who might have seen what she had, but the street was quiet. Shades were drawn, shutters were closed, and the only suggestion that the neighborhood hadn't been completely deserted were the birds flying overhead. Its manicured lawns, shrubs trimmed to perfection, and mature trees lining either side of the street were otherwise lifeless.

Celia didn't know the people who lived in that house very well. They'd moved in about six months ago and she'd attempted to be neighborly by coming around after they'd settled in to introduce herself, muffin basket in hand. The husband and wife were polite, but had made it clear that they preferred to keep to themselves. She hadn't been back since, only waving on the rare occasion when she spotted them outside. What she was certain about was the fact that they had no children.

Celia paused a moment longer. Her glance struck every window fronting the home. Each was obscured by heavy-looking curtains and wrought iron bars. The baby was growing impatient at the break in movement and began to make her distress known. Celia looked down at her and it was then that she knew what she had to do.

She told the 911 operator that the girl had mouthed something to her that she could have sworn were the words "help me." As it turned out, Celia was right to call.

"You're the responding officer?" Marshall asked as he lifted the tape wrapped around the columns of the front porch.

Katie slipped in behind him.

"Yes." The officer extended his hand. "Officer Gutierrez. I took the call."

"I'm Detective Avery and this is Kate Reid." Marshall returned the gesture. "We've been looking for this girl for quite a while. How's she holding up?"

"Come see for yourself." The officer stepped aside and allowed Marshall and Katie to enter.

The home was pristine. High-end furnishings in shades of cream and white. Dark hardwood floors. High ceilings with ornate crown molding and chandeliers. Staircases on either side of the foyer that wound their way up to the second floor. To the left of the foyer was the living room.

Katie approached the girl, who was wrapped in a blanket and looked small beneath the covering. The paramedics hovered over her, seemingly checking for signs of injury. "Olivia?" Katie asked.

The girl slowly raised her head. When their eyes locked, an image, just a split-second flash, filled Katie's mind. She quickly blinked to rid herself of the vision. A trigger. That was what Dr. Reyes had called it. It sometimes happened when she would walk a crime scene and it seemed to bring back the same vision: Katie, tied to a chair, Hendrickson inches from her face in that warehouse.

"I'm Katie Reid. Detective Avery has been in contact with your parents. They're on their way here now." Katie looked to one of the EMTs. "These guys are going to make sure you're okay." She knew not to touch the girl; she was in shock and God only knew what she'd suffered already. The paramedics were trained to handle victims in shock; she was not, but the desire to offer comfort was always there. Instead, Katie offered a warm smile and left her to the professionals.

Marshall and Officer Gutierrez were still standing in the foyer when Katie approached and listened in on their conversation.

"From what the girl said, they left her locked up for up to twelve hours a day, only to let her out long enough to do what they wanted, then put her back in the room," the officer said.

"Where is the smell coming from?" Katie asked.

Gutierrez looked at Marshall, seemingly wondering if he should disclose any information. Marshall's slight nod suggested the officer could continue. "I'm afraid there was another victim, deceased, and likely starved to death. The girl was forced to stay in the same room with the body."

Katie's expression shifted at the abhorrent news, but only momentarily. She had been working as an evidence technician for more than a year now and of course had already seen the darkest sides of humanity. This was just another glimpse into the depravity of human nature.

A year. More than a year, actually, and Katie could hardly remember what life had been like before Hendrickson. She and Marshall were still living in his apartment downtown. There had been talk of moving, but their lives were so busy that the topic never seemed to go beyond a few casual words late at night after they'd had a drink or two, ultimately deciding the discussion would be put on hold at least until Katie finished school. Her graduate degree in criminal justice was within reach now, only months left. Figuring out what to do after that would be a challenge, although she'd been kicking around the idea of becoming a cop, but it was more likely she'd find herself in the Crime Scene Unit.

Her decision to go back to school had been an easy one. Katie was the type of person who wasn't happy unless she strived for more. It seemed she always had to be working towards something. What happened when she finally reached her goal would be the real challenge.

"Olivia's been missing for almost two months. Thank God she's okay." Katie looked back towards the living room.

"Relatively speaking." On returning her glance, she continued, "Do we have an ID on the other victim?"

"No. Not yet. The team has just headed up there to secure the scene. The medical examiner is on the way," Gutierrez replied.

The first thing Katie noticed when they entered the home were all the locks on the front door. She hadn't made her way upstairs where they kept the girl, but she assumed it had been secured in a similar fashion. There were even bars on the windows; the decorative kind that gave the impression the owner wanted security, but not at the expense of tasteful exterior design. The only exception was the bathroom window upstairs. It didn't seem there were any other houses, at least in the immediate area that had bars on the windows.

"How did she make it to the bathroom?" Katie asked.

"We haven't been able to get much from the victim yet, but it seemed she got hold of a screwdriver or something similar and was able to loosen the hinge pins on the door and pulled them out. When we got the call from Mrs. Hernandez and made it on scene, the girl was attempting to escape through the French doors downstairs at the back. She knocked out a few of the glass panes and made it through to the security doors on the other side. These people had this place very well secured. My guess is, had Mrs. Hernandez not called, the girl wouldn't have managed a way out and would have suffered for it when her captors arrived back home."

"Our priority should be finding the people who took her." Marshall looked to Gutierrez. "Where are the owners?"

"The victim said she knew the man; had been treated by him at the hospital about three months ago. He's a doctor at St. Gabriel Medical Center. Not sure where the wife is. The vic thought she might be a nurse there too. That's when you got the call. I just sent a squad car down there to check it out."

"Her name's Olivia. Sixteen. Daughter to Michelle and Jerry Markham. She ran away eight weeks ago." Katie hadn't yet mastered the ability of detachment and her curt tone suggested Gutierrez ought to have a little more regard, especially considering there was another soul still lying in a room upstairs.

"I'm sorry. I meant no disrespect," the officer replied.

Marshall quickly intervened. "You said Olivia knew the man. That he'd treated her. From my interviews with the parents, Olivia had run away because they were going to send her to rehab. She'd already overdosed once before. The parents said she'd been treated at St. Gabriel's. Damn it. I've questioned that doctor." He looked to Katie.

She instantly recalled the man. "Stanton. Dr. Gary Stanton," Katie said, a hint of eagerness in her eyes.

It hit all of them in an instant and, before Marshall said another word, Gutierrez pressed down on his radio. "Unit 216, please respond." Static noise sounded from the radio.

"Unit 216, we're pulling up to St. Gabriel Med Center now."

"Dr. Gary Stanton. Detective Avery has just confirmed Stanton as a suspect. Proceed with caution."

"Kate, stay here and see if you can assist in evidence collection and take care of Olivia's parents when they get here. I'm going to St. Gabriel's."

Katie nodded and moved into the living room to speak with the crime scene investigator.

"Nice work." Marshall acknowledged the officer and took leave.

2

ON HER RETURN to the police station, Katie noticed the gilded sky was dimming. The long day wasn't over yet, despite the imminent nightfall. She considered skipping class tonight, as it seemed meaningless in light of what had happened, but if she waited for only the good days, she would never go. Days like these happened all too often.

Olivia was taken to the hospital, suffering from dehydration and malnutrition. Her parents rode with her in the ambulance. The girl had been severely abused, as had the deceased victim. The coroner's report would reflect cause of death as starvation. No identity yet.

Marshall's office was just ahead. Katie hadn't spoken to him since this morning, but knew they had taken Stanton into custody. He'd given up without incident. "This is everything I've got so far." She handed him the reports. He looked just as exhausted as she had. "I'm sure Hearn is all over you for the files. They're gonna want to push this one through to the DA as soon as possible, I imagine."

His desk was covered in paperwork and crime scene photos from the Markham investigation. Marshall grabbed the files from Katie and added them to the growing pile. "He's already been in here twice. The press conference is scheduled for seven tonight." Marshall glanced at his watch. "Gives me ninety minutes to get my shit together. I'll be home late. You'll be okay?"

His words seemed to burrow under Katie's skin. Marshall meant well, and she felt guilty for her frustration, but she didn't need his protection as much as he thought she did. Their love for one another was never in question, but she was not the same woman he had met nearly two years ago. It seemed the more she tried to pull away, regain some of her former independence, the more he tried to keep her close.

"I'll be fine. I've got class tonight, but I'm just not sure I can handle it right now."

"You know you need to go. It'll be the best thing for you." Marshall replied, folding his hands on top of the files.

"You're right." She shrugged off his assertion, knowing it was pointless to argue with him. After a momentary scan into the hallway, ensuring no one was around, Katie moved towards his desk and kissed him lightly on the mouth. "See you tonight."

◆◆◆

The answering machine blinked from the office of their two-bedroom apartment. Katie had been home for an hour or so and had tried to ignore it. Instead, she opted to take a hot bath as she waited for Marshall to come home. It seemed the bath had served to offer some relief from the day and perhaps she was ready to press the button, already knowing what would be waiting.

She pulled her robe closed, securing it with the belt, and listened to the messages. Only moments later, the front door was opened. Marshall was home. Katie turned to catch sight of him, his footfalls echoing on the tiled floor.

"How many calls today?" he asked, his arms braced against the door frame of the office.

"Only two." She pressed the delete button and moved to greet him where he stood. "They're not as insistent anymore. I think their interest is dying down, which I can't say I'm too upset about."

Robin Mahle

"Well, I've said this before, it's up to you to decide if you want to write about what happened. You know I'd support you, but I'm just not sure now is the right time, with school and everything."

Of course he wanted to put it behind them just as much as she did and although the money being offered would probably set them up for life, she just wasn't willing to relive the past for someone else's entertainment under the guise of "bringing awareness." She wasn't healed yet and was unsure if she ever would be. The scar above her left eye, although faded, served as a constant reminder every time she looked in the mirror.

Thoughts of her best friend Sam still churned in her mind on an almost daily basis. Occasionally, Katie would pick up the phone to call Sam's husband, Jarrod, but never could finish dialing his number. He'd helped her out so much and had very little reason to, but speaking to him was too great a reminder of the reason Sam, the woman who had been like a sister to her, was gone.

The media attention was slowly eroding, however, and that was a good thing. It was what they both needed to move on. Katie looked forward to finishing school and that was really all that mattered right now. Marshall had helped her to put her energy into more productive causes, letting go of the darkness that occasionally weighed her down, but she still felt like a work in progress.

"I agree with you. I don't plan on calling them back." She led the way into the kitchen and opened the refrigerator, retrieving a bottle of wine and two glasses from the cabinet. "Did you get everything over to Hearn for the press conference?"

"You didn't catch it on the news?" Marshall grabbed one of the glasses and took a large gulp.

"No. What happened?" This case had consumed the both of them for the past several weeks and Katie hoped someone hadn't made a critical mistake.

15

"Not long after you left, Hearn came in and said Stanton was ready to meet. So, I talked to him, got a signed confession. We found out there were others. Different states, but the husband and wife had done it before."

"Jesus. So what now? Is the FBI taking him into custody?" Katie walked into the living room with a plate of cheese and crackers. That would serve as dinner tonight. "What about the wife?"

"The wife's in custody too. FBI will take it from here, but I've still got a ton of reports to hand over. We're lucky to have found Olivia alive. They'll find out the identity of the other victim soon. They hadn't lived in that house for long; it was rented. According to Stanton, their victims were kids the couple had treated. Troubled ones. Probably kept track of them, maybe even supplied them with drugs. I don't know." Marshall sighed deeply, seemingly to find the strength to regain control. "So, on to happier topics." He parked himself on the couch next to her, snatching a slice of cheese off the plate and plunking it into his mouth. "How was class?"

His cheese-eating grin was an attempt to lighten the mood and it didn't go unnoticed. "Good. We're studying media coverage of crimes. Pretty fitting, wouldn't you say?"

She snuggled in next to him. The safe and comfortable feeling reminded her that maybe she still needed his protection. Not from some perceived outside threat, but from herself and the thoughts that gnawed away at her. Those thoughts and particularly the one so prevalent in her mind at this moment proved almost too much for her, but she would not reveal them; not until she knew for sure and that would have to wait until tomorrow.

◆◆◆

The room was too cold, too sterile, and Katie sat on the patient table. She was wrapped in a paper-linen gown, opened to the front. The results on the stick had shown positive a few days ago and the timing couldn't possibly be worse. She had imagined this day would come eventually, but certainly not now. The idea had terrified her. What would happen with her job, school, and what about Marshall? Would he be ready for this?

After the initial exam, the doctor had decided to do an ultrasound. Katie now waited on the doctor's return and the anticipation was excruciating. She jumped down from the table and pulled her clothes back on as instructed.

A gentle knock sounded on the door. "Katie? Are you ready?"

"Yes." She quickly slid her shoes back on as the doctor entered.

"Katie, I'm afraid you have what is known as an ectopic pregnancy." The doctor spoke routinely and wasted no time. "It's still in the early stages and since you haven't had any pain or bleeding associated with it as of yet, our best course is to treat with Methotrexate."

Katie worked hard to process what the doctor was saying. Only minutes ago, she'd thought she was going to have a baby.

"Do you understand what I'm telling you?" the doctor asked, appearing to notice Katie's confusion.

She knew what an ectopic pregnancy was and that it could never be a normal pregnancy. But her mind reeled at the idea of losing a baby she was terrified to have in the first place. "I understand, but how? Why did this happen?"

The doctor rolled her chair in closer. "I did the ultrasound because your blood work showed abnormal HCG levels. This is indicative of ectopic pregnancies. It appears that your fallopian tubes are severely damaged." The doctor proceeded to flip through her notes. "Have you ever had any problems in the past with missed periods or pelvic pain?"

Katie stared at the wall opposite her, where a poster of a baby inside a womb was hanging. "No," she whispered.

"What about any sexually transmitted diseases? Have you ever been diagnosed with Pelvic Inflammatory Disease?"

"Um." She blinked slowly as the questions worked their way inside her head. "No." Katie was silent a moment longer and then turned to look at the doctor. "I was sexually assaulted as a child."

"I know, Katie, but I can't say for sure that that could be a cause. It is possible you contracted an infection that went unnoticed. Or maybe…"

"Maybe I suffered damage when it happened?" Katie began to wonder what she had done to bring on this misfortune. Was this Hendrickson's final gift to her?

"That's really hard to say."

"Dr. Johnson, will I be able to have children?" She had wanted a life with Marshall, a family. Now all that seemed to be in jeopardy.

"Katie, there are lots of solutions for you to consider. IVF is likely the best answer. Your tubes, I believe, are just too damaged to try and repair. But you do have options. In the meantime, we need to address this matter urgently. We can start with an injection today and then we'll have to check your hormone levels every few days to ensure the treatment is working. I believe this is the best course of action. If we don't get the results we need, we can consider surgery."

Katie drew in a deep breath, her stinging eyes pleading to Dr. Johnson.

"It's okay; you're going to be just fine."

◆◆◆

The apartment was drenched in shadow, resulting from the small shafts of light that filtered around the curtains. Katie drew back the living room drapes and the bright afternoon sun shot through, filling the room with its white light. She opened the window to the sounds of the traffic below and the cool air hit her skin, making the noise tolerable. She would not return to work today, knowing that it would prove impossible to face Marshall in this moment.

Standing fixed in the middle of the room, Katie took in her surroundings. A few pictures of Marshall and her on the beach, one of her parents, another of Marshall's mother and brother. And the one that held the most meaning for her was the one in the silver frame, sitting on a shelf in the bookcase next to the TV. Sam. Smiling, happy, beautiful Sam.

Katie moved towards the picture and took hold of it. Her index finger caressed the outline of Sam's face, touched her lips. She raised up the frame and gently kissed the picture. "I miss you so much. I need you here with me now, Sam. I would have named the baby after you. Boy or girl, it wouldn't have mattered."

She set the frame back in its place. The dust outline that remained was now slightly off-kilter. Overcome with yet more grief and pain, Katie cried out, shoving the contents of the shelf to the floor. The heavy law books smacked against the tile, followed by two more pictures of Marshall and Katie, their glass covers shattering on contact. The small vase that held a single dried flower Marshall had given her hit the ground last and shattered into several tiny white pieces of porcelain. She dropped to the ground amid the broken clutter. Head in hands, she sobbed.

He did this to her. The doctor's words mattered little; Katie knew the truth. But he was gone and there was no one to make her suffer anymore, except for her. The anger that Dr. Reyes and Marshall tried so hard to expel from Katie seemed to rush back with a vengeance. She had already lost so much and now she was losing her future.

Katie remained seated in that spot for how many hours, she didn't know, but it had grown late in the day. The sun had lowered in the sky and directed rays of orange and red light through the window. She needed to clean up the mess before Marshall arrived home. He couldn't see her this way.

Her legs were asleep and, as she stood, the tingling began. The numbness sent her off balance and her right foot landed on a shard of glass from one of the frames. "Damn it!" She hopped towards the bathroom, little droplets of blood landing on the floor, leaving a trail behind her.

As she sat perched on the edge of the toilet, tissue pressed up against the gash in her foot, the front door opened. Her shoulders dropped, knowing that it was Marshall.

"Kate?" His voice echoed, followed by his footsteps sounding on the floor. "Kate? What the hell happened? Are you okay?"

"I'm in the bathroom. I'm fine." She looked up to find him now standing in the doorway, his brow narrowed in confusion.

"What happened to you? Were you trying to reach for something on one of the high bookshelves? For God's sake." He moved quickly to her side, gently taking hold of her foot.

"I told you, I'm fine." From his expression, she realized her appearance was likely telling a different story.

"Have you been crying? You must have really hurt yourself. Do you need stitches?" He looked closer at the blood still pooling around the cut.

"No. I don't need stitches. Please, just give me a second to clean myself up and put a Band-Aid on this. I'll be out in a minute."

She noticed the look on his face and knew the conversation wasn't over, but at least he'd resigned to giving her a moment alone to collect her thoughts.

Marshall pulled the door closed and Katie tended to the cut. Rising to her feet again, she stood in front of the mirror. He was right to be concerned by her appearance.

Water splashed against her face as she tried to remove the black stains left by the mascara that had run down her cheeks. Setting the cloth down on the side of the basin, Katie placed her hand over her lower abdomen. They had talked about having children in abstract terms. She knew that now wasn't the right time, not really, but she would've been happy and so would Marshall. Now, she was about to tell him that this life would end before it even got a chance to start.

Katie reemerged from the bathroom and padded along the hallway, careful not to put too much pressure on the wound. Marshall was picking up the broken glass and placing the books back on the shelf.

"You ready to tell me what happened?" He looked up at her, holding a large shard of glass in his hand.

Katie bent down to take his arm and help him to his feet. "Come on; let's sit down."

"You're scaring me, Kate. What's going on?" He tossed his head towards the pile of debris. "That wasn't an accident, was it?"

"I went to the doctor today." She quickly raised her hand. "Before you say anything, just let me finish. I was late and I'm never late. So, I took a pregnancy test and it was positive." His face was already lighting up and she dreaded to continue. "I wanted to be sure before I said anything to you, so I made an appointment."

"Oh my God."

"Please. Just wait." Her look began to convey the nature of the results and she watched as the light in his eyes diminished and his expression shifted. "Marshall, it's an ectopic pregnancy. The doctor had no choice but to treat it."

"And by treating it, you mean terminate the pregnancy?" He looked away, appearing to gather his thoughts.

This was what she dreaded most; being the one to disappoint him. "I'm sorry," Katie said.

He returned his glance. "What are you talking about? You have no reason to be sorry. I'm upset that I couldn't be there for you when you found out. I wish I had known. I would have been there for you, Kate. You know that. But, I understand these things happen and the most important thing is that you're safe and healthy." Marshall placed his arm around her shoulders. "You shouldn't have had to go through this alone, sweetheart. So what do we do now?"

"Wait. The doctor gave me an injection of something called Methotrexate. It's supposed to end the pregnancy. I have to go back in a couple of days to make sure it's working. If not, then I'll have to have surgery. But the doctor said it was caught early enough that she believed the injection would work." She decided to leave out the part about the vomiting and bleeding and all the other potential side effects the doctor had warned her about.

Katie moved away slowly, positioning herself so that she could look squarely in his eyes. "Marshall, there's something else I have to tell you."

He didn't reply, only waited patiently for her to continue.

"The reason this happened, according to the doctor, was because my fallopian tubes are damaged, severely damaged. It isn't likely that I'll be able to carry a child without the help of fertility treatments."

"Okay. Well, that's not all bad news, then. We can work around it, but from the way you're looking at me, you don't see it the same as I do."

"He did this to me, Marshall. He's the reason I can't have kids."

Marshall pushed up from the couch. "Wait; hold on just a minute. This is what the doctor told you? That the damage was caused by the assault when you were young?"

"Not exactly. She said it was possible. That maybe I'd contracted a virus as a result and it was left untreated."

"So you don't know for sure that he was the reason?" Marshall reached for her hand. "Honey, this is a slippery slope and you know it. If the doctor isn't sure, then it seems there's no way to prove the damage resulted from what happened."

"Would you please stop talking about it like this is happening to someone else? For God's sake, your baby won't survive because of what he did to me. And now you're stuck with damaged goods. You know how expensive IVF is? And how most of the time it doesn't even work? Can you honestly look at me and tell me that you're okay with that?"

Marshall walked to the bookcase and picked up the frame that now had no glass. It was a picture of the two of them last Christmas at Katie's parents' house. They stood on the porch, wrapped in coats and holding coffee mugs. The steam could be seen rising to their faces and they looked happy.

"I know you blame yourself for what happened to Sam. You blame yourself for what Wilson did too." He faced her now, holding the picture so that she could see it. "You are not damaged goods, Kate. You're looking for another reason to keep him in your head. You think if you let him go, *really* let him go, that you'll lose Sam too."

Katie stood up and moved towards him. "I don't know if I'll ever be whole again. And it doesn't matter how much you try to protect me from the world, Marshall. You can't protect me from myself."

3

THE WAITER PLACED the check on the table. Edward looked at his date, wondering if she just might reach for the check. So far, what he knew of her, she didn't seem the type. Lindsay remained still with a firm smile and arms folded neatly in her lap. She was no more going to reach for the tab than she would reach for his crotch later on.

This was what Edward had come to expect from women. Superficial, egotistical, and only interested in men with money. They'd met through a mutual friend a few weeks ago. He'd held out hope for her, but this was their second date and her true self was beginning to show. The ugliness inside.

Edward pulled his wallet out of the back pocket of his jeans. After placing his credit card inside, he pushed the black leather bill holder to the edge of the table.

"Thank you, Eddie. That was a wonderful dinner," Lindsay told him. Her paper-white teeth gleamed beneath the red lipstick she'd just reapplied. The smile seemed just as fake as she was.

"You're welcome." He'd corrected her several times already that he preferred to be called Edward, but it seemed he'd given up on that too.

The bill had been paid, his card returned, and Edward was about to slip out of the dark and secluded booth. Would he ask her here or wait until he walked her to the car? Would they go back to his place or hers?

Maybe it was better to be shot down someplace more private, like a dimly lit parking lot. He proceeded to stand and extended his hand to help Lindsay. She took hold of it gently and maneuvered herself in what appeared to be the most seductive manner she could muster.

Edward was beginning to think the night wouldn't be a total loss. He even did his best impression of gentlemanly behavior by placing her sweater over her shoulders. The weather had turned quite cool and he didn't need for her to be distracted by a chill as they stood outside.

Lindsay smiled once again and led the way through the busy restaurant. The muted lights cast a bronze hue throughout the space. The trendy Japanese fusion spot had been Lindsay's choice. As far as San Diego restaurants went, this was one of the more pricey places to eat, and that was saying something.

The two finally reached Edward's car. A charcoal grey late model Nissan sedan. The guy was, after all, a student. A graduate student at UCSD, but still, if Lindsay was looking for someone with money, she was barking up the wrong tree.

He pulled open the passenger door. "Would you like me to take you home?"

Lindsay seemed to ponder the question for some time and Edward's hopes were fading with each passing moment. "Um, sure." She began to step inside the car. "Maybe you can come in for a drink?"

Edward closed the door and, as he walked around to the driver's side, his lips spread into a thin smile.

◆◆◆

Lindsay lived in a small, cottage-style rental home in Mission Valley. The 1960s two-bedroom was shared with a roommate. According to Lindsay, the roommate was away for the night.

She fumbled with her keys for a moment, appearing to be somewhat affected by the two drinks she'd consumed at dinner. Finally, the door opened to reveal a small living room, complete with contemporary furnishings, the kind you'd find at Ikea, and a moderately-sized flat panel TV fixed to the wall above the fireplace mantel.

There was no mistaking that this was a young woman's home. Edward kept looking around, figuring there had to be a cat or two somewhere.

"Why don't you have a seat while I pour us a drink? I've got spiced rum."

Of course you do. "That'd be great, thank you." Edward sat down on the low white sofa that was adorned with various brightly colored throws and pillows. He glanced around to find several framed photos of Lindsay and what he believed must have been her girlfriends. All were very attractive. Blond hair, dyed, of course. Tanned. The only feature distinguishing one from the other was the eyes. Lindsay had brown eyes, while her friends' appeared to be blue. Unless they wore colored contacts. Either way, he was growing tired of the typical SoCal girl and longed to be back in Colorado. But he was determined not to go back alone.

Edward had moved last year and was now attending UCSD's graduate program in Criminal Justice. He was older than most of his classmates. He didn't have Mommy and Daddy footing the bill for him, which he suspected was Lindsay's story, and she was five years his junior.

"Here you are." Lindsay set the drink down on the chunky black coffee table, placing a coaster beneath it first. She lowered herself onto the couch, crossing her legs. Her form-fitted skirt raised slightly. "We've got a hot tub in the backyard. Care for a dip?"

"I don't have any swim trunks."

Lindsay stood up. "Don't worry; you won't need them."

Edward emerged with a towel wrapped around his waist. He made his way to the back patio and slipped through the already opened sliding glass door. Lindsay was there, waiting for him. He lowered the towel and stepped inside the foamy water. The heat felt good on his cold skin.

Lindsay moved closer to him and it wasn't until she dipped her head backwards into the water and raised it up again that he finally began to feel heat in the place that mattered most. He hadn't been overly attracted to her until that moment and he knew exactly why.

Lindsay's hair lay straight against her shoulders, dark and wet and it was then that she reminded him of her. The one woman he'd been drawn to. The one woman who could make him move several hundred miles just to be near. Edward closed his eyes and leaned in to kiss her.

Katie.

◆◆◆

The clock seemed to be moving in slow motion. Katie desperately needed for this class to end and hadn't been able to focus on tonight's lesson at all. Staying home would have been better, but she knew that would have meant Marshall, under some sort of perceived obligation, would have stayed home with her. Instead, she insisted she was fine, having already missed two days of work.

Marshall had left for the station this morning before she even got out of bed, which was just as well because he got to miss out on watching her get sick; one of the side effects Dr. Johnson had warned her about.

The Markham case was still being turned over for federal prosecution. Katie figured he still had a fair bit of paperwork to wrap up today and would be home late.

"That'll be all for tonight. Remember, the presentations are due next week. Thank you all and have a good night." The professor opened up his carrier bag and dropped his files and textbooks inside.

Katie stood up and put her laptop inside her own bag, but on her way out the door, she was stopped.

"Good class tonight, don't you think?"

She wasn't really in the mood to speak with Edward, but let him walk beside her along the corridor out of kindness. "Yeah. It was. How are you, Edward?"

"Good, thanks. Listen, you want to go and grab a coffee? I wouldn't mind bouncing some ideas off of you for this presentation we've got coming up."

Edward was fond of Katie. She had picked up on that early on this semester. But, it seemed he had become more and more insistent that she spend time with him. Of course, he knew about Marshall and in fact had picked her brain on more than one occasion regarding a few of their past cases. He had never brought up last year, though, and she was grateful for that.

"I'm really sorry, Edward, but I've got to get home. It's been a long day." She tried to pick up the pace, working to stay a couple steps ahead of him. "Don't worry. I'm sure your ideas are great. You always do well with these types of assignments. I'll catch up with you later?"

Edward stopped short. "Yeah, sure. No problem. Have a good night, Katie."

She continued on towards the parking lot and glanced back at him. He was growing smaller in the distance, but she could clearly see his face. Although he was smiling, something lay beneath that smile that caused her to stumble.

When she'd reached her car, she fumbled for her keys while scanning the immediate area. The shadows were playing off each other and, in an imagination as prolific as hers, all sorts of scenarios rushed to mind. Katie pressed the remote to unlock the door. The noise seemed to echo in the near-empty lot. Her breath was becoming labored under the weight of her thoughts. The steam rose from her mouth as she finally pulled open the driver's side door and slipped inside.

She shut the door of her small Toyota SUV and locked herself inside. *What are you doing? He's not following you. The guy's harmless. You're letting your imagination get the better of you.* She'd already begun sliding down that slippery slope Marshall warned her about. Edward had never been anything but kind and helpful to her.

The engine purred as she gripped the steering wheel and Katie began to laugh at her own irrationality. With her hand now on the gear shift, she noticed the light from her cell phone and reached to answer it.

"Well, hello. What are you doing calling so late, Marc? Slow news day?"

"Sort of. What's going on with you? Haven't talked in forever. You and Marshall still working on the Markham case?"

"Just finishing it up. Well, Marshall is anyway. I'm just leaving class now. What's going on?"

Katie and Marc Aguilar had remained friends since Rio Dell. He was a good guy and they often phoned or texted one another just to check in and see how the other was doing. Once in a while, Marc would ask about their cases, but if they were open, she couldn't say much. He understood. She was glad to be hearing from him now and it seemed to help pull her out of the spiral she was heading down.

"You still got a connection with the FBI? Nick or somebody else down there?"

"I haven't talked to him in a long time, Marc. Why? Hey, I'm gonna put you on speaker. I'm pulling out of the parking lot at school now. Hang on." She pressed the button to connect the call through the hands-free unit and pulled out onto Gilman Drive in La Jolla. The twenty-minute or so drive home would give them time to catch up. He had her attention now. "Okay, go ahead."

"So I wanted to know if you still talk to that guy. I don't know if you've heard about that man who's been making his way cross-country, leaving a trail of bodies behind him."

Katie had caught the news story and, so far, the count had been two women dead. It had been a couple of weeks since the first body was discovered. He was picking off random women, leaving them on the side of the road. The last victim was found in Kentucky. Marc must have wanted some sort of exclusive on the story, but Katie didn't have that kind of pull. Not with Agent Nick Scarborough; not with anyone, really.

"I've seen it on the news, but I imagine I know just about as much as you do."

"Do you think you could call Agent Scarborough? Ask him if he'll talk to me?"

Katie continued heading towards downtown. Not too much traffic, which suited her just fine. But it looked as though a storm might be heading in. Hard to tell in the dark, but when she pulled up to the stoplight and glanced through the moon roof, no stars were visible.

"I don't know, Marc. I really don't think he'd talk to me about it, much less a reporter. I know we've got history, but hell, I don't even know if he's on the case."

"Could you find out? Listen, I just want to get out ahead of this deal. If this maniac's coming our way, I want to be the first one to warn the public."

"You mean, cause a panic?"

There was no reply.

"I'm sorry, Marc. I didn't mean anything by that. It's just you know how these guys work."

"Come on, Katie. It's me. I don't ask for much."

He was right. He rarely asked her for favors and, considering her line of work, he could have easily tried to use their friendship to his benefit. "Okay. I'll try to get hold of Scarborough. I haven't talked to him in a long time, but I'll see what I can do."

"That's all I ask. Thanks a bunch, Katie." Marc paused again. "Everything else all right?"

Well, no it wasn't, as a matter of fact. Of course, she couldn't tell him that. "Everything's fine here; thanks for asking. I'll touch base with you after I contact Nick. See what I can find out."

"Have a good night, my friend."

"You too, Marc." Katie pressed the end call button on the wheel. She was glad to hear from him. It was nice to take her mind off of her own problems for a moment. That was one thing she loved about working cases, though. Her laser-sharp focus helped to keep most other problems at bay.

◆◆◆

Agent Nick Scarborough walked into the FBI Louisville field office after getting the call a few days ago from ASAC Miles Underhill that another victim had been found. The second one with the same markings, left in a similar fashion; on the side of a highway. Local authorities found the body outside of Elizabethtown, about forty-five miles south of Louisville. No guarantees it was the same unknown subject Nick was after from the murder in Virginia, but he guessed the chances were better than winning a grand on a lottery ticket.

He watched the numbers as the elevator climbed, approaching the third floor of the expansive building. On arrival, he stepped into the marbled foyer, where a security guard waited behind an information desk. Nick showed the man his credentials. "I'm here to see ASAC Underhill."

The man pressed a button and the large glass doors to his right clicked open.

"Thank you."

Inside was a handful of agents huddled near a board with notes written beside photos of both crime scenes. The first one in Virginia and now this one. "What do we know?" he asked as he approached the other agents.

"Agent Scarborough, thanks for coming down." Agent Vernon Mills handed Nick a picture from the crime scene in Elizabethtown.

Almost immediately, Nick knew this must have been the work of his guy. "We need to get down there now."

"That's what we thought. Your team here yet?" Mills asked.

"They're at the hotel, waiting for an update. I'll have them meet us down there."

Just as Nick was reaching for his phone to inform his team, an incoming call rang through. At first glance, the name on the caller ID alarmed him. "I've got to take this," he said to Mills.

Nick moved to a quieter location. The small conference room down the hall would offer the privacy he needed. "Katie. My God, I can't believe it's you. How are you?" He was genuinely surprised and glad to be hearing from her.

"Agent Scarborough. Hello. I'm fine, thank you. And you? I'm guessing you've got your hands full as usual."

Nick cast a glance into the hall. "You could say that. So what do I owe the pleasure of this call?"

"I know it's been a long time since we've spoken, but you remember Marc Aguilar from the San Diego news station?"

"How could I forget?" Nick tugged at the waist of his pants. "What about him?"

"He asked a favor of me and I, in return, am asking an undeserved favor from you." Her muffled sigh sounded in his ear. "Look, I've got no business asking this of you, but do you have any information on that—what are they calling him? The Highway Hunter?"

Nick lowered his head, groaning just a little, not at Katie's inquiry, but at the media's flippancy. He despised the fact that they often made celebrities out of these killers, giving them nicknames that only served to shine a spotlight on them, creating notoriety and fame. It sickened him. "Yes. It's my case and I'm only telling you this because I consider you a friend. Why? What does the reporter want? You of all people know that I can't go spouting information about an ongoing investigation."

"I know, and I appreciate you talking to me. I really do. It's just that Marc wants to know if you think he's coming our way. Out towards southern California?"

"Katie, I haven't got a single damn clue as to what this son of a bitch's got going on in his mind." Nick started to move towards the door of the conference room. It wouldn't be long before someone came looking for him. He had a good forty-minute drive ahead of him and he needed to get a move on. "I'm sorry, but I can't help you out. I really wish I could. We don't know much more than what the media's already reporting, save for a few details I can't disclose anyway."

"I understand. I'm sorry to have bothered you, Nick. It's just that I owe Marc a lot and I thought I'd at least try. I appreciate your time and, hey, you know who to call if things start moving our way and you need any help at all."

"Of course I do."

Three agents were working their way towards him and he knew he had to wrap it up. "I don't suppose you've changed your mind yet?" Nick hadn't talked to Katie in almost ten months. The last time he'd called her, just to check in and make sure she was adjusting well enough, all things considered. He'd jokingly reminded her of his offer, but she'd politely declined. He figured it would go down the same now, but he had to ask.

Katie chuckled at the suggestion. "No. Not yet. But if things start to go south for you at the FBI, I'm sure I can find a place for you here at the good ol' SDPD."

That brought much needed laughter for both of them. "I've gotta go, Katie. It was really great to hear from you and I am sorry I couldn't be of more help."

"No problem at all, Nick. You take care of yourself and be safe."

Nick ended the call just as the agents arrived. "You ready to go?" he asked them.

4

KATIE'S OFFICE WAS tucked away at the back of the station, near the lab. She coordinated her efforts with the other evidence technicians and forensics and didn't often leave her little hole unless it was to see Marshall. He was a senior detective now and had a big office, surrounded by windows just opposite the bull pen. A few of the junior team answered to him and Katie had grown pretty fond of the place and the people who worked there.

Still, she took pause at Nick's offhanded remark. The idea that she could be involved in such important cases was appealing. But she could never leave the family she'd come to know so well here in San Diego. And the thought of leaving Marshall; well, that just wasn't going to happen.

A painful cramp had taken hold and she cringed, placing her hand over her stomach. It was to be expected, according to the doctor, whom she was scheduled to see again later this afternoon. More blood would be drawn to determine if the treatment was working. *Treatment.* It didn't seem like an appropriate word for what was happening inside her.

The past few days had been uncomfortable and awkward with Marshall. It seemed he was unsure of how to respond to the situation and it had been unsettling for him as well as for her; neither wanting to acknowledge what was happening.

The situation had breathed life into the past and created a force that began tearing away at the walls Katie had erected around the painful memories. The thoughts wanted free of their confinement; free to spread in her mind like a disease, killing off the good memories, replacing them with the blackness they carried.

This latest blow, losing a pregnancy she hadn't realized she'd wanted, had to be pushed behind those very walls. The problem would be in opening the door to force them through. It would prove difficult to keep the rest at bay. So for now, ideas swirled and anger raged at what was happening and she hadn't the courage to lock them away.

Katie approached Marshall's office to find him still buried in the Markham investigation, although most of the files had been turned over. Captain Hearn was still on his case about coordinating with the community leaders regarding the home in which the girl had been found. Nearly a week had passed and it was still taped off, mainly because the second victim, the one who hadn't survived, still had not yet been identified and forensics was searching for anything in the home they might have overlooked.

"Hey, can I come in?" She leaned in his open doorway.

"Yeah, of course." Marshall looked up from his computer screen, his cheeks lifting at the sight of her. "What's up? Are you feeling okay?"

"I'm fine." She wasn't, not really, but right now wasn't the time to bring up the elephant in the room. Katie sat down in the orange chair opposite Marshall's desk. The department had "upgraded" its décor, although she felt little comfort in the mid-century modern revival piece of furniture. "I just got off the phone with Agent Scarborough."

This seemed to pique Marshall's interest. She noticed his eyes widen for just a moment.

"Really? Did he call you?"

"No. I called him. Marc asked me for a favor. He wanted some information on that Highway Hunter guy they're all looking for right now."

Katie made no secret of her friendship with Marc Aguilar. Marshall knew they often spoke. It seemed he'd finally relinquished any dubious feelings he might have felt in the past regarding the man. "So what did Marc want? An exclusive with the FBI?"

"Well, yes, sort of. He wanted me to ask if Nick was on the case and, if he was, did he know if the killer was heading our way." A slight cringe briefly crossed her face as a cramp took hold once again. She shifted in her seat and continued, "He's just looking to get a scoop on it before anyone else does."

"So is this the deal? Does he know anything yet? Nick, I mean."

"If he knows, he's not saying. It'd be nice if he could give us some kind of profile on the guy, though. Don't we get to know what they know, just to give us something to look out for, should a victim turn up in our jurisdiction?" Katie noticed a half-grin playing on Marshall's face. "What?"

"Nothing." He shook his head, still smiling. "It's just that you sound an awful lot like me." Marshall turned serious for a moment, placing his forearms over the top of his desk and leaning in. "You sure you don't want to go for detective? Okay, so you'd have to put in some time as a patrolman, but you've got time in already, pretty much. I mean, CSI is great, but you could be amazing as a detective."

Katie tilted her head. "That would mean we'd be working together almost exclusively. I think you'd tire of me always hanging around. Home, work. We'd never be apart."

"Would that be such a bad thing?"

Genuine. That was one trait in many that she loved about Marshall, but he had hidden meaning beneath his words. A meaning that she wasn't sure he even picked up on. It had become so automatic, he probably didn't know it was there. Protection. He had engulfed her in it for such a long time and while it was certainly well-meaning, she just might disappear entirely if it continued. She would simply become a part of him and lose herself.

"Oh, I think eventually we would get on each other's nerves. Besides, you know how much I love the research. You're the best investigator I know and I think that work is best left to the professionals." She stood up to leave, another cramp piercing her stomach. This time, a noticeable flinch ensued.

"It still hurts?"

"Not really. I promise, I'm fine." Katie moved towards the door. "I'm going in later today for more blood work. I'll let you know how it goes."

She was halfway into the corridor when Marshall spoke. "Hey."

Katie turned.

This time, his voice dropped to a whisper. "I love you."

She smiled, her lips mouthing the words. "I love you too."

◆◆◆

The big screen televisions in the bar were showing the Chargers football game, but Edward hadn't taken much notice. He wasn't much for football, and since he was from Colorado, even if he was, his support would go to the Broncos. He preferred hockey and that was about as likely to be shown in a bar in San Diego as Canadian basketball.

After a few failed attempts, he managed to get the attention of the bartender and raised his empty bottle of beer, signaling he was ready for another.

A quick nod from the guy behind the bar and he was off again, tending to the other patrons who had bellied up to it on this cool Thursday night.

"You get me one too?" Shaun Hudson, a curly-haired, blonde kid who had latched onto Edward in recent months pulled up a stool.

"I didn't think you were gonna show. It's been an hour."

"Sorry, man. Got caught up at work." He waved the bartender over. "Mich Ultra, please."

"Sure. And you were the Guinness?" He pointed to Edward.

"Yeah."

"Sorry about the wait. I'll get 'em now." The man disappeared behind the large glass display of liquor bottles and beer taps.

"Shit, man. I asked him for another beer like ten minutes ago," Edward said.

"It's ladies' night. Place is always packed. Must be nice to get drinks for a friggin' buck just because you got a vag." Shaun cast a glance to the three women hovering at the end of the bar.

"Yeah, well, you need them to keep drinking, my friend, if you stand any chance of picking off one of those three."

"Fuck off, dude." Shaun nudged an elbow in Edward's direction.

They laughed the way men do when they think they're being clever.

"Seriously, though, man, you got my shit?" Edward was finished with the niceties. He had business to tend to.

Shaun tossed a look at the bar entrance. "In my car. I still don't know what you need with that chick's file. I copied all of it, but I gotta tell you, at first glance, I didn't see nothin' that would be worth anything."

"Don't you worry about it. I got my reasons." Edward took a swig of the beer that had finally arrived.

"She's cool and all, but you know what happened to her, right? Been through a lot of shit and she's got that cop-boyfriend." Shaun poured half the bottle of beer down his gullet. "Guess it's none of my business. We square now?"

Shaun had come to know Edward through a mutual set of friends. Edward was nice to the awkward and lanky twenty-something since they had met almost a year ago. Since then, Shaun had sought the advice of the older, more experienced student. Career advice and, more often than not, advice on how to handle the fairer sex, something with which the kid had little to no experience. But it was Edward's help on a more recent matter that Shaun had found himself indebted to the man. A situation had arisen in which Shaun required some financial assistance. Edward was all too willing to help out, in return for something of substantially more value to him than money.

Shaun was about to deliver the goods. He worked part time at the school, in the registration office, and pulled the file of a certain someone with whom Edward had desired to become further acquainted, if he stood any chance of taking her from her cop-boyfriend.

"We're square." Edward retrieved his wallet and pulled out a twenty.

"Dude, I just got here. You're leaving?"

"Got a date tonight." His phone was sitting on the bar top and he quickly checked the time. "I'm late as it is. Where's your car? I wanna get the file."

◆◆◆

Edward slicked back his dark hair and tucked it behind his ears. The loose waves grazed his shoulders. If he was going for a Middle-Earth slash *Game of Thrones* look, he'd achieved it. The girls always liked his thick locks, especially when he wore them long. He figured it must have been a "bad boy" kind of thing that they liked. Whatever the reason, it served his purpose.

The knock on the door could only be coming from Lindsay. Right on time. Edward liked her well enough, for a good lay at least. Other than that, he held no real affections for the younger girl. The woman he'd wanted was, as of yet, unattainable, but that would change soon enough.

He'd followed Katie's story on the news and something about her demeanor, her strength had spoken to him in a way he'd never experienced before. It was an interview she'd done shortly after she'd gotten out of the hospital that had moved

Robin Mahle

him to take the necessary steps ensuring he could be nearer to her.

So far, Edward couldn't bring himself to do much more than say hello on occasion and ask a question or two about her work. He'd tried to engage her on a deeper level, but she was always rushing out of class. He hadn't really yet found the nerve to talk to her. The other night, as he walked alongside her after class, he'd finally managed to ask her out for a drink, just a friendly coffee, but she'd turned him down.

Still, he hadn't lost hope yet. After his date tonight, he'd planned on studying the file Shaun had pilfered from the school. He didn't know how he would use it exactly. Maybe just find her weaknesses – grades or whatever – and use them to his benefit. He regretted having to resort to such measures, but Katie had left him little choice.

Edward opened the door to a smiling Lindsay, standing at the top of the landing. His second-floor apartment was small, but located near the school and the girls didn't mind it so much. Of course, the sort of girls he went out with weren't as discerning as his Katie. "Come in, please."

He removed her coat and took in her slender figure, which was tucked nicely inside the short black dress. "You look very nice."

She turned to face him, looking seductive and needing to please, the way a young woman who hadn't quite found herself yet often did. "I bought it today, just for our date."

◆◆◆

On return to Edward's apartment, after yet another expensive dinner, he'd anticipated a little foreplay, then a roll in the sack, but as he began to kiss Lindsay, she started to pull away.

41

"I'm sorry. I really should be getting home. It's late and I've got an early class tomorrow. I had such a great time tonight, Eddie, really." She began to reach for her coat, which lay tossed over the back of the small grey sofa in his living/dining room.

"You're leaving?" He expressed his displeasure at this unexpected turn of events by placing his hand over the coat, blocking her from retrieving it.

"I know. I'm so sorry, babe, but I can't afford to let my grade slip any further in that class, and I've got to get some sleep tonight."

He removed his hand from the coat, but reached for her arm, squeezing it tighter than he realized.

"Ouch. Eddie, that hurts. What's wrong with you?" Lindsay's face was masked in surprise and more than a little discomfort.

He quickly released her arm. "I'm sorry. Please, I—didn't mean to..." Edward yanked her hair back and pressed his lips hard against hers, working to part her lips with his tongue.

She pushed him back and he nearly stumbled over the dining chair. "What the fuck are you doing, you fucking asshole?" Lindsay brushed past him and got to the door in a matter of seconds.

Edward regained his footing and wasn't far behind. He pressed his hand against the partially opened door, slamming it shut and looked down at her. His frame towered over hers. "By the way, it's Edward, you fucking bitch." He pulled the door open and stood aside.

5

THE SCENE WHERE the woman had been found the other day by a field hand had already been secured when Nick arrived. Small flags marking the spot where she had been located dotted the area. The woman's body had been moved to the coroner's office and what remained was an imprint of her small frame and flags marking the trail in which she'd been dragged off the main highway.

Word was spreading quickly about the so-called "Highway Hunter," and this victim had fit the bill. The other victim had also been placed in a manner that left exposure to the elements.

No clothes, face up, and a V carved from the chest to the navel and back up again. In the center of the carving lay flowers; dandelions, to be exact. The victim's fingers were laced together over the chest and the dandelions placed firmly between the thumb and forefinger.

Those little details had been left out of the media and Nick wondered, had they known about them, might they have tagged the killer with another, more suitable nickname? It only took a matter of days for them to coin him the "Highway Hunter," although he attributed the quick headline to the fact that it had otherwise been a slow news day in Virginia and the national media picked up the sound bite with ferocity.

The Richmond woman had last been seen at a gas station a few miles from where she'd been found. Nick was still waiting on the surveillance video, but the local police had been having trouble with the proprietor of the station. It seemed the owner didn't want to admit his facility might not be as safe as one would expect. Standing here now, looking down on the flattened spot shaped like a body, he knew this case was going to get much worse before it got better and if he had to be the one to put pressure on the owner, then that was the way it would have to be. It was becoming apparent this latest victim wasn't going to be the last.

◆◆◆

After spending the better part of the morning standing in sticky grass, studying every inch of the scene, Nick now sat at his makeshift work station in the field office, his laptop displaying the FBI seal bouncing around the screen like a pinball; the screensaver. He stared at the monitor as he replayed the conversation with the coroner, regarding the latest victim. They still needed the DNA tests to come back, but it appeared as though a similar implement had been used to make the carving and it also appeared that the body had been located somewhere else for several hours before being dragged to the spot where she was discovered. The wound had coagulated in much the same way as the previous victim's in Richmond. Nick figured the killer didn't want to soil his vehicle with blood.

"Did I catch you at a bad time? You look like you're in deep thought." Agent Dwight Jameson popped his head through the doorway of the conference room where Nick still sat in silence.

"No, not at all. Come on in." Nick's team had arrived as scheduled. He had worked with Jameson for the better part of six months and had developed a good rapport with the man.

Agent Jameson had also proven to be a good friend in recent weeks since this case was assigned, although his name always seemed to bring to mind the whiskey brand, or maybe it was just that Nick hadn't had a drink in eight weeks and was partial to the Irish malt. "What's going on?"

Agent Jameson dropped a file onto the table. "It's the surveillance video from the gas station in Richmond."

Nick swelled with excitement. "Great! Let's see what we've got." He opened the file and found a small flash drive. "I swear if they make these things any smaller, we won't be able to see them anymore!" He plugged the tiny silver square into the USB drive and waited for it to load. "Have you seen this yet?"

"No. Just got it in from Richmond police." Jameson pulled up a chair.

Nick waited patiently for the files to load. He spotted the video file icons and clicked on the first one. "These are labeled by the time of day?"

Jameson glanced at the screen. "Doesn't look like it. Damn. It's going to take a while to go through these. Why don't you copy them over to me and I'll start looking at the back half and you can take the front half."

Agent Jameson left and Nick began dividing the task.

"Okay." Jameson reemerged with his laptop. "Let's do this."

Nick welcomed the help and as he began opening file after file, reviewing the gas station's surveillance of the prior three days before the victim was discovered, he hoped he would find something of value. He had a name and the woman's family had already been notified. According to the husband, Carla Atkins had left for work as per usual the day she disappeared. He'd filed a missing person's report the following day with local authorities. Carla's credit card hadn't been used again after filling up her Chevy minivan the morning she went missing.

As he uploaded each file and watched the stillness of the cameras focused on various areas of the station, he began to think of Katie. How she'd asked for some insight into this current investigation. Okay, so it wasn't for her exactly, but for that guy, Aguilar, he'd met in Rio Dell.

It brought to mind how strong she'd been. How she refused to take a back seat in finding Hendrickson, even if it meant risking her safety. Nick admired her greatly for that and for what she'd suffered through, coming out perhaps even stronger than before. He'd given her a chance, an offer to take her skills and talent to the next level, but in retrospect, it had probably been too soon to propose such an offer.

He wondered now, though, if she was ready. If she might reconsider. Time offered distance and allowed healing. It wasn't often he came across such a determined individual that had the knack for developing theories and testing out those theories with tremendous detail.

"Hey, I think I've got something here." Agent Jameson turned his laptop towards Nick.

"What's that?" He was pulled back into the moment and turned to see what Jameson had found.

"That's the minivan, right?"

"I do believe it is." Nick patted the agent's shoulder, pleased with the man's attention to detail. "And I believe that," he pointed to a dark spec in the black and white image off in the distance, although it would require the computer analysts to scrutinize the video, "may be our suspect."

◆◆◆

Once again, Katie found herself sitting in a blue paper gown on a table lined with paper. She shifted uncomfortably as her feet dangled beneath her, the blood rushing to her toes, her feet turning purple.

Today would see the results of the final blood test to determine if treatment had worked and if Katie was officially out of danger. The past week had been harder than she could ever have imagined. Dreams of sitting in a rocking chair in a dark room with a bundle of blankets haunted her more than once. In one of the dreams, she had pulled down the blankets to reveal a heap of body tissue, hair, blood, and tiny fingers; a malformed ball of human bits and pieces.

The way her mind worked often frightened Katie. It found ways to bring forth her deepest fears, forcing her to face them head on. What she had discovered, however, was that those fears could be conquered and she could learn from them. Dr. Reyes had once told her that it was Katie's gift and she should not squander it. Most who faced their darkest secrets, fears, and desires would choose to run from them. Katie's mind and soul would not allow her to run, at least, not for very long.

"Okay, Katie. I've got the results back." Dr. Johnson entered the room, seemingly pleased with what she had read on the chart. She raised her head and cast a pleasant smile in Katie's direction. "Everything is back to normal. You will be just fine."

These were words Katie was glad to hear, but reverberated the single thought that continued to trouble her; she would not be able to conceive naturally. "What are the risks that this could happen again?"

"It is, of course, possible, Katie, especially considering the extent of the damage. However, I'm reluctant to suggest removal of one or both of your tubes. I just don't feel it's necessary. I would suggest, though, that you remain on the pill until such time as you and your partner are ready to conceive. We can then talk about IVF or other options that are available. On the off-chance it occurs again, we can discuss preventative measures." Dr. Johnson placed her hand on Katie's knee. "I am sorry you have to deal with this, but it isn't the end of your future hopes of becoming a mother. Now why don't you get dressed and we'll get you out of here."

Dr. Johnson left Katie alone to dress.

A mother. Before this, she had rarely considered the possibility, although the scenario had seemed much more viable in another life. A life that involved Spencer — and Sam.

If she was being honest with herself, motherhood seemed a distant dream, unattainable to one like her. She wasn't even sure now if that was what she really wanted. Motherhood meant love, of course, but it also meant pain and possibly loss, and Katie wasn't sure she had any more room for those feelings.

◆◆◆

The night sky had already shrouded the sun and the clouds obscured the stars as the tide rolled in. It was Marshall who had greeted her at the door on her arrival home and it was Marshall who would be the one to offer comfort. As always.

Katie was relieved that he was home and gladly returned his greeting.

"How'd it go?" He gently removed her coat and placed it on the hook attached to the wall.

"It's done. Over." He had expressed a desire to be there for her today, but she had refused. Katie walked towards the kitchen and inhaled deeply. The apartment smelled of pasta and garlic and offered solace. "You made dinner?" She cocked her head and unveiled a smile masked in genuine surprise as she turned back to him. "Thank you."

Marshall wouldn't press her, as he knew she would talk when she chose to do so. Instead, he dished up their dinner, poured a generous glass of wine for each of them, and they simply enjoyed each other's company for a rare few hours. Uninterrupted by calls, texts, or emails, they shut out the world around them. They finished the night intertwined in the warmth of each other's bodies, remembering the love they had for one another. Whatever prospects the future held for them could wait.

◆◆◆

The vibrating cell phone sounded in her dream like a swarm of bees diving straight for her. When the noise erupted again, her conscious mind was awakened enough to bring her out of her sleep.

Katie lifted her head, still heavy and foggy. The light from her phone stinging her eyes, she squinted to see the screen more clearly. Marc. She noticed the early hour and wondered if something must be wrong. They didn't speak all that often, let alone at this early morning hour that masqueraded as night. She pressed the silent button so as not to wake up Marshall.

The stone tiled floor felt icy on her bare feet as she stepped out of the bed. A quick glance to Marshall. Still asleep. Katie shuffled towards the door, the call having already gone to voicemail. She reached for her robe and wrapped it around her chilled body.

On approach to the second bedroom that served as an office, Katie slipped inside and closed the door. A small lamp on the corner of the desk illuminated when she pressed the button at the base. Her eyes still hadn't quite adjusted and she turned away from its harsh light.

The sun was working its way up in the west, shining a dull, pale light through the slats in the window blinds. Katie sat down in the chair behind the desk and began to listen to the voicemail.

She rubbed her eyes and listened to Marc speak of the "Highway Hunter." It seemed he'd found himself another victim. This time in Hudson, Colorado, northeast of Denver. Katie had never heard of the place, but Marc relayed his discomfort at the nearing proximity to California.

The idea that he simply wanted to capitalize on the story entered Katie's mind. It wasn't really Marc's style, but she couldn't quite work out his intense interest. It didn't seem likely the Highway Hunter would happen upon them.

Agent Scarborough had made it clear he didn't have any useful information, or if he did, wasn't inclined to share it. She knew how these things went down. The FBI didn't let on more than they had to. Still, she would return Marc's call out of respect and friendship, but remind him that it was far too early an hour to rouse her from sleep and set herself to feelings of anxiety over the message.

"It's me. I just got your voicemail." Her tone was gruff, not out of anger, but because she hadn't yet soothed her throat with the warm, welcoming taste of coffee that signaled the official start of her day.

"I'm sorry to have called so early, Katie. It's just that I've got a real bad feeling about this. They found another victim yesterday, only this morning issuing a press release that it was a suspected victim of the Highway Hunter."

"Marc, I already told you…"

He abruptly cut her off. "I know, I know. Scarborough doesn't know anything. But, Katie, you gotta talk to him again. This psycho's moving west and we need to get a handle on the situation."

"What are you planning to do, Marc? Warn everyone in San Diego to lock their doors and don't pick up any hitchhikers? Most people already know that. Hell, they stand a better chance of getting killed on our streets by gang members than getting picked off by some hitchhiking killer." Her severe tone wasn't intentional, but she was beginning to feel frustrated and it was much too early. "I'm sorry. Look, I know you want the scoop on this, but I'm telling you, Agent Scarborough is being tight-lipped about all of it and probably for good reason."

Marc was quiet on the other end of the line. "You're right, Katie. I shouldn't have called you so early. There's nothing you can do. I understand that."

Katie's head fell and rested against the back of the chair. Marc knew her well enough to know what buttons to push and it seemed he'd pushed the right one. Telling her she could do nothing, that her hands were tied, was a great way to piss her off. "Fine. I'll call him again. But I can't promise you anything."

"That's all I ask. I swear I'll drop it if he says no again."

"Yeah. Yeah. Can I go now? I need some coffee."

"Thanks, Katie. It means a lot to me. I'll talk to you later."

She ended the call without another word and shook her head. On the one hand, Katie appreciated that Marc believed her to have some sort of influence. But on the other, her work with the department kept her busy, not to mention school, and so to begin to get involved in something she had no business being involved in wasn't a proposition she wanted to explore, intriguing though it may be. Unfortunately, she would be required to keep her word and once again call on Agent Scarborough to ask for any insight he might have. Marc wasn't the type to accept no for an answer.

Resigned to the fact that she was now completely awake, Katie padded softly to the kitchen and put on the coffee. A quick glance at the clock on the bookshelf and she noticed that it wouldn't be long before Marshall would be up. She also took notice of the now vacant spot on the shelf above where a picture once stood, remembering that it had been shattered into several pieces on the ground. Katie cast her eyes down, regretting her intense reaction.

She wondered, though, if Marshall would really be accepting of the fact that having children would be no easy task, if it happened at all for them. Then there was the flip side of it. The thought of the Markham case, of the young girl who found the courage along with the opportunity to seek help and escape her captor came to mind and so did the child who didn't survive.

Katie's work showed her the evil inherent in this world and especially the sort that took the most innocent as its victims. She was beginning to believe the risk of bringing a child into the world in which she had now become entirely too familiar was too great. She'd seen pain in the eyes of parents, devastating pain that she herself would likely be unable to bear if she was in the same situation. So, perhaps it was for the best. For her, at least. Marshall might yet find difficulty in accepting such a fate.

With a hot cup of coffee in hand, Katie returned to the den and put herself to task. Getting a jump on the day would be the only benefit to having risen so early. Too early to call Scarborough just yet, although she suspected he would not be sleeping much these days.

The laptop hummed and began to wake from its sleep. Katie sipped her coffee and turned towards the window. The sun was now exposed just over the horizon and she opened the blinds a little to bring in the natural light. Her caseload seemed to be winding down, but that never lasted for long. In a city the size of San Diego, it would only be a matter of days before the next case file would be tossed on her desk, or she would find herself on another crime scene. She didn't work with Marshall on every one of his cases and that was preferable. They had three different tech teams that rotated with each of the different units.

Katie punched in her password and the emails began filling her inbox. It seemed that she would have reason to call Agent Scarborough after all. He'd sent her an email late last night, already in Colorado and mentioning the need to speak to her. She set her coffee down on the desk and reached for her cell phone.

"Good morning, hon." Marshall was standing outside the door, his robe opened, revealing his boxers. "You're up before me? That can't be good." He started in towards her.

"Good morning." Katie rose from the chair and moved to greet him. The call would have to wait. It would be a challenge explaining to Marshall why he had contacted her. Of course he already knew about the initial conversation and seemed unmoved, but this particular email suggested further involvement; to what extent, she didn't yet know and until she did, it would have wait to be discussed further with Marshall.

"I've already got the coffee on. How about some breakfast?"

6

IT HAD BEEN almost a week since the Kentucky murder and it seemed this latest victim, a woman in her thirties outside of Denver, was also a casualty of the man of which Scarborough was growing increasingly wary. His style was erratic, his movements too unpredictable, but Nick had no doubt of the connection.

The victim was a professional woman with manicured nails and hair color not of the bottle-type variety, her makeup elegantly understated. Even in the condition in which they found her, naked and marred by her attacker, she was different from the others.

That was why Nick and his team had arrived on the red-eye last night when he got the call from local authorities. Some of the staff were still on scene, but the victim had already been transported to the local morgue and was awaiting autopsy. This was, of course, standard procedure, but Nick didn't need the results. He knew it was his guy. What he didn't know was the significance of the dandelions or the carving. What the hell did a dandelion have to do with any of this?

Nick wasn't a profiler, but the woman who had been assigned to work with him had been assessing the information. As of now, she had a few theories, nothing concrete. She needed more time, but time was a precious commodity in these situations. He had a string of murders that was growing and a supervisor hungry for answers. Not to mention a ravenous media for which he had little tolerance and despised the notoriety they had already given the killer.

It was approaching eight a.m. and Nick wondered if Katie had read his email yet. She was an hour behind, but he figured her for an early riser. He didn't know why for certain he had asked if she wanted to help. His team was extremely qualified and he didn't lack for resources. But when he spoke to her the other day, that idea she had triggered in him more than a year ago, that she could quite possibly be an excellent federal agent, still lingered in his mind.

She'd gone after a killer. She'd gone after him and found him as if it was in her nature to do so. And she'd accomplished it with exquisite resolve. Maybe it was because he'd been up nearly all night, only catching a few zzz's on the plane, but he wanted her input and her unique insight. Katie had been in the belly of the beast and fought her way out. Maybe that was what he needed now.

Time was ticking away. It was urgent that he get to the morgue and talk to the coroner, then head back out to the scene.

Nick placed his cupped hands beneath the faucet and threw water onto his face. His wet hands pushing through his hair, working to tame it. The blue oxford shirt hung haphazardly in the closet of his hotel room. It was in desperate need of a press, but there was no time. He slipped on the shirt, fingers fastening the buttons. The single-breasted jacket lay across the desk chair and he pulled it on. After one last glance at his cell phone, he pocketed it and left his room of the hotel.

◆◆◆

Ready to leave for work, Katie approached Marshall as he brushed his teeth in the small bathroom adjacent to their bedroom. She looked at his reflection and unveiled a smile. "I'm heading out now. Don't forget I've got a class tonight, so I'll be late. Call you later?"

Marshall nodded, a white foamy smile crossing his lips.

Katie stepped out onto the landing of their apartment, the noise of downtown filling her ears. It was seven a.m. and the cold air settled on her skin. The short walk to the parking garage meant she would have to brave the crisp fall morning, foregoing the jacket tossed over her forearm.

Upon sighting her car, nestled between a Mercedes and an Audi, she pressed the remote to unlock it. Her small SUV paled in comparison to the much more expensive vehicles flanking either side of her. This building was home to many wealthy individuals who had purchased their units when the market was at its peak. She had to snicker a little. The mortgage on their two-bedroom was likely a paltry figure compared to what these people faced.

Pulling out onto E Street, Katie contemplated making the call to Scarborough. She thought a private conversation would be in order in this particular case. Katie was housed in a cubicle at work where ears listened intently and with great interest. She was not immune to the hushed conversations that still sometimes occurred at the proverbial water cooler. Although most of the people she worked with empathized with her past, others remained envious of her position and the fact that she had attained it so quickly. So, eavesdropping on a conversation with the FBI on what had become an increasingly noteworthy case wasn't an option for Katie. It would quite possibly be used against her by those who pressed on others as rungs on a ladder.

Katie made the call.

After more than a few rings, a voice found its way through. "Agent Scarborough."

"Nick, it's me, Katie. I got your email this morning..."

But before she could continue, he spoke. "Thanks for calling, Katie, but listen; now's not a good time. I'm in Colorado and heading to the coroner's office. I'll keep this brief. If you're interested, I'd like to send you some information on the case. Just to get a fresh pair of eyes on it. It'll have to be off the record, you understand?"

"Yeah. Okay. I'd be happy to see what you've got. But Nick, why me?"

"You know why, Katie. My intuition hasn't failed me yet and it's telling me you could be a vital part of this investigation, but no one can know about it. Not yet anyway. As much as my ASAC likes you, he wouldn't appreciate me going to you with this. But, I just got a feeling."

"Okay, well, I was going to ask you if I could relay any information to Aguilar."

"Can't talk about that now, Katie. Gotta run. But, for now, let's just keep this between you and me. I'll send you what I've got later and I'll be in touch."

"Okay." Katie was unsure of how else to respond. He'd mentioned in his email that he wanted to run a few questions by her, but taking a look at his files? That seemed way outside her wheelhouse, but before she could inquire further, Nick had disconnected the call.

"Okay. Guess I'll talk to you later then."

◆◆◆

A knock on Edward's door at this early hour couldn't be good. He shuffled towards the front room and pulled on a pair of shorts that had been tossed on the couch.

He peered through the peephole where two uniformed officers stood. One was standing as if at attention. The other appeared more relaxed. Edward assumed he was the senior partner, but what eluded him was the reason for their presence.

"Edward Shalot? This is San Diego County Sheriff's office." The officer knocked on the door again.

"Shit," he whispered and began unlocking the deadbolt. An immediate surge of adrenaline made its way through him, sending him a little shaky. "Good morning, officers. What can I do for you?" Edward fixed on his most charming smile, which he had called on in many different scenarios, mostly involving women. Whether it would work in this particular situation remained to be seen.

The junior officer looked to his mentor, dispensing with any thought that he was the one in charge.

"Mr. Shalot, I'm Deputy Jackson and this is Deputy McGuire." The man held out an envelope. "We had a Lindsay Brown come in with her attorney yesterday afternoon. It seems you and Ms. Brown had an incident the other night?"

"I'm not sure what you're talking about. Lindsay and I had a date and, at the end of the date, we had a minor argument and she left. Nothing else happened, sir." Edward felt a rise of panic in his stomach.

"Mr. Shalot, this is a Temporary Civil Harassment Restraining Order filed on behalf of Ms. Brown. This will remain in effect for not less than three weeks, at which time Ms. Brown will be notified by a judge as to the permanent status of the restraining order. Mr. Shalot, you are not to contact Ms. Brown in any way, including email or texting, nor go to her home or place of business. You will be served with the permanent restraining order once it has been approved by the judge." Deputy Jackson handed Edward the envelope.

"I don't understand. I didn't do anything. That stupid bitch. This is going to be on my record now."

The deputies already began to turn away, but stopped short when Edward continued to run his mouth.

"I'm sorry?" Deputy Jackson laid a hand on the butt of his holstered gun. "Are we going to have a problem here, Mr. Shalot?"

Edward tossed a glance at the gun. "No, sir. I'm just— surprised; that's all. Have a good day." He closed the door and thumped his head on the back of it, wondering what the hell had just happened.

"A restraining order. A fucking restraining order." Heat began to rise in his cheeks. Edward couldn't let this bitch ruin everything. If she was capable of this, he wondered what else she might do.

The only hope he had of making this thing go away would be for him to try and make amends first. Withdrawing the order wasn't possible, but at least when it got to court, she could make a statement and try to convince the judge to cancel the order.

"I have to see her."

It was a risky proposition to say the least, but Edward believed his charms could hold sway over her. Lindsay was a young and naïve girl. Showering her with a little affection and maybe some flowers and all would be forgiven. The belief that he held such power over women had been confirmed by previous efforts and he felt he could draw on those experiences to get him out of this situation as well.

Edward couldn't risk Katie finding out about any of this. Chances that the two of them, Lindsay and Katie, would cross each other's paths were slim, but if she caught wind from the law enforcement pipeline or from another student in their class and decided to look it up, his story would unravel in a hurry. This would have to be nipped in the bud. Today.

◆◆◆

The knock on Lindsay's door was gentle and non-threatening. It was midday and Edward knew she stopped by her house for lunch before her two p.m. psych class. His only concern was if the roommate was home too. If she was there, he wouldn't stand a chance of getting through that door.

The dark-haired, chain-smoking political science major had moved in with Lindsay at the beginning of the year. She didn't like Edward much. Thought he was narcissist. At least, that was what she had expressed to Lindsay and she'd relayed the information to him one night over the phone. "You know, she thinks you're a little full of yourself," Lindsay had said, following it up with a drunken snort.

Edward waited for the door to open. Maybe she wasn't home yet. He double-checked the time on his watch. *She should be here by now.* A second knock was followed by a press of the doorbell. He could hear it echoing inside. "Lindsay? Laura?" Edward pressed his ear against the door. "Dammit."

Edward started to turn away, working through his plan as this attempt seemed to have been a bust. As he moved towards the front window, a small opening through the otherwise closed curtains allowed him to catch a glimpse inside. The scene forced him to pull back quickly, gasping at the unexpected sight. "What the fuck?" He dropped the flowers and pressed his face to the window for a better look.

Inside, the living room had been ransacked. The white sofa, overturned, the black table collapsed, tilted on its two remaining legs. Papers scattered, figurines lying shattered on the ground. Empty bookshelves and table tops. "Jesus!" Edward shot a glance behind him and to either side. No one was around. The neighbor's houses were quiet and the street was barren.

He started to walk towards the side of the small house and in between the narrow opening between the homes. A window had been broken. It was Lindsay's bedroom window. A sudden jolt of fear passed through him as he leaned back, his pulse quickening.

Edward was not a man of compassion. He was not charitable, nor did he consider his fellow man in any manner other than how he might benefit from them. But as he stood in the three-foot gap, his shoes settling in the damp soil, he felt genuine concern for the woman who had seemingly set out to destroy his plans. Or perhaps it was primarily concern for what would be perceived as his role in the present situation.

He stepped forward, landing on the fallen ruins below, pushing them into the ground under his weight. Edward leaned further until his head was inside the opening.

Lindsay lay sprawled out on the floor, her face covered in blood. His legs wobbled beneath him. His hands trembled so much so that his left palm sliced open on impact against the broken glass still hanging inside the window frame.

He could not look away and devoured every inch of her body with fear and fascination.

Edward's attention was focused on what she held in her hands. He narrowed his eyes to gain a better view. Yes. Dandelions, but what was more concerning to him was the symbol left by her killer. "Oh my god." He reached for his cell phone.

Only after ending the call that had taken much longer than he'd expected, did Edward finally call the police.

"911, what is your emergency?" the voice on the other end asked.

"I'm at my girlfriend's house. She's dead. Someone killed her."

◆◆◆

"Marshall?" Katie jogged to catch up to him in the hall. "Do you have a minute? I wanted to talk to you about Agent Scarborough. I asked if I could get some information on the 'Highway Hunter.' He said he'd welcome a second set of eyes on some of the files, but it has to be off the record." She was struggling to keep up with him. It seemed he was on his way to somewhere in a hurry.

Marshall tossed her a sideways glance. "Well, you might get a chance to see him in person very soon. A call came in about an hour ago. Someone found a woman's body in her home. According to Captain Hearn, it could be related to the man the FBI is looking for."

Marc's words came to her in an instant. *"We need to get ahead of this thing, Katie, before the killer ends up at our doorstep."*

Was it possible? She'd only spoken to Nick this morning and he was heading to the scene of another possible victim in Colorado. That would mean the suspect would have had to take a flight in order to get to San Diego so quickly. From what she knew of the case already, days or almost a week would pass before another victim would turn up.

"You say she was found in her home? From what Scarborough knows about the killer, he says that the guy tosses the bodies onto the side of the highway. Something's not adding up." Katie was already thinking like a detective. She began to feel energized by the news and was ready to go all in and do what she could to help.

"The captain knows more about this than I do and, by the sounds of it, so do you." A measure of discontent seemed to prevail in him.

The tone was not lost on her, but she continued, "Who's the lead on the case?"

"If it turns out to be the guy the FBI is looking for, they'll handle it. But Hearn has assigned Gibbons for the time being. He's heading out now." It appeared that Marshall was feeling a twinge of guilt for his earlier comment. "Look, if you want in on it, you'd better talk to Harris to get on his team."

This case would be outside Marshall's area and so Katie knew his involvement would be limited at best. The differing units in the department crossed paths once in a while and Marshall was senior to many of the other detectives. They often came to him for advice or to run on a lead, if needed. It came as no surprise that he was already aware of the call. She was glad to have his support, even if it seemed somewhat reluctant.

"Thank you, Marshall."

Rather than return to her office, Katie took Marshall's advice and headed straight to see Dr. Harris. As the Crime Scene Supervisor, he assigned the investigators and evidence technicians. It wasn't often Katie requested to work on a case, but she hoped he would give her an opportunity now.

"Dr. Harris?" Katie tapped on his opened door.

The scene in his office depicted a man quite literally obsessed with the history of forensics. He held a Ph.D. in Forensic and Behavior Science, so this hadn't come as much of a surprise to Katie. Textbooks, certificates, even a DNA model were all on display on the several bookshelves that lined the walls.

"Katie? Please, come in. What can I do for you?" He removed his glasses, placing them neatly on his desk and rubbed his hands along the top of his freshly-shaved head. As a man nearing what Katie assumed to be about fifty, he was in remarkable shape. His button-down shirt revealed slightly bulging pectoral muscles and broad shoulders. What he lacked in vision and hair, he more than made up for with a well-toned frame.

"I understand that Detective Gibbons is handling the case of the victim over near Bay Park that was called in this morning."

Dr. Harris leaned in, as if waiting for her to continue.

"I was wondering if you've already assigned your techs to the team."

"Are you interested in this particular case?" Dr. Harris seemed curious by the special request.

"Well, yes, actually. I hear they think it has something to do with this 'Highway Hunter,' and well, I know the FBI agent working that case, and I just thought maybe I could help."

"We don't know if any connection exists between the two, not that Gibbons has relayed to me anyway. But if you want in, you're in. If there is a connection, you won't be in for long. The FBI will pull it from us in the blink of an eye."

"I understand. Thank you, Dr. Harris. Who will the CSI be that I should report to?"

"Sanderson is at the scene now, or will be within minutes. Call him. Tell him you'll be assisting in the collection of the evidence." Dr. Harris placed his glasses back on his face, signaling the end of the conversation.

"Thank you again, Dr. Harris." Katie nodded gently and, as she turned to leave, a wide grin spread across her face.

7

IT SEEMED LIKE a quaint neighborhood. Green lawns, trimmed hedges, 1960s architecture. Katie took in the picturesque scene, finding it hard to believe a murder had just been committed inside one of these small bungalows.

Stepping out of her Toyota and into the organized chaos of the crime scene, Katie looked for Gibbons and Sanderson. Three patrol cars and the coroner's van were parked out front. Neighbors had been held back by barricades and tape. Some appeared to return to their homes, while others remained fixed by their own morbid fascination.

On approach to the lead detective, Katie immediately recognized the man to whom he was speaking. "Edward?"

Detective Gibbons turned to her, appearing confused by her familiarity. "Katie? You know Mr. Shalot?"

"We're in the same class at UCSD. Criminal Justice," Edward replied.

"Yes, that's right. What's going on?" Katie asked.

"Mr. Shalot discovered the victim earlier this morning and made the 911 call." Gibbons hesitated for a moment before continuing. "Sanderson is inside. Why don't you touch base with him, see what he needs?"

Gibbons appeared reluctant to share anything further regarding Edward. The brushoff was fairly apparent and not just to her. "Of course."

Sanderson was in the living room, scribbling notes on his tablet. Lights flashed as photographs were being taken. Evidence was carefully being placed in bags and those inside were documenting and collecting with precision.

"Officer Sanderson? Dr. Harris assigned me to assist you."

"Katie. Great. Glad you're here." Sanderson turned up and caught sight of her. "We could use your help transporting the evidence to the vehicles." He looked towards the man photographing the upturned coffee table. "Crawford? Reid is here to help. Put her to work."

◆◆◆

Detective Gibbons stood on the porch, huddled with another officer, while Shalot remained as he was directed, leaning over the thick wood railing on the opposite end.

"You're telling me this guy had a restraining order filed against him just yesterday? Son of a bitch." Gibbons stood with arms folded and legs shoulder width apart. He towered over the other officer by a good foot. "We're gonna have to bring him in." He cast a brief look to Shalot.

"What about the FBI? This girl was carved up just like the others. And the weeds?" The officer shook his head.

"The media doesn't know about that. I don't see how we could be dealing with a copycat. I'll put a call in to the captain now. Why don't you go and tell our friend over there that he's gonna be coming in with us?" Gibbons raised the cell phone to his ear.

"Ten-four."

"Oh, and one last thing." Gibbons turned back. "We need to have a word with Reid. She knows this guy."

◆◆◆

The lab was inundated with evidence from Lindsay Brown's home. Katie, along with the rest of the evidence team, finished unloading the boxes.

Word had reached Katie that Gibbons wanted to speak with her. "Is there anything else you need from me?" She waited patiently for Sanderson to look up from his computer and offer direction.

"We're good for now, Katie. Thank you. You were a big help this morning."

She took leave and headed for Detective Gibbons' office. The desire to call Scarborough and let him in on the present situation ate away at her, but stepping over that line wasn't advisable. Not yet. She would wait to see what Gibbons had to say.

Seeing her classmate there was unexpected, to say the least. She was sure this was why Gibbons had called on her. "Knock, knock." Katie rapped her knuckles on the door frame of the detective's office.

He turned his attention from his partner, appearing to have been in furtive conversation. "Come in, Katie. Please, close the door behind you."

Gibbons was junior to Marshall, but only by a few years. He had worked Homicide at the department for the past three, coming from SWAT. He was a good cop and well respected.

He sat perched on the edge of his desk. Katie took a seat, feeling his guarded eyes fall on her.

Gibbons' partner, Detective Garza, was fairly new to the department, having transferred from Riverside. Katie knew little about him, but he appeared even less approachable than Gibbons. Maybe that was due to his unfamiliarity or maybe it was due to the grave look on his face. Katie suddenly began to feel as though she was under suspicion.

"What do you know about Shalot?" Gibbons' straight-for-the-throat method was well known, although Katie had never experienced it first-hand.

"He's in my Criminal Justice class that I have twice a week, Tuesdays and Wednesdays. I've talked to him maybe a handful of times. That's it." She began to shift uncomfortably, as if a spotlight had been trained on her.

"You don't know if he was dating anyone or where he lived or anything other than the fact that he was in your class?"

"I'm sorry, detective, but no. Like I said, I hardly spoke to him."

Gibbons looked to Garza and continued. "I understand you have a friend at the FBI. An Agent Scarborough?"

"Yes." Most people in the department knew what had happened to her and she didn't feel the need to elaborate on the relationship.

"Can you tell me what you know about the so-called 'Highway Hunter'?" Gibbons moved to his desk chair and sat down, looking Katie squarely in the eyes.

"Not much. I've got a friend at Channel Nine who asked me to put a call into Agent Scarborough. I wasn't even sure if he was on the case, but it turns out that he was." Katie thought back to the Nick's words, knowing she needed to honor his request to keep things off book. "He said he couldn't divulge any more than what the media already knew, so I thanked him and left it at that."

"And that was it? He didn't mention any of the specifics of the case?"

"Well, no. He didn't. I wouldn't say that he and I have a particularly close relationship. We're friends in the loosest sense of the term. He and I had been through a lot in the past, but that was in the past. We don't hang around the same circles." She was working to read Gibbons, wondering why the pointed questions. Could Shalot have said something to make them believe she knew more than she was letting on? For that matter, what the hell did Shalot know anyway?

"Were you aware that Edward Shalot was dating the victim?"

"I'm sorry, no. I wasn't aware of that at all." Hadn't she already stated she hardly knew the man?"

"Okay." Gibbons rose again. "Thank you for your help, Katie. We appreciate it."

Katie pushed up from the chair. "Do you believe this was the work of the 'Highway Hunter'?"

"The captain's put a call into your Agent Scarborough. He's on his way here."

Although she hadn't known this, it didn't come as a surprise. *They must believe the murders are connected.*

On her way out, she retrieved her phone and noticed several missed calls and a few text messages. Most were from Marc, but two were from Scarborough. It seemed he wanted to tell her he was coming down. His flight was due to land in a few hours.

This morning, Katie thought her only involvement in this case would be to take a look at a few of the files. Backgrounds of the victims and such, looking for any connection. She didn't believe for a moment that Scarborough really needed her help. Instead, he was giving her another chance. A chance to see that this was the type of work she should be doing, but things had now changed dramatically. With her personal knowledge of the man who called it in, her involvement had just become compulsory.

Katie reached Marshall's office. He looked as though he was expecting her.

"Close the door." Before she had a chance to say anything, he started in. "What the hell's going on, Kate? You know this guy?"

"It's not like he's a personal friend of mine. He's in one of my classes. That's it. I didn't know he was the one who called it in." Word had clearly already reached Marshall.

"Did you know the victim had filed a restraining order on the guy just yesterday?"

Katie was taken aback by this little tidbit of information that Gibbons seemed to gloss over. "No. I had no idea. I'm telling you, Marshall. I really don't know the guy from Adam. He's talked to me a few times. Asked me out for coffee after class. That's it."

"You never mentioned going out for coffee with a classmate."

"That's because I never accepted the offers." Her brow creased in response to his critical tone. "Come on. I would have told you if I'd socialized with anyone from class."

"I know." Marshall didn't seem to want to believe she had somehow become a reluctant participant in the situation. "I was just surprised to find out you knew this guy. He shouldn't have been there this morning. He had a restraining order against him. That's the part that scares me. I don't know, Kate. I don't like how this is going, and now Scarborough's coming? Did you know about that? You said you'd talked to him recently."

"I didn't know he was coming until Gibbons said something. Then, when I left his office, I found a message from Nick on my phone. He's gonna be here in a few hours. I just can't help but think there's no way this could be the same guy, not after Nick had just found a victim in Colorado. Not to mention this woman was killed in her home and not dragged onto the side of the highway like the others."

"Yeah, well, there seem to be too many other similarities. I guess we'll know more when Scarborough gets here." Marshall paused for a moment, appearing to study Katie's expression. "You sure you can handle this? I don't know if this Shalot is involved or not, but I can't say I'm happy about you getting dragged into this thing."

"I can handle it, Marshall. Just, please, don't worry so much about me. I'm not as fragile as you think I am."

"I know you're not, Kate. But with everything that's happened over the past few weeks..." Marshall cast his eyes towards her midsection. "I just want to be sure you're up for this—physically, you know?"

Katie put on a thin smile. "I'm fine. Besides, wasn't it you who said I'd be better suited as a detective? Well, I may get the chance to prove my skills."

♦♦♦

The plane rolled to a stop and Nick immediately turned on his phone. He began scrolling through his emails when the flight attendants finally opened the doors. The woman sitting next to him nudged his shoulder.

"I'm sorry to bother you, but would you mind opening the overhead bin and taking down my bag for me?"

Nick took notice of the bump in her belly and figured he should help her out. "Of course." He rose to retrieve her bag along with his and placed it in the middle seat.

The other passengers began filing out of the aircraft, and as Nick made his way through the concourse, his felt his phone buzzing in his pocket. He swiped the screen and began to read the text from Katie. *"I know the guy who called it in. Come see me as soon as you can."*

Protocol had to be followed and that meant a briefing with the Chief of Police first. She wasn't likely to be happy about his arrival. The last thing any local law enforcement wanted was a serial killer in their city. It was only a matter of time before the connection, or possible connection was leaked to the media as well, adding further fuel to the fire.

Nick still had his doubts. This one just didn't follow the killer's MO. Agent Myers, who was due in on the next flight with Jameson, had begun to put together a fairly extensive profile of the killer now that they had three bodies to deal with. She and Jameson were all he had at the moment and they were both desperately trying to wrap things up in Colorado. The video from the gas station in Richmond hadn't led anywhere, not yet. All of this was happening too fast and they couldn't keep up with the killer.

Nick needed Myers' expertise to determine if the San Diego victim was likely the result of the same person thought to have taken the other three lives. It was possible, of course, that the two crimes could be committed inside such a short period of time, but from what Nick knew of the unsub so far, it was that he preferred to take his time with this victims. The precision with which the incisions were made, the careful placement of the body and the flowers. It was as if he'd been preparing the victims for a formal viewing, however gruesome the display.

Now he would have to deal with this one in San Diego. It seemed the likelihood of a copycat killer was becoming increasingly probable. It would have to be someone who had a contact on the inside, though, if that was the case. No one knew about the flowers or the v-shaped carvings. No one outside law enforcement.

The customer service rep behind the rental car counter handed Nick the key to his mid-sized sedan. "I hope this will be all right for you."

Nick grabbed the key. "It'll be fine, thank you." His was a little disappointed, though. It was the same mid-sized car most of the agents drove now and he was kind of hoping for something a little sportier.

He reached the parking lot and pressed the remote to unlock the door, tossing his bag in the back seat. It was a short drive to the station. Nick wondered what would await him there. The victim would have already been transferred from the scene and so he would find himself at yet another medical examiner's office. The idea of working on something like white collar crimes sounded very appealing to him at this particular moment.

Nick pulled into parking garage of the station, leaving his bag inside. He'd have to check in at the hotel later, having no idea how long he'd be in San Diego. At this rate, he expected another body to pop up at any time.

It seemed word had already reached the media as Nick spotted a handful of reporters hovering in the lobby. They twirled their visitor badges while on the phone, looking as though they had very important information to share.

He approached the front desk. "I'm here to see Chief Wyatt. Special Agent Nick Scarborough." Nick showed the woman his badge. It appeared she had been expecting him.

"I'll let her know you're here. Please have a seat."

Nick had no intention of going near the reporters and instead meandered a few feet away, waiting to be called up.

It took several more minutes before the chief was ready to see him. Nick was escorted through the building and into Chief Wyatt's office.

She stood behind an oversized dark walnut desk, her back turned, peering through the window. Chief Maureen Wyatt had been in the job for two years. She presided over nearly three thousand staff, an annual budget of almost half a billion dollars and all while maintaining a political neutrality, which proved challenging on a daily basis. Today, she would be forced to concede control, and when Nick walked into the room, it was apparent that she was not happy about it.

"Agent Scarborough?" She moved from behind her desk, hand extended, and greeted the agent. "I'm Maureen Wyatt. Very nice to meet you."

Nick returned the greeting. "Chief Wyatt, the pleasure's mine." He took a seat at her suggestion.

"I'm sorry to be here under such unpleasant circumstances, chief. I trust you're already well aware of the situation?"

Wyatt pulled her chair out and sat down. "Unfortunately, yes. I've been briefed by my assistant chief and captain. Have you been to the scene yet?"

"No, ma'am, I haven't. I'm hoping to get out there as soon as possible, though."

"Of course. If it turns out that you believe this is the work of your suspect, I'd still like to offer any assistance you need for as long as you're here. I have to tell you, though, I hope it isn't. I've got a lobby full of reporters looking for a sensational headline and, once that happens, these things tend to take on a life of their own."

"I'll know more after I get out there. Can I see the detective working the case? I'd like to get started right away."

"Understood. Detective Gibbons is waiting for you. I'll have someone take you to him."

Nick stood up and turned towards the door.

"Agent Scarborough?"

"Yes?" Nick turned on his heel.

"My officers are extraordinary men and women who put their lives on the line every day. They do what they can and by the book as much as they can. If this turns out to be the work of your guy, don't yank the rug out from under them. They deserve every consideration and you'll get it in return tenfold."

Nick expected something of this nature to be said. This was usually where the local guys felt the need to defend their cases and how they'd been handled. "Chief Wyatt, I have no intentions of trying to make your people look bad. I know exactly what they do because I'm in the trenches with them. Thank you for your time, ma'am." He walked through the door, gently pulling it closed behind him.

8

THE AFTERNOON SUN was disappearing behind the white clouds as Nick stepped off the front porch of Lindsay Brown's home. Lack of sleep and general mental exhaustion made his eyes overly sensitive, even in the muted light, and so he placed his sunglasses on his face.

"So what do you think?" Detective Gibbons asked.

"Until we see the coroner, I won't know what exactly we're dealing with here. But I can tell you that it appears as though this woman likely knew her killer. The broken bedroom window? Unless you're familiar with the layout of a house, how would you know to pick that window? Not to mention that it seems an odd choice to break in through when most people would choose to enter through a room in which they believed no one was present. Ms. Brown would have heard the window break and probably would have had time to get out through the front door by the time the person climbed over the frame and entered her room."

"I gotta agree with you on that point. The man who found her is still down at the station." Gibbons noticed the time on his watch. "At least, he will be for a little while longer. The son of a bitch had a restraining order against him from this woman. It just doesn't make sense that he'd be the one to find her and call it in."

Nick struggled to come to terms with the idea that Edward Shalot could be the killer. "We need to see the body; talk to the examiner. If the man you have did it, he would have to have known some very specific details about my investigation."

"We've got an evidence technician who knows him. She says he was in a class with her, but she had never said more than a few words to him."

"I'm aware. Katie Reid and I go way back. I'd like to have a word with her when we get back to the station."

"Okay. Hop in." Detective Gibbons unlocked his car.

◆◆◆

Agent Scarborough and Gibbons arrived at the County Medical Examiner's office, where Lindsay Brown's body had been transported.

Gibbons approached the front desk. "Detective Gibbons and Agent Scarborough here to see Dr. Napier."

The receptionist buzzed the office of the ME, Dr. Sheila Napier. "I have an Agent Scarborough and Detective Gibbons here to see you." A short pause, and then she resumed. "Thank you. I'll send them right over." She placed the phone down. "Go to the end of the hall and take the elevator down to lower level one. You'll find Dr. Napier in the room labeled 'Private: Staff Only.' She's expecting you."

A latch released and Gibbons pushed the door open. Nick followed closely behind, walking inside the large and sterile room. He'd seen far too many of these places already, especially in more recent days.

Along the back wall was what appeared to be a cooler; a steel frame, housing six smaller doors where Nick figured they kept the bodies. The highly polished tiled floor bounced the overhead fluorescent lighting around the room and off of the stainless steel tables. He counted ten separate stations, each with its own storage, sink, and table.

"Dr. Napier, this is Special Agent Nick Scarborough with the FBI," Gibbons said.

"You'll excuse me if I don't shake your hand, Agent Scarborough. We've already begun our external examination." The doctor continued taking photographs of Lindsay Brown's face. Her assistant pulled down the sheet that covered the body to capture additional photos. "Good to see you again, detective."

Dr. Napier continued on. "I don't normally see the FBI down here. Although Detective Gibbons has informed me that there is reason to suspect this victim may be linked to a series of deaths?" She handed her assistant the camera and began removing the plastic bags that had been tied around Lindsay's hands to preserve evidence.

"That's what we're here to determine. Would it be possible to see the incision on the victim's chest?"

Dr. Napier looked up at Nick, appearing annoyed at the request. She was meticulous and took steps in their necessary order, but reluctantly obliged his request. "Well, as you can see," the doctor aimed her gloved pinky at the "Y" incision that examiners use as a dissection technique, "this individual began the incision. However, rather than the traditional 'Y,' this person carved out a 'V,' ending at the navel." Her finger gently grazed the skin along the wound for emphasis. "It's a haphazard attempt at precision. Clearly, whoever did this did not use a medical instrument or, if he or she did, the instrument was blunted. My guess right now would be something along the lines of a pocket knife. And, the instrument did not penetrate the tissue completely; it merely reached the superficial fascia. No muscle or bone has been breached. This was not how the victim died and, until I get to the internal exam, I'm afraid that's all I can tell you for now."

"How soon will you have results back?" Gibbons asked.

"This shouldn't take more than a couple of hours. However, you'll have to wait for labs. I'll be scraping for DNA under the nails and such, but getting the results back will take some time."

"I think I've seen enough for now, Dr. Napier. Thank you, and I'm sure Detective Gibbons will be waiting for your call."

The doctor returned to her work, but raised her head again as the men were leaving. "Agent Scarborough, from what you've seen here, do you believe it is the work of your Highway Hunter?"

"If it isn't, it's a damn good imitation. Thank you for your assistance, Dr. Napier."

◆◆◆

Gibbons pulled his car around the corner of the police station. Night had already settled in and still several media personnel skulked about as if waiting for their prey. "I got a feeling it's gonna be a long night."

Scarborough peered through the passenger window as they rolled on. "I'm used to it." He turned to Gibbons. "You still got Shalot in custody?"

"I spoke to my partner earlier and he confirmed Shalot will be staying overnight, but if we can't bring charges by end of day tomorrow, he'll be released." Gibbons turned the wheel, driving into the first floor of the parking garage.

"I'd like to talk to Reid, if possible. I'm having trouble thinking Shalot's our guy. You remember what Dr. Napier said about the depth of the cut?"

"Yeah."

"The other victims' were much worse. They'd been carved much deeper, even penetrating some of the organs. And, the others had been cleaned up. Minimal blood had been found at the scenes." Nick paused for a moment, considering the possibility. "Someone leaked information. There's just no other answer that makes any kind of sense. They leaked it and now we've got someone out there trying to get in the spotlight. I don't know if Katie can give us any more insight into Shalot than she already has, but I'd still like to speak with her."

"I'm sure Detective Avery will want to be in on that conversation. He doesn't let her out of his sight much. I don't think he's gotten over what happened to her last year." Gibbons stepped out of the car and glanced over the rooftop as Scarborough emerged. "But then, you know all about that, don't you?"

◆◆◆

Katie caught sight of Marshall walking down the corridor towards her cubicle. She'd spent most of the day entering a portion of the evidence collected on scene from the Brown investigation into the database for the lab. She thought his approach meant that Scarborough was here and ready to talk. It would be a welcome break from her present task.

"Hey. Scarborough and Gibbons just came in. You wanna come over to my office so you can talk with him?"

She hadn't seen him in a long time and only recently had heard his voice again. It brought back a lot of memories; ones she wasn't prepared to recall. There were others, however, that outweighed those and she called on them now to help settle her nerves. Nick had seen her through a great deal and that thought was what propelled her from the chair, allowing her to follow Marshall back to his office.

The two passed by the captain's office, where the FBI agent and Detective Gibbons were presumably briefing Hearn. Scarborough noticed Katie and tipped his head in acknowledgment. Katie picked up on his subtle smile and returned it in kind. He'd been reluctant, she recalled, during the Hendrickson investigation, but had come to see Katie for who she really was: an intelligent and intuitive woman who had proven herself to be more than useful.

On arrival at Marshall's office, he closed the door after Katie stepped inside. "They'll be finished soon, I'm guessing. Has Scarborough contacted you today?"

"No. I sent him a text after you and I talked about Shalot. I let him know that I knew the guy, but he didn't respond." Katie dropped into the seat and pushed her fingers through her hair.

"You look tired," Marshall said as he took a seat behind his desk. "You sure you're feeling all right?"

"Yes. I'm fine. I promise." Her eyes crinkled as the corners of her mouth upturned slightly. "I'm just having a hard time processing this whole Shalot thing. Do you think he killed that girl?"

"I don't know, Kate. I can't wrap my head around the fact that she'd filed a restraining order against him, then he just shows up and finds her dead?" The familiar grunt that had become his trademark of frustration sounded. "Just doesn't make sense, but I suppose we'll know more after Scarborough and Gibbons arrive. I'm sure Scarborough's team is already knee-deep in Shalot's background."

The men appeared outside the glass door and Scarborough waved to make their presence known.

"Nick." Katie rose from her chair and pulled the door open, greeting the man with a temperate hug. "It's so good to see you."

"It's great to see you too, Katie. You cut your hair?" Scarborough replied.

"I guess I needed a change." She took a section of her brunette locks, which were now shoulder length, and pulled it out to emphasize her new look.

"It suits you very well." Nick turned his attention to Marshall. "Detective Avery. How the hell are you, man?" He extended a greeting. "Last time I saw you, you were just getting out of the hospital."

Marshall took hold of the agent's hand and patted his shoulder with the other. "Good to see you, man." He began to smooth down his shirt. "Yeah. Let's just say I'm doing a hell of a lot better now. Take a seat, please." He looked to Gibbons. "I'll go grab another chair."

"No, no. I'm fine. I'll just park it over here."

"So, Katie, what do you know about Edward Shalot?" Nick began.

"Not much, I'm afraid. I told Detective Gibbons that I have a class with him, but that's about it really."

"So you've gone back to school?" Nick asked.

"I'm getting my graduate degree in Criminal Justice. I've just got a few more months left."

"Well, congratulations. I'm glad to hear it." Nick returned to the more pressing situation. "Have you talked with this guy much? Have you had any other contact with him, apart from in class?"

"No. Not really. He's approached me maybe two or three times about studying after class, grabbing a coffee, but that's it. I gotta tell you, though, he doesn't strike me as a killer."

"No. He doesn't," Gibbons interrupted. "Brown's roommate talked to my partner earlier today. Said Shalot threatened Brown the other night at his apartment. Brown wasn't going to do anything about it, except the roommate convinced her to file a restraining order against him. She said she had a bad feeling about the guy. We're still digging into his background, but haven't turned up anything that would raise any red flags. No priors, hardly even a speeding ticket."

"So we're going to release him then; is that right?" Marshall asked.

"Unless we get the ME's report indicating differently," Scarborough started. "But I doubt that'll be ready before tomorrow. Hell, I'm still waiting on the tox screen and DNA from my Colorado victim."

"We'll put surveillance on him until we get something definitive from the lab." Scarborough continued. "Whoever did this had to know the roommate was out of the house, but the timing of this is what really gets me. The victim in

Colorado was most certainly killed by the person I'm looking for. What I can't figure out is, if this guy is a copycat, how the hell did he know the details we kept from the media?"

"Speaking of details, you plan on letting us in on your investigation?" Gibbons crossed his arms as he leaned against the filing cabinet. "If we got the Highway Hunter in town, might be nice to know what exactly we're dealing with."

Katie was reluctant to mention the fact that Nick had emailed her the files late last night. She'd only had time to save them to her flash drive and had planned on reviewing them tonight. But that was before Shalot. Now, she was unsure of where she stood on the matter and needed to speak to Nick in private.

That might prove difficult with Gibbons, who was hungry for a good collar, and Marshall, who had difficulty letting Katie run on matters of this nature. She'd given him reason to be nervous, of course. It seemed he still hadn't quite forgiven her for taking off to Sacramento and meeting up with Aguilar without his knowledge. But it had been the only way, in her mind, to find out what Chief Wilson had been hiding. In the end, she was right to do what she did, but sometimes, she didn't think Marshall believed it had been.

Nick lifted his cell phone from his shirt pocket. "The rest of my team should be here by now. We need to speak with Agent Myers. She's put together a detailed profile of what we know now. I expected her to meet us on scene this afternoon, but I haven't heard back from her." He scrolled through his calls and messages, double checking that he hadn't missed her call. "Damn. Excuse me for a minute while I put a call in to her to find out what's going on." Scarborough stepped out.

"So what do you think, Avery?" Gibbons asked. "You think he's gonna take this over?"

"Once his team arrives, my guess is they will. I don't know what more information we can provide. And, to be honest, I'm not sure we really want to be handling this one. The media's been all over it. Calls have already been flooding the front desk. I'd just as soon they get what they need here and move on."

"You know the guy, Katie. What's your take on it?" Gibbons asked.

She looked to Marshall. "I, for one, would like to know more about Shalot. We've got a connection to him. Me. Can you get me in to talk to him while he's still in custody?"

Katie expected push back from Marshall straight away. Instead, she watched as he seemed to be considering the proposition.

"I think it may be our best chance to determine what we're dealing with before Scarborough and his people take over," Marshall replied.

Did he just agree with her? That definitely came as a surprise. It felt good to have him on her side, instead of keeping her in the background. "Great." Katie looked to Detective Gibbons. "Let's not waste any more time."

"What do you think our FBI agent is gonna say about this?" Gibbons replied.

Katie made a move towards the door. "He'll support it. So long as he gets to listen in. Scarborough's a good man. He'll take whatever help is offered and, right now, Shalot is still in our custody, not the FBI's."

The two men followed her out, lagging behind a little. Gibbons grinned at Marshall, slapping his back.

"That's quite a woman you got there."

They caught up to Agent Scarborough and filled him in on the idea. Katie was right. He agreed without hesitation and they now stood outside the interrogation room.

Marshall placed his hand on the door knob, knowing Shalot waited on the other side. "Gibbons will be in there with you. So just keep your cool, ask him what we discussed, and if it starts to go south, he'll get you out of there. Got it?"

"Got it," Katie replied.

Although Shalot hadn't been officially charged with anything as of yet and was considered "a person of interest," it was still the first time Katie had been allowed to question a potential suspect.

Marshall opened the door for them and Katie thought, just for a moment, that he might be reconsidering his earlier hasty agreement.

"Katie." Shalot stood from his chair. "What are you doing here?" His eyes shifted between the two of them.

"Ms. Reid works for the department, in forensics, but since she knows you, she wanted to come and have a word and ask you a few things about Ms. Brown."

"Katie, I swear to you, I didn't kill Lindsay. You know me. I just went to her house to tell her I was sorry for the other night."

"No one's saying you killed her, Edward. These guys just need to be sure you don't have any other information pertaining to what happened to her." Katie sat down opposite Shalot while Gibbons stood behind him.

"You know Katie from a class at UCSD?" Gibbons asked.

"Yes." Edward returned his attention to Katie. "I knew you worked here, but I thought you were like a clerk or something."

"'Or something' pretty much sums up what I do here. I'm an evidence technician. But I've worked here for a while now and these guys have put a great deal of trust in me." She placed her forearms on the table, lacing her fingers. "You don't have to say anything, Edward. You haven't been charged with a crime and you have no lawyer present." Katie glanced at her watch. "And by this time tomorrow, you'll probably be home."

Gibbons' eyes sharpened as he appeared to focus on one of the cameras in the corner.

In the adjacent room, Marshall and Agent Scarborough sat in front of the monitors and picked up on Gibbons' concern.

Scarborough folded his arms and waited.

Marshall seemed to have the same sentiments. "She's good."

"That she is," Scarborough replied.

Katie gauged his reaction. She attempted to put him at ease, wanting to convince him that she was on his side and was no threat. It seemed her technique might have worked. "They need to find the person who killed Lindsay and they think you can help. Can you help us, Edward?"

Shalot's eyes softened and his face relaxed. "I don't know what more I can tell you that I haven't already told Detective Gibbons."

"You've always been very kind to me, Edward. I can't imagine a reason why Lindsay would have filed a restraining order against you. Is there anything you can tell us about that?"

He seemed to stiffen at this inquiry. "I don't know why she did that. Sure, we had a little argument last week, but no harm done. She went home and that was that. Then the sheriff's department shows up at my door, handing me a restraining order." Edward began to shift in his seat. "Look, I just went to her house this morning to see if I could clear things up with her. That's all." His sigh was audible. "You know what having this on my record will do to my career, Katie? I just had to convince her that I was sorry for the disagreement." His shoulders fell and his head dropped into his hands. "Christ. I didn't kill her, Katie." He closed his eyes for a moment. "You should have seen her body. Who the hell could do that?"

Katie looked to Gibbons, who seemed to be thinking the same thing. Was Edward Shalot just at the wrong place at the wrong time? There was still one question that Katie needed to ask.

"I don't know, Edward, but that's what we're trying to find out." She paused for a moment. "Can you tell me, did anyone else know you were dating Lindsay? Any of your friends or other classmates?"

"We'd only gone out a few times. I hadn't mentioned it to anyone that I can recall. Her roommate knew, of course." He seemed to turn a shade darker. "I know she was the one who told her to file that damn order against me." Edward looked straight into Katie's eyes now.

"You gotta help me, Katie. My career will be over before it has even started if my name isn't cleared. Just please get me out of here."

"I'll do what I can, Edward. I promise." Katie looked to Gibbons, signaling that she was finished. "Just hang in there, okay? This will all be over soon."

Gibbons held the door open and Katie did a final turn to Edward. "Thank you for talking to me, Edward. You've been a great help."

They walked into the monitoring room, leaving Shalot on his own.

Katie wasn't sure if she'd accomplished all that had been set out, but she felt as though the others would see what she had seen.

"That was very well executed, Kate. I don't think I could have done a better job," Marshall said.

"Yes. Very impressive, actually." Scarborough looked to the other detectives. "I don't know what you two think, but I don't think Shalot's our guy."

"No." Gibbons stared at the monitors and watched Edward. He was shifting, knocking his knees, and maybe even had a little sweat building on his forehead. It was clear the man was nervous and terrified. "He didn't do it. He'd have to be a complete idiot to kill her after a restraining order, then show up the next morning to call it in. But I still think he's holding something back from us. Did you see how he reacted at the mention of the roommate?" He cast his glance to the others once again. "Any chance we can get into his house before he's released?"

Marshall looked to Scarborough. "The guy had a restraining order filed against him from the victim. We had cause to bring him in. We're not going to need a warrant to get into his house with probable cause."

"You're right, but we need to act with extreme caution here. Get a judge to issue one anyway. I want to be sure our bases are covered. No charges have been filed against him yet. It might be a gray area, since he won't be present at the time of the search." He looked to Gibbons. "My team is here and I've got to meet them on scene in thirty minutes."

"Okay, boss," Marshall began. "Gibbons and I will handle the warrant. In the meantime, Kate, why don't you accompany Agent Scarborough, since you're already familiar with the scene. I'd still like to have a local presence there for the time being."

"I agree," Scarborough replied. "Would be glad to have you with us, Katie."

9

A RUNDOWN MOBILE home perched on top of rusted jacks was one of only a handful still remaining in the otherwise abandoned trailer park on the outskirts of town. The men inside, two millennials who were still wandering through life, assuming that the world had given them the shaft, sat on a stained floral couch amid a cloud of smoke.

"We gotta go soon if we're gonna do this tonight." Ty wrapped his lips around the joint again and inhaled deeply.

"Yeah, all right. You're not too fucked up, are you? Can't screw around with this shit, you know that." Marcus extinguished the joint, waving the smoke away from him. "Let's get the hell out of here, then."

There were no street lamps along the adjacent road and only a couple of windows were illuminated from the other derelict trailers. When they stepped outside, the air was still warm, hardly cooling at all from the heat of the day.

"Jesus, I don't remember it staying as warm as it has this late in the fall." Ty walked the few steps over to their car and inserted the key into the door lock. "You ready to do this?"

"I'm ready." Marcus yanked on the door, its hinges squeaking loudly enough for everyone in the park to hear. "Let's go."

◆◆◆

They'd been following her around for the past couple of days, learning her routine, deciding on which spot would be the best place to make it happen. They didn't know if the woman had a family, didn't know if she had kids, and didn't care either. She had been chosen and that was just her dumb luck.

"I see her; there." Ty pointed as the woman emerged from her office in the strip mall, locking up the small dental clinic where she worked as a hygienist. "Wait till she's closer to her car."

Marcus wiped his brow as sweat formed. He wasn't sure if it was from the heat or just nerves. He knew the deal. It had to be done. They had all agreed. But now that the moment was actually here, he was apprehensive; scared shitless, more like.

"We do it like we talked about, Marcus. I'll approach her from the front, then you come around the back."

Marcus nodded and they both stepped out of the car.

The woman turned her head at the screeching sound in the distance. It was the car door that caught her attention. Her eyes widened as she attempted to see what lay ahead in the darkness. She began to pick up her pace and was now only a few feet away from her car.

"Goddammit!" Ty whispered. "Now we gotta go after her."

The men began their approach and she spotted them emerging from the dark. They were just feet away from her. She dropped into an all-out run, trying to make it to her car.

"Go on. Take her from the right, I'll head straight," Marcus said. His adrenaline was pumping fast now, fueling his desire to catch the woman, all fear evaporating.

The woman screamed. But only for a moment.

◆◆◆

"She's gonna wake up, man. Come on; don't be a pussy." Ty secured the woman to the bed. It had already been lined with rubber sheets and plastic as had the walls and floor. There could be nothing left behind. That was the deal.

Marcus pulled the knife out of the drawer in the kitchen. They'd agreed that it had to be that one. He walked back into the bedroom where the woman lay comatose. Ty had hit her hard and she'd been out for almost five minutes. He would do it again if she stirred. "I got it."

"Good. You know what to do." Ty stepped aside. "It's gotta be like the others. We need to show all those fuckers out there that they're living a lie. Religion, politics; none of that shit matters. We're part of the Five. They'll see what chaos really is."

He leaned over the woman. Bruises were already forming on her face and arms, and even on her thighs where Ty had gotten too rough. "The Five is all that matters." Marcus closed his eyes and upon opening them again, began to press the knife into her chest, just below her breast. As soon as the knife pierced her skin, she woke up and began to scream. Ty did exactly as he was supposed to so Marcus could continue.

Marcus sliced open her pale skin, down to her navel and up the other side. Blood spilled out over her chest and stomach, pooling onto the plastic sheet beneath her, eventually dripping onto the floor. She would not awaken this time. The pain would have been too much for her body to take.

When he was done, the grotesque symbol was complete. Now, they had to wait. Wait for her to lose enough blood and eventually die. Then, Marcus and Ty would make the early morning drive up the I-10 and place her as carefully as the others had been.

No telling how long it would take before she would be discovered, but they'd call it in themselves if it took more than a few days. The body wouldn't last long in this heat. The animals would have a field day and they would need to be sure their masterpiece wasn't destroyed.

◆◆◆

It seemed that getting the warrant was presenting itself to be a greater challenge than the two detectives believed it would. The hour had grown late and it was questionable as to whether the judge would even get off his couch to fulfill the request. But in the end, they had convinced him of the urgency of this situation as media attention had grown considerably and the sooner they could rule out Shalot as the Highway Hunter, the better—for everyone.

Edward Shalot's apartment building was tucked away in an older, less desirable neighborhood about twenty minutes from the college campus. Marshall and Detective Gibbons drove up along the street side of the building. Only a few of the windows were still illuminated at the late hour.

"Let's see what we can find." Marshall stepped out of the vehicle.

They walked along the concrete path towards the arched opening. The old Spanish architecture had begun to crumble with age and lack of proper maintenance. Inside the opening was a courtyard dotted with a few benches and the centerpiece was a pool.

Marshall and Gibbons stood in the middle of the courtyard in search of apartment 2741.

"Over there." Gibbons pointed to the second floor in the right corner of the complex.

The pathway was sparsely lit and, in fact, the moonlight offered better illumination as they made their way up the stairs to the second floor.

"Don't suppose you've got an old credit card handy?" Marshall asked. "Otherwise, we're gonna be busting out a window."

Gibbons pulled out his wallet and retrieved a misshapen card that had obviously seen its share of locks. "As a matter of fact, I do." He finagled the card in between the lock and the door jamb, working to open it.

Marshall scanned the area, ensuring no one was watching. A moment later, he heard the click of the lock.

"We're in." Gibbons pushed the door open, exposing a darkened room. He felt along the wall for a switch, finding it near the front window that he was grateful had been spared.

The room lit up, revealing a sparsely decorated space, leaving no doubt that a single man lived there.

"I'll go back to the bedroom," Gibbons said. He began walking through the hall towards the single bedroom and, once inside, he spotted the files spread along the small desk in the corner. Gibbons approached the desk and began pushing around the files. Immediately, his stomach dropped. It was then he realized what they were dealing with.

"Avery, I think you should come in here." Gibbons opened one of the files.

"What'd you find?" Marshall entered and headed towards him. He felt his heart sink at the sight of the pictures of Kate. It was then that he realized he might have misjudged Shalot, now believing that the man might just be after her. "What the hell is this?"

Gibbons expression was veiled in regret at the unsettling discovery. "This guy might not have killed Lindsay Brown, but I think we have another problem." Gibbons pointed to the file header. "This looks like it came from the university."

Marshall began reading the contents of the file. "Christ, these are her school records. Schedule, grades, former addresses. We need to figure out how he got his hands on these files."

"Look, man, you better let me talk to him. This may be the way keep him in custody a while longer until we get forensics back."

That old feeling began to resurface. The unsettling one that suggested Kate was in danger once again. His head began to spin at the possibility that he could have missed something so obvious.

Gibbons must have picked up on his thoughts. He placed his hand on Marshall's shoulder. "Why don't you go and have a look in the kitchen for anything else. I'll gather these files and bring them out."

◆◆◆

Katie lingered in the conference room at the station along with Agent Scarborough and his team. The hour was nearing dawn and she began to wonder why Marshall and Detective Gibbons had not returned.

Scarborough was listening to his senior agent discuss the profile of the killer they were looking for. "Have you determined the significance of the dandelions?"

Agent Myers had worked for the FBI for more than eight years, only last year becoming one of the senior agents at Quantico. During that time, she had compiled many different profiles, but she had never come across something or someone of this nature. "I consulted with a few botanists and they have determined some significance to that particular flower. First of all, it is extremely hardy and can survive in any area. Some of the more symbolic meanings are that the flower or weed symbolizes faithfulness, fertility, and abundance."

"So we are dealing with someone who believes in the nature of faithfulness and fertility." Agent Scarborough turned to Katie, seemingly wanting her input.

Katie immediately thought of her recent loss, but pushed it away just as quickly. "And yet this person who believes in faithfulness is taking lives?"

"Maybe, but there's also another meaning." The agent typed on the laptop and pulled up a poem that flashed on the screen. "My contact pointed me to this poem about the flower. Take a look at the final two lines."

And when I'm gone, please don't show sorrow.
I'll be back again tomorrow.

"'I'll be back again tomorrow,'" Agent Scarborough repeated. "This seems a little more relevant."

The idea struck Katie hard. This was not about faithfulness or fertility. This was about the nature of the flower's ability to come back. Over and over. Never to be eradicated. As she looked to Scarborough, it seemed he was thinking the same thing.

This, however, did not explain whether or not Shalot killed Lindsay Brown. "Agent Myers, do you believe the man we have in custody could have killed your victim in Colorado, then traveled here to take the life of Ms. Brown?" Katie asked.

The team had spent several hours at Ms. Brown's home after reviewing the items Katie had already collected and entered into the database.

"Anything is possible, Ms. Reid; however, this does seem an unlikely scenario." She looked to Nick. "Agent Scarborough, after interviewing the ME, what are your thoughts?"

"I don't believe Shalot is our guy. Someone found out about the flower and the carving. Someone who had a connection to one of the previous cases and got the details. Lindsay Brown was different, though, so it was someone who didn't know everything."

"Unless Detectives Avery and Gibbons turn up something in Shalot's apartment, I don't see as we have much choice but to let him go. The killer's still out there and we may now have a copycat out there as well."

Scarborough noticed the time. "It's late. We all could use some rest. Why don't we stop for tonight and get in a few hours? We'll plan on meeting back here at seven?"

Katie waited for the room to clear before approaching Nick. "They're all wondering what the hell I'm doing here, Nick."

"Look, you were on scene, collecting evidence. No one should question your involvement. At least not until this is officially declared an FBI matter. Your Captain Hearn doesn't have a problem with you being here and neither should my team. Besides, no one else here has a personal relationship with Edward Shalot. That alone gives you the right to be here."

"I wouldn't call it a personal relationship." Katie felt slightly embarrassed by the term. As if she had known the guy all her life.

"You know what I mean," Scarborough continued. "You should go home. Get some rest."

"I haven't heard from Marshall, have you?" she asked.

At that moment, Gibbons and Marshall appeared in the doorway of the conference room.

"Did we miss out?" Gibbons asked.

"My guys needed some rest and I sent everyone back to the hotel. We're meeting up again at seven. What did you find?" Scarborough asked.

Katie recognized the look on Marshall's face. She'd seen it before. It was the same look he'd given her at the hotel back in Rio Dell. The look that meant she was about to be shut out because he was afraid for her.

Gibbons tossed the files onto the conference room table.

Katie's mouth dropped at the sight of her name on several of the papers. "What the hell are these?" she asked, leaning in to get a better look.

"We found these in Shalot's bedroom. We don't have a clue as to how he got his hands on them."

"These are my school records. Every class, every grade I've received. The professor's notes. My God, everything is here. Why?"

"We need to charge him with something, fast," Marshall began. "The warrant only allowed us to search his apartment in connection with the Lindsay Brown murder. We found nothing of hers at his place. Nothing that would suggest he was involved in her death. We've already got her computer and the computer lab is searching that and her phone records. So far, they haven't turned anything up as it relates to Shalot. It appears as though he didn't harass her, or send her messages other than relating to their dates."

"And yet she filed a restraining order?" Scarborough said.

"Yes. According to the order, he had threatened her on their final date a few days ago," Gibbons replied.

"Look, if I could just talk to him again; ask him why he had my records," Katie began.

"Hell no," Marshall said. "Are you kidding me? A woman he dated is dead and we find a bunch of files having to do with you in his apartment? No. Absolutely not."

Katie reddened with embarrassment. She felt as though she'd just been scolded by her father. It seemed the others had taken notice as well. Scarborough quickly looked down at the files again, appearing to pretend he hadn't heard the reprimand.

"If we can't bring charges against Shalot, he's going to be going home in a few hours," Gibbons said. "I'll talk to him. I think it's a good idea if you three observe in the back room." Gibbons turned to Marshall. "I don't want you in there, understand?"

Marshall tossed a reluctant nod in his direction. He wasn't happy about any of this.

◆◆◆

One of the officers brought Shalot into the interrogation room. The man appeared exhausted as if he'd just been awakened, which he likely had, given that it was almost four in the morning. His hair was disheveled and his clothes were wrinkled.

The officer began to shackle him to the hooks embedded in the concrete floor, but Gibbons waved him off. "We won't be needing that, will we, Mr. Shalot?"

"No, sir," Edward replied.

Gibbons sat down in the chair opposite and nodded to the officer to take leave. He turned his attention back to Shalot. "We found some very interesting items back at your apartment, Mr. Shalot."

Edward's expression hardened. "How the hell..."

Gibbons didn't bother letting him finish. "How did you come by the files of our Ms. Katie Reid? Why would you have possession of her school records, Mr. Shalot?"

"I thought I was here because of Lindsay Brown? You people think that I killed her, isn't that right?"

"The FBI is here to determine that, Eddie. But right now, I'm very curious as to what your interest is in Ms. Reid. Care to enlighten me?"

"Look. I know my rights. I don't have to say anything to you. Are you gonna charge me with something? 'Cause if not, then I have a right to leave."

Katie, Marshall, and Nick stood behind the desk in the observation room, staring at the monitors.

"I don't like where this is going," Marshall said.

"No, neither do I," Scarborough replied.

Katie didn't know exactly what they were suggesting, but she was getting the sense that the law was not on their side this time. It was a frightening revelation to hear that Edward had somehow obtained her school records, but she hadn't a clue as to why. The man hardly said but a few words to her.

What interest was she to him? More importantly, why was he becoming increasingly defensive at Gibbons' questions?

The detective cast a subtle glance at the camera in the corner of the room, behind Shalot. It seemed he had honed in on Marshall's and Nick's concern. "You realize the prosecutor has forty-eight hours to bring charges and we can hold you for the duration. At last check," Gibbons turned his wrist to check the time, "it's hardly been twenty-four."

"Look. You know I didn't kill Lindsay. Why the hell would I have stuck around and called 911?" Edward leaned against the table. "I didn't kill her, goddammit. So what? Now you think I'm gonna go after Katie Reid?"

"Why the hell did you have her school records in your goddam bedroom, Eddie?"

Edward closed his eyes. "I want a lawyer."

And that was it. Gibbons' could ask the man as many questions as he wanted without charges, but as soon as he uttered those words, the game was changed. Now, Shalot could get a court-appointed lawyer.

Gibbons began to rise. "That's your right, Eddie." He started to walk out of the room.

"It's Edward!" Shalot rose up.

"Calm yourself there, Eddie. You're starting to act like you got something to hide." Gibbons opened the door, but before leaving, ensured he got in one last jab. "You picked the wrong girl to stalk, my friend."

Edward turned his face upwards and looked into the camera. "Katie, if you're listening, I swear to you, I didn't kill Lindsay. Please, you have to believe me."

He was quickly interrupted by the same officer who brought him in. "Come on. You're done here." The officer grabbed Shalot by the arm and twisted it behind his back.

"Please, just let me explain, Katie. Please talk to me."

Katie watched as Edward was escorted out of the room. She turned to Marshall. "The only way we're going to get any answers is if you let me talk to him. You know that as well as I do."

Marshall shot a glance to Scarborough. He looked as though he was in agreement with her.

"You can't protect me all the time, Marshall. You have to let me do my job." Katie was pleading now. It was as if this past year hadn't even happened. All of the gains she'd made in her career. All of the nights spent working through what had happened with Hendrickson. All of it seemed to have been erased by Shalot's words.

"When do you expect the labs to come back?" Marshall asked Scarborough.

"We should know something later today, or this evening. We may not have everything, but I think we'll have enough to know whether or not we can charge Shalot with anything. Relating to Brown anyway. This other issue, well, it's opened up a whole new can of worms. The problem is, I still have a serial killer out there."

"You're convinced it isn't Shalot?" Katie asked.

"Everything in my gut says he didn't kill Brown. I've got three other victims miles from each other. Shalot couldn't have killed all of them. For one thing, he was in class with you the night that my victim in Kentucky was killed. And as for the woman in Colorado, seems our Mr. Shalot was on a date with the now deceased Ms. Brown."

Scarborough paused for a moment. "The more likely conclusion? Someone got wind of the details and decided to make it look like the Highway Hunter killed Lindsay Brown, maybe even going so far as to frame Shalot for it. We need to find out who. The only way may be for Katie to have a chat with our friend, Eddie. It's gotta be someone he knows or who knows of him. Someone who knew he was dating Brown. Someone who has access to police records or knows who does. Avery, we don't have much choice. I can't have a copycat out there and, if we have an in, then we need to use it."

Katie looked to Marshall once again. It seemed he would resign to the fact that she needed to do this.

"Okay. Let's get her to talk to him again."

10

THE LACK OF sleep from which Katie now suffered could have easily been blamed on the morning light that was forcing its way beneath the drawn shades of their bedroom window. Instead, it was the idea that burrowed its way into her mind. The idea that Edward Shalot was at best a stalker and, at worst, a killer and she had had no idea.

Any sense of privacy Katie might have had prior to Hendrickson had all but vanished as a result of the high-profile case. She'd become a reluctant celebrity and with her newfound status came the admiration of people whom she'd never met. Even now, more than a year later, some people still recognized her and stopped her on the street; coming out of a store or a post office, it didn't matter. Men and women alike approached her, took hold of her arm or her shoulder, telling her how brave she was, that she was a hero. Katie never felt like a hero.

For all the accolades and admirers, there were those who took it a step too far. After she'd returned home from Rio Dell, after Hendrickson's death, she had received letters at the station, sometimes emails, if the people got hold of her email address, which wasn't that difficult, considering the standard format the department had for email addresses. That, however, changed quickly at Marshall's insistence and the ones that posed a threat were filed and the people tracked down by their IP addresses.

It was all so unexpected and frightening. She often had to remind herself, *This will all die down, don't worry about it.*

And it did, mostly. Until now.

His body shifted and a guttural moan escaped him. Marshall was awake.

"You okay?" he asked as his eyes squinted, appearing to focus in on her shadowed face.

"Can't sleep. Did I wake you?"

"No. I've been drifting in and out mostly. What time is it?" He raised his head slightly to catch sight of the clock on the bedside table, then quickly dropped back down. "Guess we'd better get up now anyway." Marshall sat up, tossing his legs over the edge of the bed. "You don't have to do this, you know. Everything doesn't rest on your shoulders, Kate."

"I know that, but we both know that there have been people out there, since the incident, who've been drawn to me. If Shalot is one of them, then I should be the one to get what I can from him."

He looked over his shoulder towards her curved frame, which was still beneath the covers. "I'm sorry for what I said yesterday; earlier this morning, that is. I just worry about you. I know you're completely capable of handling yourself and I'm sorry if I treat you otherwise." He turned back. "I love you and I'm scared to death of losing you."

Katie reached across the bed, resting her hand against his back. "You're not going to lose me, Marshall, and no one is going to hurt me again. Hendrickson is gone and I don't think for one minute that Edward Shalot has any intention of harming me. *That was a lie.* I think he, like some of the others, are just fascinated; nothing more. Besides, I've got the entire department at my back, not to mention a few good FBI agents. I just need to feel useful. You know that."

"You're right. I'll go hop in the shower." Marshall pushed up from the bed. "Care to join me?" He smiled.

"Well, I think that's the best idea I've heard all week." Katie soon followed.

◆◆◆

The substantial glass doors of the police station reflected the sun's early morning rays into Katie's eyes as she approached. She waited for Marshall to catch up and looked out onto the street, noticing how quiet it was. It had finally occurred to her that it was Saturday morning and that was the reason for the empty roads. The days were slipping by almost completely unnoticed.

This morning was the first time she hadn't felt nauseated. The doctor said it would take a while, but it too would pass. Maybe it was because she'd had other pressing matters that required her attention, but she was grateful to be through the worst of it now.

The conference room where they were to meet with Scarborough appeared more chaotic than the rest of the station. Scarborough had set up three separate workstations, tied into the department's AV system and displayed a map on the wall-mounted screen of the Highway Hunter's crime scene locations.

"Did you get any sleep, Nick?" Katie asked, marveling in all that had been accomplished in such a short period of time.

"Not exactly. Got back to the hotel, then got a call from the Virginia office. They've been able to further analyze the video from the gas station where the Richmond victim was last seen. I'd spotted someone taking cover in the trees adjacent to the facility and asked that they work to identify the individual. Unfortunately, the cameras were fixed and only took intermittent shots in various locations. Not a very high-tech system, but it was better than nothing. We can only assume that person made his way into the victim's minivan while she was paying for fuel inside. They've come up with a few possibilities. I'm going over them now."

Katie set her coffee down and moved towards Scarborough, who was studying the images on his laptop. "So, you're trying to get an ID?"

"Yeah. I came back down here about an hour ago and recruited some of your people to help me get set up. When can you get in to talk to Shalot again?"

Katie looked to Marshall. "We need to know if his lawyer has arrived yet, right?"

"Let me get with Gibbons and find out." Marshall quickly made his way back out into the hall.

"You sure you're ready for this, Katie?"

She pulled out a chair and sat down next to Scarborough. "I think this will be the only way to get answers out of Shalot. I know we tried before, but we didn't know what he had then."

"You mean anything and everything pertaining to you?" Scarborough appeared almost as troubled by that fact as Marshall had.

"Yeah. Although if his lawyer is present, I don't know how much he'll say. We really need to get forensics back."

"I've already got a call into the ME." Scarborough continued analyzing the data on the screen. "What I find interesting is the geographic locations of his victims." He proceeded to walk towards the TV monitor and began tracing with his finger the locations of the victims as marked by large red circles. They had all been discovered in remote locations – all small towns, and what emerged was a pattern that related to the highways. "Why is he choosing these particular areas? The chances these victims would never be found seems fairly high. Travel along these roadways is sparse at best."

The exception to this was Lindsay Brown.

Marshall appeared in the doorway, pressing against the wall as he leaned in. "His lawyer has arrived; we can go ahead and see him now. Let's go." He tossed a nod in Katie's direction.

Katie and Nick followed a few steps behind Marshall and she considered the questions she would be asking Shalot. The first question that came to mind was how he got his hands on her files in the first place.

"I'll be in the observation room with Agent Scarborough," Marshall said. "You need anything, just look into the camera and nod."

Katie tilted her head forward in acknowledgment as the officer opened the door and allowed her into to the interrogation room.

At her entry, the pleading look from Edward's face softened Katie's demeanor. No one seemed to believe he killed Lindsay Brown; it was appearing too much like he'd been set up. But the question remained: what was he after?

"Good morning." Shalot's lawyer rose from his chair, extending a hand to Katie. "I'm Nathan Bender and I've been assigned to represent Mr. Shalot."

"Katie Reid. I'm an evidence technician here at the department and I have a relationship with Mr. Shalot. We both attend UCSD." Katie pulled out her chair, sitting down in a more hesitant manner than she'd wanted to come across.

"I understand charges have not yet been filed against Mr. Shalot as it relates to the death of Lindsay Brown," Bender began. "Can you tell me why my client is still in custody? And where is the arresting officer?"

"Detective Gibbons has already spoken to Mr. Shalot. In fact, it was Mr. Shalot who asked to speak with me. From what I understand, Edward has obtained some personal information as it pertains to my student records. Detective Gibbons and Avery searched your client's apartment as allowed by warrant and discovered files that should not have been in his possession." Katie looked to Edward, surprised that he had appeared ashamed by her revelation.

"I'm sorry, Katie. I just wanted to get to know you better; that's all. I tried to talk to you after class a few times, but you never seemed to have time for me."

Bender raised his hand to pre-empt his client from further elaborating. "Mr. Shalot, you are not required to answer any questions. We are here only to ascertain if the prosecutor will be filing charges against you. As per California law, they can only keep you in custody for forty-eight hours without charges. I believe we have now advanced beyond the twenty-four-hour mark." He returned his attention to Katie. "Ms. Reid, as you are not the arresting officer, nor are you an officer of any kind, I think it best if your superiors take over this interview."

Gibbons had entered the small monitoring room. "How's it going in there?" he asked Marshall.

"Not well. That damn public defender won't allow Shalot to answer Kate's questions. Now he wants her out of the room, insisting only the arresting officer continue with the inquiry."

"Goddamn lawyers." Scarborough knew the drill, but still disliked it.

"That's what he wants? Then that's what he'll get."

Gibbons immediately proceeded to the adjacent room. "I'm Detective Gibbons. You know, we were trying to keep this civil, let Mr. Shalot explain why and how he had possession of personal files of a member of our staff. Considering he knows Ms. Reid, we thought he might better explain himself, but I can see that won't be possible now." Gibbons turned to Katie. "Ms. Reid, if you'd like to get back to your work, I'll take it from here. I appreciate your help."

Edward quickly stood. "Wait!"

"Mr. Shalot, sit down please," Bender said.

"Katie, I'm sorry. I really am. I just wanted to get to know you. I know what you've been through and I thought maybe I could be a shoulder to lean on."

Marshall zeroed in on the monitor. His pulse began to rise as Shalot continued to speak.

Katie's brow furrowed as she listened to Edward insist that he knew her on some personal level. "What is it that you think you know about me, Edward? What you read in the papers? What you saw on TV?" She shook her head and smiled. "That person is not real. The person standing in front of you now; this is me. I'm a real person, with real feelings."

Katie stood there for a moment longer, wondering how she could use this situation to her advantage. There had to be a way to make Shalot talk. She wanted to appeal to him personally. Katie glanced into the camera, then turned her head towards Gibbons.

He seemed to know what she was going to do and wasn't about to stop her.

Katie sat back down in her chair. She placed her arms on the desk, folding them carefully. She looked at the attorney, who seemed to be waiting for her to continue, and then back to Shalot. "Edward, we could have been friends. You didn't need to go behind my back and violate me in that manner. Can you tell me, how did you get my school records?"

Edward cast his eyes down and was silent for a moment, then continued, "I got them from someone who works in student records. The kid had a penchant for gambling and needed some money. In return for payment, he pulled your file for me. I thought that if I learned more about you, you might think of me as more than just a friend."

Marshall gripped the edge of the desk, which caused the monitors to shake a little. Heat had begun to rise beneath his collared shirt.

"You gotta cool down, man. I know what you're thinking, but let her do this," Scarborough said.

Katie's face softened. "You understand that I am not available?" Katie inhaled a deep breath, pondering her next question. She needed to point the conversation into a different direction. Get him to answer the real question and that was how he got the files. "Edward, this friend of yours in records, what's his name?"

For the first time, Edward looked to his attorney for guidance. Of course, anything that might point the light of accusation to another would only serve to help his client, so Bender nodded in reply. "Just some kid I know: Shaun Hudson."

Edward looked directly in Katie's eyes. "I thought you might see that I could make you happy. We're so much alike. If only you'd have let me show you. I could have protected you too, you know; make sure no one would ever hurt you again."

That was enough for Marshall. He yanked open the door and headed immediately into the interrogation room before Nick could stop him. Marshall held the door handle, his hand trembling with anger, then remembered what he'd said to her just this morning. She needed to do this on her own.

The chair screeched beneath Katie as she pushed up from the table. "I don't need anyone's protection, least of all yours." She opened the door to the sight of Marshall. "Jesus, you scared me."

"You all right?"

"Yeah. I'm fine. I guess we need to talk to Shaun Hudson." Katie began walking along the corridor.

Marshall quickly caught up to her. "Hey."

She stopped and turned to him.

"You did great in there, Kate. I mean it. I would have lost it on the guy. I'm really proud of you."

She eased a little at the comment. "Thanks. I don't think it went as I was expecting, but at least we have a name. Now, we just need to get something back from the medical examiner; prove one way or another what we've got on our hands here."

◆◆◆

Bender had kept a short leash on his client and Detective Gibbons had gotten no further than Katie had. It was approaching midday now and Scarborough's team continued their work on the other cases and remained in the conference room, waiting for something, anything from forensics.

Documenting the final pieces of evidence from Lindsay Brown's apartment was the first priority for Katie. The crime scene photos were always the hardest to catalog. It was the first time she'd seen the body of the woman, as it had been covered prior to her arrival on scene. Katie looked at the monitor, the image so vivid, and it was the dandelion that caught her attention amid the lacerations Lindsay had suffered. It had been placed with extreme care inside the victim's laced fingers.

Katie studied the flowers; only some of the white fluff remained attached to the stems while one still flowered with yellow pedals. She began to think of the poem. *"I'll be back again tomorrow."*

A dandelion was essentially a weed that could grow anywhere, its seed carried by the winds when the flower turned to white fluff. Countless children have yanked them from the ground, made wishes, and blown them away, scattering the fluff into a million different directions, chaotic in nature.

"I'll be back again tomorrow," Katie whispered. She carefully studied Lindsay's face. She had suffered blows to her cheek, lips, and right eye. Her hair had been yanked out in places. Lindsay had tried to fight back; defend herself from her attacker, as evidenced by the cuts on her forearms. The knife that had been used to carve her skin left marks on them.

The events of Katie's past were so deeply ingrained in her identity now that it was impossible not to think of what Lindsay Brown would have done to defend herself. Was it possible to believe Edward had done those things? Would he have done them to Katie as well, given the chance?

Katie turned away just for a moment, searching for meaning. "The flower is a weed, spreading its seeds, giving life to new ones." She dropped her voice, hoping no one was listening as she rambled away, trying to make sense of the thought that was beginning to form. "I'll be back again tomorrow." And then it came to her. They were not dealing with just one killer and it didn't seem possible to her that this could have been the work of a copycat. She didn't know how many, but it was the flower that convinced her. "If one was caught,   others   would   be   back   tomorrow."

11

KATIE HURRIED TO the conference room, where Scarborough was just ending a call on his cell phone.

"That was the ME. She's got the labs back," Scarborough said, spotting Katie as she entered. He turned to his team. "Myers, come with me. We need to know what she's got."

"This wasn't Shalot, Nick." Katie blocked the door. "I know we've already assumed that to a degree, but I also don't think this was a copycat killing. A copycat just couldn't have known the level of detail of the other murders. Look, I think we're dealing with more than one suspect and I think they're working together."

Nick appeared impatient, folding his arms as he waited for more on her theory.

"It's the flower. The poem. That's what gave me the idea." Katie looked to Agent Myers. "This isn't about faithfulness, this is about a weed. A weed that spreads its seeds, creating new ones." She returned her attention to Nick. "I'd like to come with you to the examiner's office. Please, Nick. I know that we're not dealing with a single killer."

"We have tossed the idea around, in abstract terms," Agent Myers began. "The logistics of the killer arriving here from Colorado in that time frame and finding Brown, it's just not plausible. I know you and Ms. Reid have history." She looked to Katie. "Let her come with us. Hell, it can't hurt."

As the three prepared to leave, Marshall and Detective Gibbons arrived. "Gibbons just got DNA back from Lindsay's apartment from our lab. There were no hits in the database.

We need to get Shalot to give us a sample for cross-reference," Marshall said.

"I just got a call from Dr. Napier. She's got lab results for us too. Let's get down there. See what we're dealing with and if we're going to have to let Shalot go," Scarborough replied. "Katie's coming with us."

Marshall didn't object, but his expression turned to that of someone who'd begun to see the writing on the wall. It was in his eyes and Katie could feel it when he acknowledged the idea, nodding reluctantly. She sensed that Marshall thought she was slipping away.

◆◆◆

"We're here to see Dr. Napier. Agent Scarborough, FBI." He again showed the woman at the front desk his badge.

She pressed a button on her headset. "Dr. Napier, I have Agent Scarborough with the FBI here." She paused for a moment. "Thank you." The woman looked at the others and then to Scarborough again. "Go on down; she's waiting for you."

Dr. Napier buzzed them inside. "Welcome. I see you brought some people with you?"

"Yes," Nick proceeded. "You remember Detective Gibbons, this is Detective Avery, Katie Reid, also with PD, and this is Agent Myers. She's been working on a profile of our suspect."

"Please, come in." Dr. Napier walked to one of the autopsy stations and retrieved her tablet. The victim's body remained under cover of a heavy white sheet.

Katie had been through this before. She began to recall the moment she saw Sam's body laid across the cold metal table. She recalled the precise locations of the stab wounds, the contusions on her face and body. Everything came back in such detail, she nearly reeled back as the doctor lowered the sheet that covered Lindsay Brown.

"I've determined the cause of death to be asphyxiation. We found high levels of carbon dioxide in the victim's blood." She pointed to Lindsay's eyes. "Of course, the bloodshot eyes is a telltale sign as well. Finally, we found trace elements of plastic in the lungs. It appears she either tried to pull away at the bag or plastic sheeting that had been placed over her face and inhaled small pieces of it, or there were loose fragments that she'd inhaled."

"What about any DNA under her nails, any fibers? Anything that we can use to find out who did this to her?" Katie asked, a little surprised by her own questions. It seemed she'd picked up on a fair bit working in Evidence.

"I was just about to get to that," Dr. Napier replied. "First, let me just say that the carving on the victim's body happened post-mortem. The instrument was dull and had a small blade, like an old pocket knife."

"Not nearly the precision of the previous victim in Virginia," Scarborough interjected. "According to the ME there, she bled to death from the wound and the suspect used an extremely sharp implement. Possibly even a scalpel. I haven't received confirmation yet on the body in Kentucky, but it appears she had suffered the same, bleeding out from the wound. Both victims were essentially drained of all blood and had been moved later. That at least partially explains the lack of blood on scene."

These victims were in stark contrast to that of Lindsay as well, Katie thought. Those women had families and were quite a bit older. Her theory didn't seem so far out in left field right now.

The doctor returned to her tablet and began typing, appearing to open up a file. "We did get something back from the lab that you might find of interest. Foreign DNA was found in the victim's mouth. It appears she may have bitten down on her attacker."

Scarborough turned to Avery and Gibbons. "We need to cross reference this sample with what you were able to pull from the scene and get Shalot to submit to that swab test. Dr. Napier, could you please email your results to me and Agent Myers? We need to get back to the station quickly. We have someone in custody and before he's due to be released, we need to know if these samples match."

"Of course."

♦♦♦

The CSI lab back at the station was overcrowded with FBI agents, detectives, and the technicians, all working to get the results before the forty-eight-hour mark when they would be forced to release Shalot.

Katie was leaning more and more on the theory that Edward wasn't the culprit. It seemed Agent Myers was on her side as well. They would need to convince the others and cross-referencing the DNA from Lindsay's apartment with the sample from the medical examiner would prove it one way or the other. Shalot had willingly submitted to a swab test, which was another reason to believe he wasn't Lindsay's killer.

Dr. Harris, the man in charge, didn't like his team being put under such pressure. People under pressure made mistakes. And in his line of work, mistakes meant someone guilty could go free or someone innocent could go to jail; neither scenario worked for him and so he hovered protectively over his team. "I'd prefer if you let us do our work, Agent Scarborough. I can assure you that you will be the first to know when we get our results."

Katie approached Marshall, who stood only steps from Agent Scarborough. Both loitered as if it would make a difference. "I'm not going to be of any use here. I'll head back to my desk and get to work. See you later?"

Marshall seemed surprised by her sudden departure. "Kate, what's going on? You wanted to be in on this and now you're just going to leave?"

"I just think we're wasting time in here. Shalot isn't the guy. We know it. The FBI knows it. So, I can't just sit here waiting for the labs to come back, telling us what we already know."

Marshall held her gaze for a moment, appearing to try to read her intentions. "I know that look in your eyes, Kate. We got half a dozen people that want the same thing as you do. Don't go off thinking you need to run on some idea all alone. Last I checked, we were partners."

"We are. I understand that. I just need to get back to work."

She'd been too harsh. It wasn't intentional, but as she made her way back to her desk, it occurred to her that he might perceive it as such.

It was the nagging feeling that set her off, as if she and everyone else were missing something. Katie began to wonder why it was that Marc Aguilar contacted her only days before Lindsay Brown turned up dead. It was as if he knew what was coming. The timing couldn't be coincidental.

The story was already headlining on every news station. The reporters offered conjecture as to whether or not the authorities were dealing with the Highway Hunter and working to keep it quiet. They would take every advantage to sensationalize the story.

Aguilar had seen it coming, though. What had he known that she or the authorities hadn't? Maybe it was time to meet up with her old friend.

◆◆◆

There he was, Marc Aguilar, Channel 9 News, sitting at the restaurant booth and scrolling through his phone. Katie spotted the perfectly coiffed hair and tanned skin immediately. She respected Marc for what he'd done for her when she felt as though there was no one else in whom to confide. He'd come through for her on occasion since Hendrickson too. They'd become good friends, but he was still a reporter and reporters were always looking for a scoop on a good story.

He noticed her on approach and flashed his bright white smile, which stood out even more against his bronzed cheeks. "Katie." He greeted her with a peck on the cheek. "It's been too long. Please, sit down."

"Thanks for taking the time to see me, Marc."

His expression quickly turned serious. "I understand you know the man they have in custody for the murder of Lindsay Brown?"

"He's just a person of interest right now. Nothing more. But yes, I am acquainted with him." Katie grew suspicious that he had obtained this as of yet undisclosed information.

Marc took a sip of his iced tea. "I can't imagine that makes Detective Avery very happy."

His inference had not gone unnoticed. "No. Not very happy."

"I've done some digging into this Edward Shalot's background," Marc began. "Don't look at me like that. You know when I've got a feeling about something that I'm not going to just let it go."

"The FBI and the San Diego police are looking into Shalot's background. Marc, this is already a very difficult situation." Katie had made her point, but she knew it would not deter him. The same as it would not have deterred her.

"I understand, but I think you might change your mind once you see this." Marc slid a manila folder across the table.

Katie flashed her eyes between him and the folder for a moment, then decided to take a look. This wasn't expected. In fact, her question had as of yet remained unasked.

Upon opening the file, her lips pursed until they turned white. "Oh my God." She looked to Marc. "What the hell is this and how did you get it?"

"It seems your acquaintance might not have been completely honest with you or the authorities."

Inside were photographs of Edward Shalot, capturing him hanging around various places of ill repute, mostly from security cameras around the locations. In and of themselves, these were not that disconcerting. What was, however, were the print-outs of several blogs, Facebook, and Twitter posts about him. It seemed he had a reputation for frequenting strip clubs and venues that catered to alternate lifestyles. But as Katie began to read some of the posts, she grew even more troubled.

Most of the blogs and posts were complaints by women. Some were exotic dancers, some were women who had also frequented what appeared to be something akin to swingers clubs, but all seemed to validate the same thing: that Edward Shalot had posted unauthorized pictures of these women and that when some had confronted him, had found themselves on the receiving end of his rather nasty temper.

Of course, none of them reported these assaults. At least, according to the posts. They were either too afraid of losing their jobs or of their personal lives being exposed. So, they chose to spread the word about him online. Even going so far as to post pictures of him so people would know what he looked like.

"First of all," Katie began, "how did you even know that we had Shalot in custody? His name hasn't been released to the public. Hell, we haven't even charged the guy with anything. Secondly, when you called me the other morning, you already knew something about this Highway Hunter, didn't you? Something more than what the FBI told the media.

Why else would you have asked me to talk to Scarborough? How did you get this information, Marc? Look, it's me. You gotta tell me what you know."

The fact that Marc hadn't been straightforward with her up until now was more than a little upsetting, but she supposed if he had a contact who was feeding him information, that person would fall under a protected source. It didn't seem to matter that lives could be at stake.

"Did you know that Shalot had stolen my school records? Had my address, phone numbers, my class schedule; everything that someone would need to keep tabs on me."

Marc leaned back in surprise. "Katie, I'm sorry, I had no idea. Look, these posts weren't exactly hidden. Anyone who knows how to use Google would be able to find them with little effort. Frankly, I'm surprised no one else came across them."

"Who are you talking to, Marc? Come on. You didn't just come across this stuff. You didn't just call me at five in the morning on a hunch. Who's your source? Someone who's trying very hard to convince everyone that Edward Shalot is the Highway Hunter is playing you. And whoever this person is knows far too many details about the investigation. Jesus, Marc, we're dealing with a killer here."

"Katie, I—I can't..."

"Are you kidding me? Your source deserves more protection than I do? What the hell, Marc?" Katie banged her knee on the table as she stood up in anger. "Don't ever ask me for a damn thing again. You hear me?"

"Wait!" Marc raised his voice, drawing unwanted attention from the other restaurant patrons. "Katie, I'm sorry. Come back and sit down, please."

She returned to her seat under protest.

"He didn't give me a name, okay? Just called me up at my desk one day last week and said he knew there would be a killing here, a Highway Hunter killing. Didn't know when or where or who the victim would be. Believe me, if he had told me that, I would've gone straight to the police. You know that.

"So that's why I called you. For all I knew, the guy just wanted attention and was talking out of his ass. I thought if I could talk to Scarborough or have you talk to him, maybe he could give me something to go by. You know, information that I could test this guy out with. Find out if he was for real or not. Then make the call to the authorities if it panned out."

Marc took a drink of his tea, the weight of Katie's eyes bearing down him. "When Scarborough declined, he didn't leave me much recourse. The guy called me again and told me to pick up an envelope from some nearby location. Said I would be convinced that the serial killer was here, in San Diego."

"For God's sake, Marc. Why didn't you tell me?"

"It's not like I knew Lindsay Brown would turn up dead. Jesus. You think I would have kept that to myself if I did? Give me a little credit. Anyway, you ended up calling me first. I just got this today and I figured you needed to see it. Katie, I didn't know Shalot was the one in custody until I got this and it wasn't until just now that you told me about the nature of your relationship with him..."

"There is no relationship, Marc. Let's just get that clear."

"I didn't mean..." Marc waved his hand, brushing off the comment. "I meant that I didn't know you knew him before now."

"All right." The anger that she felt towards Marc was beginning to dissipate. She understood now why he did what he had done. "I'm honestly just shocked by this." She thumbed through the pictures and blog posts. "Maybe he did kill her."

"If something happens – you guys bring charges against him – will you tell me first? I know you're restricted from saying much, but Katie, the public has a right to know if they have the Highway Hunter, or if he's still on the loose and there's someone pretending to be him."

"Marc," Katie began with pleading eyes.

He held up a preemptive hand. "I'm not going to release anything. But when the time comes, you promise me I'll get the news first."

Marc spotted the waitress coming and immediately closed the file, pushing it towards Katie.

The waitress placed two glasses of water on their table. "Are you both ready to order?"

"I need to get back to work, Marc. I'm sorry, but I can't stay."

"Of course. I'll talk to you later?"

Katie slid out of the booth and excused herself to the waitress. "I'll be in touch."

◆◆◆

Blue skies had finally emerged as the day progressed. The wind, however, still brought with it a chill. It was either that, or the fact that this new information Katie now held in her hands had turned her blood cold.

She approached Marshall's office. His door was closed. Never a good sign. "Knock, knock." Katie slowly opened the door, unsure of what she would find. The blinds covered his windows and there were no assurances he was actually inside.

Upon opening the door further, he appeared, casting his eyes up to her, and what Katie saw in his face frightened her more than what she was about to reveal to him. "What's wrong? What happened?"

"Close the door and sit down," he began. "Where have you been? I checked your cubicle and was just about to call you."

Katie slowly sat down in the chair opposite his desk, bracing her weight against its arms. "I was having lunch with Marc Aguilar. Well, we didn't actually get around to eating. I left after only a few minutes. Will you please tell me what's going on?"

"The sample Gibbons took from Shalot matches what the ME found in Lindsay Brown's mouth. Scarborough and Captain Hearn are going to be speaking to the media in a few hours, bringing official charges against him."

The samples matched. How was that possible? There wasn't much more any of them could do. That type of evidence was almost impossible to refute. Scarborough would remand Shalot. The case would be over, as far as the San Diego Police Department was concerned.

Everything she had considered was just wiped away. Would the files she now held matter or would they solidify the case against Shalot even further? "Well, Agent Scarborough knows what he's doing. I guess they got their guy," Katie said, still skeptical.

"Not exactly."

What was Marshall holding back? He'd wanted this result and should be thrilled that it was over. What was the real reason for his gravitas?

"There's been another killing. Scarborough got word shortly after speaking to the medical examiner."

"But we've got Shalot in custody," Katie started. "Then there is more than one of them."

12

AGENT SCARBOROUGH APPROACHED Gibbons as he stood near the interrogation room. Edward Shalot was inside along with his court-appointed attorney. "Guess we should give him the good news?"

Gibbons opened the door and followed Scarborough inside.

"I didn't kill her, I swear to you. I'm being set up. I'm not this damn Highway Hunter," Shalot pleaded.

"I see your attorney has informed you of the charges?" Scarborough replied. "Then I guess you know you'll be handed over to the FBI until your court appearance?"

"I'm telling you, I did not kill Lindsay!" Shalot's actions were becoming erratic. His hands trembled and his face had grown pale.

"Calm down, Mr. Shalot." Bender placed a hand on Shalot's forearm.

"What kind of goddamn lawyer are you?" He yanked his arm away. "You haven't done shit for me and now I'm going to prison!"

"Don't fuck around with me, man," Scarborough started, his eyes in a deadlock with Shalot's. "You killed that woman and you and whoever else you're working with have killed other women in exactly the same way. The sooner you tell us who your friends are, the better off you'll be." Scarborough walked towards the detention officer. "Please, uncuff him from the floor."

The officer pulled the key ring off his belt, kneeling down to unshackle Edward. Scarborough reached for the man and led him into the corridor, where Agents Myers and Jameson waited.

"Let's get him to the field office," Scarborough said.

Agent Jameson took hold of Shalot and proceeded to lead him to the front of the station.

Along the way, Shalot spotted Katie still inside Marshall's office. He threw himself at the window. "Katie, please. I'm innocent. I didn't kill Lindsay. You have to help me. I'm begging you. I shouldn't have taken your file. I'm sorry. But that doesn't make me a murderer."

Katie hadn't yet revealed the contents of the manila folder to Marshall, still holding it in her hand. Instead, she leapt to the door and pulled it open. "What the hell is all this, then, Edward?" She flipped it open and showed him the pictures.

Scarborough eyed the photographs and quickly looked to Katie. She didn't acknowledge him, only continued staring directly into Shalot's eyes. "Avery, what the hell is this?"

Marshall's mouth opened, but nothing came out. He seemed at a loss as to why she had not shown him this first.

Edward lowered his shoulders. "Nothing. It's nothing. I go to clubs once in a while, okay? I didn't do anything to any of those women. I know they post shit about me, but not once was I charged with any crime!" He must have realized his voice had risen considerably and lowered it once again. "I can explain all of this." Shalot tried to reach for Katie's shoulder, but cringed as Jameson pulled back on the cuffs.

"All right. You've done enough damage here. Let's go." Jameson pulled Shalot along, nearly tripping him up as they disappeared around the corner.

She watched as he was dragged away. Confusion settled in her mind. She didn't know what the hell had just happened. Here was a man who stole personal information about her, frequented strip clubs and other places where he harassed women. How was she supposed to believe he didn't kill Lindsay, or that he was at least a part of the Highway Hunter killings? They had his DNA.

Katie turned to Marshall, who now stood directly behind her. "I don't think he killed her, Marshall."

He threw his hands up and returned inside the office. "You mind explaining to me what the hell all that was about? Where did you get this?" Marshall pulled the file from her hand. He tossed it onto his desk and began sifting through its contents.

Scarborough moved in to get a better look, appearing to disbelieve what he was seeing. "My God, Katie. When were you going to let us in on this little bit of information?"

"I was about to tell you, Marshall. That's why I came in here. I met with Marc Aguilar."

"The reporter?" Scarborough asked. "The one you asked that I speak with the other day?"

She was beginning to feel as if trapped in a corner. Her intention was not to withhold this information. It simply hadn't yet been revealed. When she saw Edward in the hall, a switch had gone off inside her and she lashed out, demanding an explanation.

"Look, I was about to hand that over to Marshall. I'm not trying to impede the investigation, I'm trying to help! Marc knew we had Edward in custody. He's got a source. This source told him that the Highway Hunter was on his way here. This same source contacted him again and said he had something for Marc. It was this file. Marc and I just met up a short time ago and he told me everything. He said he had to be sure the guy was for real. That's why he wanted to talk to you last week. He'd gotten some vague information and wanted to know what you knew."

Katie started to feel a sense of betrayal by the men who had both taught her so much. She was being treated as if a child under threat of a scolding. "Now, if you'll both get over yourselves for just a minute, we can figure out who killed Lindsay Brown because I can tell you, it sure as hell wasn't Edward Shalot."

Agent Scarborough was the first to concede. "Katie. I'm sorry. I overreacted." He stepped away from the desk and began to pace the small office. "We have Shalot's DNA. How can you possibly think he didn't kill that woman? Yes, she was different than the others, but we've already discussed the possibility that we're dealing with more than one person. We just got a call about another victim. So what we've got is a man whose DNA was found on a victim's body, who killed her in a similar fashion as the others that we've found so far, and you're insisting it wasn't him."

Marshall said nothing, only waited for her reply.

"Because he wants me." Katie looked to each of them. "That would clearly not be possible if he was in jail for murder. I believe it was made to look like he did it for reasons that remain unclear and what's in that file there? Just more evidence to stack up against him." She looked at the photos and papers spread across Marshall's desk. "Why else would Marc's source bring up Shalot's history? He is not a nice man – that's become very clear to me – but someone who knows him well is working pretty damn hard to see him put away for life."

Marshall appeared to study the information. "That doesn't explain why he had your records. You're so sure he didn't kill Lindsay Brown, but what if she was like you? What if Shalot had become obsessed with her, same as you?"

"I don't know how all this ties into the fact that this poor woman died at the hands of someone either trying to emulate the Highway Hunter or was a party to the other murders, but what I do know is that someone else is dead now and we'd better figure out who gave this shit to Marc Aguilar. Shalot's going to take the blame for the Brown murder. What I want to know from you, Agent Scarborough, is will the FBI tell the public there's more than one killer out there?"

Nick shifted to his feet. "Myers, Jameson, and I need to get to Phoenix. The reports are starting to filter in from the other medical examiners. We'll figure out pretty quickly how many we could be dealing if we get any hits in the system. As far as Shalot goes, we've got too much on him now to consider anything other than what that evidence shows. He's in custody and, as far as I am concerned, Katie, you are safe from him. Your reporter-friend has uncovered interesting information, but nothing more." He began to step towards the door. "That being said, the cooperation and help of the San Diego Police Department is critical to this investigation. If you, Detective Avery, or Detective Gibbons believe we have not reached the bottom of Ms. Brown's death, then I will leave it in your very capable hands to continue on. I'll be in contact once I've had a chance to see what we've got in Phoenix."

Katie looked to Marshall as the door clicked behind her. Agent Scarborough was gone and the two were now alone.

"I was out of line earlier, Kate, and for that I am very sorry." Marshall leaned back in his chair, crossing his legs. "Scarborough was right. He said to me earlier that you weren't the same person he met last year. Not the same as the quiet girl who walked into that meeting when I first met you, absorbing information, learning. It took some time for me to see it. All you needed was a push in the right direction.

"Kate, you are an extraordinary woman. I've always known that, even if I haven't always shown it. It has proven difficult for me at times, letting you go; letting you do the job. Please know that it was not for lack of confidence, but my own insecurities. My fear of losing what has become the single most important thing in my life. I do fear for your safety. I do fear that you will be hurt. I tried to instill in you the ability to let go of the past and I have not followed my own advice. And for that, I am truly sorry."

It was those words that she longed to hear from him. Even now, almost eighteen months into their relationship, he rarely spoke of himself, or his feelings. He had been so guarded for so long, she figured he simply didn't know how to bare himself to anyone.

Law of Five

"I'm not going anywhere, Marshall. Nick thinks he sees something in me and that makes me feel very proud of how far I have come, but he doesn't know me, not the way you do. He wasn't there after it all happened. You were the one who wiped away the tears at night months later. You were the one who held me close when the pain became unbearable. You were the one who made me see who I really was."

"But you could be a great..." Marshall began.

She raised her index finger to her lips, respectfully requesting that he let her continue. "What makes me a great anything—is you." Katie turned away for a moment when the stinging in her eyes threatened to spill tears. "I had hoped, in return, to someday give you all you have ever wanted. A happy life full of love and children." She returned to him, catching the briefest glimpse of regret that had crossed his face. He could hide behind his wall better than anyone she knew, but that tiny crack revealed his true feelings.

"I have no doubt that you and I will have everything we've ever wanted and we will be happy," Marshall replied.

Her thin smile conveyed what he wanted to see; her acceptance of the hand they'd been dealt, but she was almost as good a master of concealment as he was. "Nick's gonna call us after he makes it to the scene. I think we need to find out who Shalot hangs around with in the meantime."

Marshall appeared to take notice of the shift in conversation. "We also need to get Aguilar to tell us who he's been talking to. Shalot's got to have some friends at the school as well. There might be something there. I'll do some digging around on the people named in this file. Maybe talk to Vice and see if any one of them know the women in the pictures." Marshall took to his feet. "In the meantime, if you hear from Scarborough, let me know. I'll do the same."

Katie stood up to meet him. "Okay. I've got a class tonight. I'll ask around, but as far as Marc goes, I already tried to get a name out of him. He says he doesn't know. I believe him, but there has to be a way to find out." She reached for his hands.

"Thank you." She touched his lips with hers in a brief but tender kiss. A kiss that conveyed what they both could not fully express in that moment. It was enough, for now.

13

THE CLASSROOM WASN'T one of the larger lecture halls at the university, but rather a moderate-sized room with about forty or so students. Most were professionals, working towards a graduate degree as she was and were now packing up.

However, rather than listen to the professor's lecture, Katie spent the better part of the hour studying each and every one of her classmates, working to determine who might be friends with Shalot, if in fact he had friends. Most likely, they were simply acquaintances. Still, she needed more insight into the man.

Marshall had succeeded in identifying a couple of the women in the pictures. He was already working with Gibbons to speak to them. Now it was her turn.

In her observations, three people stood out as possible "friends" of Shalot. Pinpointing her reasoning for why she suspected as much was difficult. It was just a feeling, but better than nothing.

Katie jogged to catch up with Will Mathers. She didn't know him well – she didn't know any of her classmates well, least of all Edward Shalot. "Will?"

"Katie? What's up?" He stopped in the corridor and waited.

"Listen, you know Ed Shalot? He's in our class?"

"Edward? Yeah."

"Do you ever talk to the guy? I mean, do you two ever hang out or anything?"

He tilted his head as if he hadn't understood the question. "No. I—I don't know him. We aren't friends. Why do you ask?"

It wasn't a secret that Katie worked for the police department. Everyone in class knew exactly who she was. Sometimes the professor would ask for her opinion, as she was in the rare position of working in the industry in which they were all studying, although most were sensitive to her past and never questioned what she had been through.

Now, she felt as though she had been too transparent with her question and had given away the fact that her inquiry was likely based on something the department wanted to know.

Will Mathers took pause.

"It's just that I didn't see him in class tonight and I wondered if you might have an email address for him that you could use to get him the notes from tonight's class." She stepped back. "I didn't realize you weren't friends. Sorry about that." She began to walk away.

"Wait."

It appeared she had read him correctly. Of course he knew Shalot. He gave it away the second he called him Edward, a preference Shalot had made known to those with whom he was acquainted.

"I don't really know him that well. I mean, you wouldn't call us friends by any stretch of the imagination. But I caught up with him a few times at the sports bar not too far from here. He goes there every now and again after class, but I don't have any contact information for him."

"Alone?"

"What's that? Oh, you mean go to the bar alone? Mostly. But I saw him with this guy, um..." Will turned up his eyes in search of the missing information. "Shaun Hudson. That's right. He's an undergrad. Met him once or twice, I think. Apart from that, Edward usually sat by himself, tossing back a few drafts. He might have Edward's email."

A surge of recognition welled up in her. She recalled Edward mentioning that name. He was the guy who copied her records for him.

"Listen, I gotta go. I'm sorry I couldn't be of more help to you, Katie. Maybe someday you'd like to have a coffee or something? Talk, you know?"

"Sure. That'd be great." Katie smiled, waving as Will walked away.

◆◆◆

On the drive home, Katie pressed the call button on her steering wheel.

"Katie. Thanks for returning my call."

"Sorry for the delay, Nick. I just finished class. How's it looking in Phoenix?"

"Not good. So far, it appears there are two distinct characteristics in these victims. Two distinct styles."

"So we're looking for two people, aren't we?"

"I'd like to think we've already got one in custody. This victim, the marking in her torso was the same as all the others. Something similar to a scalpel or very sharp knife had been used, but the cut went deep, not like with Brown. The woman bled out before she was dumped off the I-10, in the desert, heading towards Tucson."

Katie could hear the frustration in his voice. "We're working on a few leads on our end. Detectives Avery and Gibbons are questioning a few of the women in the photographs and I just talked to a classmate who says he's an acquaintance of Shalot's."

"Any luck there?" The speaker cut out for a brief moment, then returned.

"Maybe. He said Shalot hung out with that guy who sold him my information. Shaun Hudson. Said he saw them at the sports bar near campus a few times. He thought they were friends."

"Listen, Katie. If you're going to be talking to people, do me a favor and just be cautious of what's around you. Don't go off someplace secluded. So what about Aguilar? Is he gonna talk to us?"

"I put a call in to him, but I haven't heard back yet. He doesn't know who's giving him the information, but I'll talk to him again. Shalot may have been charged and won't be going home any time soon, but that doesn't mean we're out of the woods yet, clearly, or you wouldn't be in Phoenix right now. Tomorrow, I'm going to look up this Shaun guy and figure out how I can meet up with him. I'll be sure to let Marshall and Detective Gibbons know what's going on."

"All right, all right."

If Nick was standing in front of her, Katie could swear he would be holding up his hands in surrender.

"Thank you. Listen, you be careful yourself. It sounds like this thing is far from over."

"You got that right. I've got the media and my bosses breathing down my neck, wanting to know why the hell we've got Shalot in custody and people are still dying. This shit's gonna hit the fan soon enough. There'll be an all-out manhunt for this bastard, or bastards. I'm just pissed I let it get this far."

"You're doing your job, Nick. You and your team." Katie turned into her building's parking garage. "Listen, I gotta go. I just got home. Call me tomorrow?"

"Will do. Be safe."

The call ended. Katie cut the engine and stepped out of the car. Her heeled footsteps echoed in the otherwise quiet parking garage. Pressing the button, she waited for the elevator to return to the bottom. Her thoughts turned to Shalot. His pleading eyes, begging for her to believe him. Still, he was clearly not a nice man, something she had missed during previous conversations after class. He was clever at hiding his intentions.

The apartment was dark when she opened the front door and that was when Katie noticed the time. It was 10:30 and Marshall should have been home by now. Her phone showed no missed calls or texts. Last she had spoken to him, he and Detective Gibbons were leaving one of the clubs that Shalot had frequented. That was before class, almost two hours ago.

◆◆◆

The woman appeared apprehensive, drawing deep on the cigarette between her fingers. Marshall loomed over the petite, disproportionate exotic dancer. Her shimmery bikini top covered only a very small portion of her enhanced breasts. He wondered if she might topple over at any moment. This prospect was further heightened by the six-inch acrylic platformed stilettos on which she was balanced.

Standing in the darkened hallway between the dressing rooms and the bathrooms, Marshall asked again, "Can you tell me if you believed Edward Shalot might harm you in any way?"

The woman darted her eyes back and forth, seemingly in search of anyone that might be lurking and might overhear the conversation. She inhaled again on the cigarette, its glowing cherry end illuminating her face, further exposing her distress. "The guy paid me for a private dance. I gave it to him. He got a little too handsy and was tossed out on his ass by security."

"And then he returned after your shift," Marshall pressed on.

"I was walking to the bus stop. He came up behind me and asked if I'd be interested in going to a party with him. I guess he was into some group shit or something, I don't know. I meet a lot of people with fetishes. Anyway, I told him I needed to get home. I got a five-year-old, you know, and I'm trying to give him a better life."

Marshall raised a hand. "I'm not here to pass judgment. I just want to know about Shalot."

She pursed her lips and continued. "He kept on, you know? Telling me how much I'd enjoy it and it would only be a couple hours. He said he'd pay me for my time. Well, that was when I lost my shit. I'm not a goddamn prostitute, you know? So I told him to fuck off." She turned away for a moment, lowering the hand that held the burning cigarette. The side smoke still wafted into the air. "He flipped out. Grabbed me by my shoulders, threw me up against the wall of the building." She now looked directly into Marshall's eyes. "He put his hands around my neck and started squeezing. So, yeah, I thought he was gonna hurt me. I screamed. There were a couple of men, I don't know, maybe fifty feet away. They heard me and came running. That's when he let go."

"And you didn't think to call the cops? Report the son of a bitch?"

She rolled her eyes. "What were they gonna do? He didn't hit me, I didn't have any marks on me. He just took off when he saw the men coming." The woman puffed a final time, then pressed the end against the metal trash can behind her. "Besides, Edward has always been a good client. He probably had too much to drink or something. Most men who come in here and think because I'm nice to them and I get them all turned on that I'm theirs, you know? They don't seem to get that it's the money I'm after. Some do. But most don't." The woman adjusted her top. "We done here? I gotta get back on stage in a minute."

"We're done. Thank you for your time."

Detective Gibbons and Marshall walked out of the strip club and onto the sidewalk that was still dotted with several people hanging around; some on their phones, some talking with friends, clearly intoxicated. Little clouds of smoke, remnants of cigarettes and visible breath in the crisp night air, billowed out of their mouths as they shared stories between themselves.

Marshall pushed his hands into his jacket and pulled it closed. "Why do I get the feeling that there's much more to our friend Shalot than we originally thought?"

Gibbons cast a sideways glance as they approached his car, which was wedged between two large SUVs. He pressed the remote to unlock the doors. "From what I gathered, the guy's into some kinky shit. Maybe Lindsay Brown knew it and it freaked her out. We know he's got a fondness for exerting his force, particularly against women."

They both stepped inside the black Chevy Impala SS, circa 1995, Gibbon's pride and joy that he got hold of at a police auction last year.

Marshall sank into the fully restored black leather upholstered bucket seat. "We need to know who was in his circle, including whoever Aguilar is talking to. I don't know if Kate got anywhere with her classmates; I'll find out soon enough. We've got all the evidence we need on the bastard, but something just isn't sitting right with me, his fascination with Kate aside. Why would he so profusely declare his innocence to her? It's as if he doesn't want her to think badly of him." Marshall turned to view the passersby on the sidewalk as Gibbons maneuvered out of the parking spot and back onto the main road.

"And it doesn't explain the connection to this goddamn Highway Hunter. Shalot's a creature of habit. Hitting the strip clubs every week; school, work," Gibbons began. "This guy isn't a serial killer. He's social – goes to college at night – not exactly what I would call your typical reclusive killer. He's a dick, but I don't think he's part of this deal Scarborough's handling."

"That's probably what they said about Ted Bundy," Marshall replied.

◆◆◆

Katie finally had a moment to take a look at the files Scarborough sent to her a few days ago, although she probably already knew everything in them. A great deal had changed in the last couple of days.

She carried a glass of wine with her into the office and flipped on the light switch. The rest of the apartment had remained dimly lit and so the bright flash of the recessed canned lighting above caused her to squint briefly.

Her eyes soon adjusted as she made her way to the desk and opened the lid of her laptop. The chair offered comfort and familiarity as she pivoted back and forth, waiting for the machine to finish loading, sipping on her glass of rosé. The hour had grown late and fatigue was setting in. However, she would not retreat to her bedroom until Marshall arrived home.

In that moment, she began to recall the conversation Marshall had shared with her some time ago about his former fiancée, how she couldn't accept the danger he would constantly face in his chosen line of work. It had occurred to Katie on more than one occasion that, although becoming increasingly accustomed to the hazards of the job, Marshall could in fact suffer harm as a result. The thought frightened her. But the allure of the job, finding the ones who caused harm to others, seeing them to justice – all that far outweighed the risks. Except on nights like these, when she hadn't heard from him and he was later than expected.

The email from Scarborough downloaded and Katie opened the files, immediately saving them to her hard drive. He'd sent her the profile Myers had compiled, along with geographic summaries and profiles of the victims. She wondered why, for a moment, that he would send her these details of an investigation that, at that point in time, had nothing really to do with her or the San Diego PD.

Had her earlier call to him served as a reminder that he'd once offered her a position alongside him? Was this an attempt on his part to lure her in? Give her a chance to sink her teeth into something substantial? Not that the work she did was not. On the contrary. But nothing she had done in the past year could come close to the scale of this investigation. Inside, she felt a thrill, a rush of adrenaline that bolstered her confidence.

Her first inclination was to review the profile Agent Myers had assembled. The level of detail was astonishing. She seemingly had left no stone unturned. Nick was right; the woman was extraordinarily talented. This was like nothing Katie had ever come across before.

As she delved further into the text, she came across Myers' interpretation of the carving in the victims' torsos. The "V."

"An iconic symbol," it began. *"A symbol that reaches as far back as the 1600s, with a variety of meanings. Not simply as the victory sign or symbol for peace that we know today, but, in part, as a symbol of the 'Law of Fives.'*

"The Law of Fives states that: All things happen in fives, or are divisible by or are multiples of five, or are somehow directly or indirectly appropriate to five. The Law of Fives is never wrong.

— Malaclypse the Younger, Principia Discordia, Page 00016

"This idea is the basis for Discordianism, a religion based on the worship of Eris, the Greek Goddess of Chaos. The Principia Discoria is essentially their holy book or 'bible.'"

Katie was captivated by Myers' theory.

"The references to five and multiples of five are what's key in this investigation. Although this religion worships chaos, it is also consistent with respect to heaven and hell, God and Satan. All things relating to five. Jesus and Satan have five letters, the holy number 23, 2+3, digits on human hands. The examples are infinite," Myers went on to conclude.

"*However, the interpretation of the Law of Fives and Discordianism, in general, is integral to the religion in and of itself. Interpretation is left up to the individual.*

"*In my research into the origins of the symbolism of 'V,' and as produced by Illuminati founder, Adam Weishaupt (incidentally, there were five original members of the Illuminati), who taught that human history came in five stages; (1) Chaos, (2) Discord, (3) Confusion, (4) Bureaucracy and (5) Aftermath. I believe we are dealing with an interpretation of this religion as Order from Chaos.*

"*The person or persons we are looking for are believers and will interpret the meaning to suit their needs. I believe what they seek is to create chaos, the first of the five stages of the cycle of human history.*"

Katie heard the front door open and the sound proved startling as she nearly leapt from her seat. "Marshall?"

"It's me." His voice carried down the hall and into the office.

Relieved, she took to her feet, padding her way into the living room to greet him. "You're home late."

"I'm sorry. I should've texted you." Marshall leaned in to kiss her. "I'm surprised you're still up."

She turned back towards the hall for a moment. "Oh, I got caught up looking at a few files that Nick sent over to me the other day. Can I get you a glass of wine?" She headed into the kitchen.

"I don't think so. It's late and I'm exhausted." Marshall removed his jacket and placed it over the dining chair. "How did class go? You talk to anyone who knows Shalot?"

Katie returned, raising a bottle of water to her lips. "I talked to this guy named Will Mathers. He knows Edward, but not well. It seems he may not have had any close friends." She moved to the couch, tucking one leg beneath her before taking a seat. "But, he did mention Shaun Hudson." There was a spark of recognition in Marshall's eyes. "Yeah, I thought you might find that interesting. Will had seen the two of them together a few times at a bar near campus. Said they seemed pretty chummy."

Marshall soon joined her on the sofa. "So you think Shaun Hudson was more involved with Shalot than simply accepting a payoff for your file?"

"I think it's worth talking to him to find out what he knows about Shalot." She looked again to the light emanating from the office. "I gotta tell you, after what I just read in the files Agent Myers put together, I think they've got their hands full with this one."

Marshall nodded; a thin smile appeared as he seemed to be in agreement. "What did she say?"

"Well, I only heard them talk about this dandelion they've found on the victims. Myers went on to explain the significance of that detail and it, in and of itself, suggested that more, maybe a lot more people were involved in these killings than they want to let on. In the profile I was reading, she goes on to say that the killer or killers are possibly connected to some religion or cult I've never heard of. Discordianism, or something like that. Myers concluded that the symbolism of the 'V' carving in the victims, for these people, anyway, means the Law of Five. It's pretty fascinating stuff." She took another sip of water. "Scary, actually."

"Well, there's a hell of a lot more to Edward Shalot than we first thought. Gibbons and I talked to a few of the women that had been posting online about Shalot. The posts Aguilar found."

Katie nodded, knowing that Marshall still had a chip on his shoulder as far as Marc and that whole situation was concerned, but kept silent.

"It seems Shalot roughed them up a little when they rejected his offers to go to his 'parties.' Or, at the very least, scared the hell out of them."

"Parties?"

"Yeah. The kind that involve several people in a room, apparently without clothing."

She couldn't help but chuckle just a little at Marshall's interpretation, although guilt immediately surfaced. After all, a woman was dead. "Sorry." Her reddened face began to cool again.

"Ah well, to each his own, I guess. I just want to punch Shalot in the face for being an asshole to those women. Son of a bitch deserves it for what he did."

14

NICK HUNCHED OVER the top of the bar, shaking his empty glass at the bartender. He was sweating his ass off. It was coming up on mid-November and it was still too damn hot here. He couldn't believe they didn't have the air conditioning on in this place. Just doors propped open. Everyone said the breeze felt nice. *Nice? Guess I should have packed shorts and a t-shirt.* That seemed to be the attire of the other patrons.

Instead, Nick wore a suit with a wool jacket, immediately shedding the coat as he entered the establishment. It was much more modern than he had expected. Not at all like the southwest décor he had envisioned. Phoenix was completely foreign to Nick. He'd never been there, never wanted to go there, but somehow, now found himself immersed in the death of yet another woman dumped on a God-forsaken deserted stretch of highway.

He'd spent the better part of the day at the local field office, coordinating with other agents as well as the Sheriff's department. The woman had been dumped outside the city limits and so it fell under County jurisdiction.

Everyone was very helpful, as expected. He held great respect for all law officials and never felt that he was somehow superior because of his federal status. The deal was to catch the bad guys and that required cooperation from all law enforcement.

"Hey, this seat taken?" Agent Myers approached and sat down to the left of him.

"Nope. Have a seat. Thought you were already back at the hotel, tucked up in bed?" Nick pressed the button on his phone to see the time. "Shit. It's only 9:00?"

Agent Myers smiled, waving to the bartender. "Yep. Feels a lot later, though, I'll give you that."

The bartender approached the two of them. "What can I get you?"

"Bourbon—neat," Myers replied.

"Whoa." Nick felt himself waver a little too much, figuring he ought to slow down on the drink. But one more wouldn't hurt. It had been almost nine weeks since his last drink. A personal best. He guessed he'd have to get back on the wagon tomorrow. Then again... "I'm impressed." He said to Myers. "I'll have a Jack and Coke."

The bartender acknowledged the order and moved onto the next patron, the numbers of which seemed to be dwindling.

"It's not like back east, is it?" Nick cast a glance around the bar. "I mean, look at these people? It's friggin November and they're all in shorts." He looked back to Myers. "There's something seriously wrong with that."

Myers tossed her head back, laughing. It seemed she had picked up on the fact that Nick might have had one drink too many already. His speech was slurring. "Remember, we need to be at the County Examiner's office at eight tomorrow. You might want to reel it in a bit."

"Pshaw! I'm fine!" He creased his brow, realizing he had just said "pshaw." This was probably going to be his last drink of the night.

The problem was, Nick had been traveling so much over the past several days that he hardly remembered what time it was, how long he'd been awake, or sometimes which victim he was seeing. They were all beginning to fuse into one. Varied eye colors, different hair, all of it matted. Body shapes from thin to overweight. It was a sea of bodies, amalgamating into one great Frankenstein-esque being. He squeezed his eyes tight to clear his mind. But since that wasn't working, fortunately, the bartender had just set a drink down in front of him.

"Here's to your theory of Chaos. I sure as hell can't make any sense out of it." Nick held up his glass, waiting for Myers to toast with him.

"To Chaos." She clinked her glass against his and tossed back the bourbon with ease.

"You've done that before." Nick smiled.

"Maybe. Just once or twice." Agent Myers placed her hand on his forearm, casting her eyes on him and brandishing a sensual smile.

Nick might have had a little too much booze, but he knew when a woman wanted him. He never had any trouble in that area, although once they found out he had never been married, nor had any kids at his age, they figured something must have been wrong with him. They would sleep with him anyway, which was fine by him. And he figured that Agent Myers wanted to sleep with him now, a possibility that had crossed his mind prior to this moment.

"Georgia." Nick looked to her, anticipation surging through his body. "That's a really beautiful name." It wasn't a cheap line. He wasn't a cheap man. Nick let his eyes fall, taking in the beauty of her red silky hair, which rested perfectly over her shoulders in soft, billowy curls. During the course of business, she wore her hair in a tight bun, making her features appear hard. Now, her cheeks disappeared behind the waves of hair, highlighting her green eyes. Or maybe they were blue.

"I was named after the peach. You know, Georgia peach? My dad said I reminded him of a peach when I was born. Soft, pale, and fuzzy." She laughed again.

He liked her laugh. In fact, tonight might have been the first time he'd actually heard it. She'd been assigned to work with him on this case when the first victim was discovered in Virginia. Nick recalled his boss summoning him into his office after local authorities discovered the body of a woman, thirty-three, single, with one kid. It was as if the killer was making a trial run. Seeing if he could do it. The acts had become more brazen, the locations planned carefully, and seemed to be occurring with a frequency that scared the hell out of him.

When his ASAC assigned the team, Myers was at the top of the list. Nick knew who she was, of course. There weren't that many "profilers," as they'd become known, although that wasn't actually an official FBI title. He agreed to the team and here they all were now, almost four weeks later and not much closer to knowing the identity of the killer, or killers, as Myers believed. He was becoming more convinced by the minute of her theory and was very impressed with her skills.

Nick finished his drink and set down the glass. This was probably a bad idea. Well, there was no "probably" about it. It was a bad idea, but Nick didn't care. His thoughts were so consumed by this case that he desperately needed to focus on something else. And right now, that something else was a pretty redhead who seemed to have similar feelings.

"Come on." He began to rise from the barstool and retrieved his wallet, dropping two twenties on the glass top.

She tossed back the last of her bourbon and followed him.

◆◆◆

A call had come in to the station earlier this morning and Captain Hearn wanted to see Marshall first thing.

"I'll let you know what's going on after I talk to Hearn," Marshall started. "Captain said they got a call from a frantic wife. Her husband hadn't made it home last night and no one had seen him since he left for work. I'm gonna find out what's going on. You heading into the office soon?"

"I won't be far behind you," Katie replied, still lying beneath the warm covers of their bed. "Be careful."

Marshall bent down for a kiss. "Always. Love you."

Katie watched Marshall leave their room and listened as he left the apartment. She rolled over to see the time. 6:30 a.m. She should have been up already, but the hour had been very late before the two went to sleep last night. And, like most nights when an idea delved its way into her mind, she found it difficult to find rest.

As daylight continued to surface, she tossed her legs over the edge of the bed and sat up. The idea spread like a fire and it would not be stopped now. It seemed likely that Marshall was about to be assigned a new case. Lots of people went missing and that didn't stop because one was busy on another case. Gibbons would still be working on the Shalot investigation, though. He too believed something wasn't right. But first, Katie would take her own path, as she so often did, and work to find Shalot's inner circle. That meant talking to Shaun Hudson.

◆◆◆

Upon arrival at the station, Katie took to her habitual routine, which included checking in with Officer Sanderson, the lead CSI on the Brown case. Then she proceeded to the kitchen for a cup of coffee, and finally sorted through the various emails that had made their way to her inbox over the past eight hours. There were surprisingly few today, but that was fine by her. She had other things to work on.

The expected call from Marshall hadn't yet arrived, but Katie assumed he must have still been in with Captain Hearn. This gave her some pause. The captain was generally brief and to the point. Some might mistake his personality as curt, but Katie knew better. He'd been there for her, stood up for her when she had come forward with the revelation that she recalled the identity of Hendrickson.

The media, including Marc Aguilar, took to tearing her down quickly after that. Hearn shielded her from the brunt of it. He also saw the potential in her and gave her this job. She would be forever indebted to the man.

Still, she worked to put the concern to the back of her mind and instead focus on finding Shaun Hudson. He was a student and so the best place for her to start was social media. Twitter, Facebook – either one would likely reveal his whereabouts, as people were consumed with informing others of their daily activities and locations. Although Katie was only slightly older than those who took to offering such information, it was something she could not understand. Maybe it was the type of work she did. Maybe it was the fact that one could be so easily tracked down through the internet. Whatever the reason, she knew the risks and what happened when bad people wanted to find you.

A fake Facebook account had already been set up. She was not new to the usefulness the platform offered in her line of work. Logging in, she entered Shaun's name in the search bar. And, again, like most twenty-somethings, his profile was public and there for all to see.

Twenty-one years old, third year undergrad, majoring in History. *I'm sure his parents must be thrilled.* By his most recent post, she figured his classes ended by early afternoon, where he then went off to work in Administration for the remainder of the day. *"Trying to keep myself awake during Euro History lecture. Def gonna hit Starbuck's before work!"*

Katie shook her head, having already ascertained his itinerary for the day. She checked the time on her computer. Ten a.m. She had time yet to continue perusing the internet for more information: who his friends were, where he liked to hang out, whether or not he was dating anyone. So much could be discovered. Almost made a detective's job obsolete.

Her cell phone buzzed with a text message from Marshall. *"Just got new case. Need to talk to the wife of missing man. Call you later."*

People went missing every day and today seemed to be no exception. Until there was a body or a crime scene, she would not be asked to become involved. Her place in the collection of evidence, not finding people, and since she was busy with the Brown case, Marshall, who would sometimes ask that she accompany him as a form of training, she would not be able to do so today.

Her first inclination was to phone Nick and let him know that she had a chance to look at the files he sent. She was a little surprised not to have heard from him yet and wondered how deep he was in it with the Phoenix victim.

The phone lay still on her desk. She stared at it, pondering the decision. Finally deciding that a quick call would be okay, she opened the screen to her contacts and pressed on Nick's number.

"Yeah," he answered.

"Nick, it's me; Katie. You got a minute?"

"Just a quick minute. Agent Myers and I are on our way to the ME's office. What's up? Everything all right?"

Katie could tell that she was on speaker and recalled what Nick had said about keeping her receipt of the files under wraps. Yes, the situation had changed, but she wouldn't risk it. So, rather than divulge the fact and possibly get him into trouble, she decided to fill him in on their progress instead.

"We've been able to get a little more information on Edward Shalot. You remember the pictures and blog posts Marc Aguilar handed over?"

"Yeah."

"A few of the women in the surveillance pictures and posts talked to Detectives Gibbons and Avery last night. Turns out the guy leans a little too heavily on the side of aggression. He's done a pretty good number of some of those women."

"Okay. That doesn't help me out much, Katie. He's being held for murder. What else you got?" Scarborough replied.

The line was turning to static and so her next words came across in spurts. She essentially indicated her intention to talk to Shaun Hudson. For a moment, Katie was concerned he hadn't heard any of it. Either that, or he was considering her idea.

"Is Gibbons going with you?"

"I'm going to the campus. I'm pretty sure I'll be safe there." She paused, waiting to see if he would continue to dissuade her, but he remained silent on the other end. "I just want to know how close he is to Shalot. If he has any personal information on him. That's all.

"You're on the right path, Katie. I think we know what we're dealing with now. Agent Myers and I have had a chance to come together on a few of her ideas. Geographically and methodically, we are not dealing with one individual and Lindsay Brown may have been some sort of payback for Shalot. We don't think she was supposed to be part of the five. There's going to be another one; we just need to find out when and where. It can't hurt to get a handle on who Shalot is. He's tangled up in this shit; we just don't know how yet."

The five. Katie recalled Myers' profile, realizing they must have discovered more information leading them to believe there'd be another. "I think so too."

"One last thing. Please be sure you let Avery or Gibbons know where you're going. We've got to go now. Talk to you later."

"Thanks, Nick. And thank you, Agent Myers."

Nick ended the call.

"She calls you Nick?" Myers asked.

He turned his head slyly for a moment. "What? You jealous?"

"Not at all." Myers returned her eyes to the road. "Just didn't realize you two were chummy like that."

"Georgia, Katie has been through a shit storm and back again."

"I know. I'm familiar with her case and the fact that you were lead on it."

"Then you know that it was me who put that bullet in her. I've never forgiven myself for that."

"Christ, Nick, everyone knows what happened down there in that cellar. It was dark and the situation turned bad in a hurry. It was an accident. Plain and simple."

"There's nothing plain and simple about that day, Georgia. Or what happened after that." He paused for a moment, staring at the lines on the road. "Katie is an amazing woman. Knowing what she went through and how she handled it, well, I respect the hell out of her. And yeah, we're on a first-name basis. I consider her a friend. Even though before this, we hadn't spoken much. Nothing can change the way I feel about her and the fact that I think she made a huge mistake not coming to work for us."

"You asked her to join?"

"I did. She turned me down. Maybe she wasn't ready, I don't know. But I'm guessing Marshall Avery had a lot to do with her decision. And that's okay. She deserves to be happy."

"Well, maybe after getting a taste of it again; working with you, I mean. Maybe she'll reconsider?" Myers said.

"Doubtful." Nick pulled into the parking garage. "Let's find out what the ME's got. Hopefully, something that will help us catch these people."

15

AS PER AGENT Scarborough's request, Katie informed Detective Gibbons and Marshall of her intentions. Gibbons insisted on accompanying her, but she made a good case as to why it would likely scare Hudson off. If he believed he was being questioned in connection with Shalot, knowing he'd taken a payoff to copy her files, the guy probably wouldn't answer anything. Not without a lawyer anyway.

Katie's way, she convinced Gibbons, would make it appear to Hudson that he was helping to further indict Shalot. He had to know that the cops would find her file in Shalot's possession. She would make it seem as though Shalot had used Hudson's position to get information about her.

"Remind me, Ms. Reid, to never underestimate you," Gibbons replied. "That being said, you need to contact me the moment you're finished. Got it?"

"Understood."

◆◆◆

The sun hadn't yet burned off the coastal clouds that were still looming overhead. Katie removed her sunglasses under the shade they offered. Ahead of her, about fifty feet or so, was a large industrial-looking building. She disliked contemporary architecture and preferred the Spanish-Colonial buildings that were prevalent throughout much of southern California. But this was a large campus, appealing to a world-wide student base and preferred to boast of its energy-efficiency and modern conveniences.

Katie continued her approach to the Administration building, where she would seek to find Shaun Hudson. Already somewhat familiar with its internal structure, as a result of attending registration, Katie knew that Student Records was on the third floor.

The elevator doors opened to reveal a sea of beige. Walls, tile, and even much of the hanging artwork consisted of varying shades of beige. The only splash of color came from the vase full of beautiful fall foliage, exploding in hues of orange, yellows, and fiery reds that sat on the front desk in the records office.

"May I help you?" A young woman, probably a student, greeted Katie with a pleasant smile.

"Yes, can you tell me if Shaun Hudson is working today? I needed to ask him if he could look up my file. I've misplaced last semester's report card and I wanted to get another copy."

"Oh sure. I can help you with that." The girl began typing something into her computer. "What's your last name?"

Shit. Katie needed another excuse, clearly overlooking the fact that others could offer assistance. "Um, actually, I kinda wanted to see Shaun, if I could."

The girl raised an eyebrow, tilting her head as if somehow this would make her understand what Katie was saying.

"I mean…" She leaned over the raised reception desk and dropped her voice. "I'm sorry. It's just that I met Shaun the other night and we seemed to hit it off pretty well. But I lost my nerve to ask for his cell number and he seemed a little shy too." Katie darted her eyes as if confirming secrecy. "He mentioned he worked here in the afternoons. Do you think you could get him for me?"

The girl smiled wide, acknowledging Katie's predicament. "Of course I can. And, don't worry; I won't say a thing." She raised the receiver of her phone and dialed an extension. "Could you send Shaun up here for a moment? There's a girl

Robin Mahle

here who needs some assistance." She replaced the receiver and looked back to Katie. "He'll be right up." The girl raised her shoulders and displayed a thumbs-up sign with each hand. "Good luck."

Katie took a few steps back, glancing down the hall where she expected his approach. She would recognize him from his Facebook profile picture.

And it seemed, as Shaun Hudson walked down the corridor, he might have recognized her as well. Color drained from his face and he slowed his approach considerably.

Don't spook him. "Shaun?" The most pleasing and non-threatening of smiles crossed her face as she moved towards him with an extended hand. "I'm Katie Reid."

He cleared his throat and looked at the girl behind the front desk. She still had the enormous grin plastered on her face. He returned his attention to Katie and looked down at her hand. It seemed to have occurred to Shaun that he would have to respond and could not simply run away. Not with the girl at the desk watching so closely.

"Yes. Hi. I'm Shaun. What can I do for you?"

"I'd like to talk to you for a minute, if you've got the time?" Katie replied.

"Um, yeah. Sure. We've got a small conference room down the hall, if you'd like to follow me." Shaun cast another glance to the girl at the desk and led the way to the room. "Right in here, please." He stood aside to let Katie enter first.

Shaun closed the door behind him. "So, Katie, how can I help you?"

He was still pretending he hadn't a clue as to who she was. Katie waited for him to sit down. "I understand you're friends with Edward Shalot?" she asked.

"I, um, hung out with him a few times, but I wouldn't exactly call us friends."

Katie would have to let him in on what brought her to him if she wanted answers in a timely manner. "Look, Shaun, I know Edward took some files from you. My files. I'm not here

151

to blame you. I'm just here to find out what you know about him and why he would want my personal information." She had to ensure he felt she wasn't hurling accusations at him. That she believed he had been taken advantage of. It would be the only way he would talk. She was learning the art of manipulation with tremendous speed.

Shaun dropped his shoulders, sighing as he sat across the table. "I don't know how it happened. He seemed pretty cool. We had a few beers a couple of times."

Some of the color had returned to his face, but as Katie watched him speak, she noticed he was working hard not to make eye contact with her. If she was going to get any real information out of him, she would need to convince him she was on his side.

"Shaun," she began, "did he steal your password? Is that how he got into the school's files?"

That was enough to capture his attention. He was looking at her now, appearing hopeful that he wasn't about to lose his job, or worse.

"I'm sure you know that Edward's been arrested for the murder of Lindsay Brown." She paused for a moment, assessing his reaction. Of course he had known. Everyone on campus knew. Everyone in the city knew now that Scarborough and Hearn held the press conference yesterday before Nick left for Phoenix. "Shaun, what I need to know is why Edward wanted my file." Katie called on a look of fear, as if she was in danger. "Do you know if I was to be next?"

He lowered his gaze. "I don't know. I don't think so. He just—really liked you, I guess. He wanted to know more about you." Shaun leaned in. "Edward wanted you more than he wanted Lindsay Brown. She was just a distraction. She wasn't even his type. Do they really think he killed her?"

"They've got some pretty compelling evidence, Shaun. That's why I'm here. I need to understand Edward. Who he is. The things he likes. What he is into."

At this, Shaun pulled back again. "What do you mean, 'what he is into'?"

"The man is no angel, Shaun. He's a murderer. But with no prior record, nothing to indicate this pattern of behavior, I know we're missing something. And I think you, as an acquaintance, maybe even a reluctant friend, might be able to shed some light on him. Clearly, he displays obsessive behavior. Shaun, please. What do you know about him?"

The stocky, blonde-headed man flexed his biceps, appearing almost as if it had been a nervous tick. His fists curled, turning his knuckles white, as he began to shift his head slowly back and forth.

Katie had gotten to him and now she had to wait. The silence continued. She would not break it and used the quiet to make him even more uncomfortable.

Shaun inhaled, preparing to speak. "I don't know much about him. I really don't. Except that he stole my password and broke into the school's files to get information about you. Look, I don't want to get fired, okay? I need this job. I'm not one of those privileged pricks whose moms and dads pay for everything."

"I'm not going to tell anyone what Edward did, okay? That's not why I'm here. You won't get fired," Katie reassured him.

"He asked me once, after we'd had a couple of beers, if I'd ever had a threesome. I told him no and he said he had — a lot of them. He said he went to this swingers club or something like that and wanted to know if I'd be interested in that sort of thing. What man isn't, right? I mean, at least as a fantasy, but that just isn't me. I told him no. After that, we didn't hang out as much. I saw him a few more times, but he was distant. Well, until a couple of weeks ago when he asked me to come down and meet him at the bar.

"I figured he just wanted to hang out. And it started out that way at first, but then he started asking about my job. The kind of information I had access to."

"So, somehow, he got a hold of your password and found my file?"

"I guess."

There was no truth in his eyes. Katie had given him an out and he had latched onto it. Edward hadn't stolen anything from him. Shaun had given it willingly and she had to know why. It was more than money. There had to be another way. So far, she had only gotten information already known to her. What was Shaun hiding?

Katie thought for a moment about Agent Scarborough and about the profile Agent Myers so diligently crafted. The poem came to mind. *I'll be back tomorrow.* And her theory of the Law of Fives. Order from chaos.

All these things swirled in her mind, trying to fit together, but the pieces weren't matching up. Four weeks, four murders, four different locations, except for Lindsay, Nick was sure she was an anomaly. Another one was coming and, somehow, Edward had become entangled in it. He knew someone or someone knew of him. This obsession he had with her didn't seem to fit anywhere in the equation, unless she was to be number five.

Katie dropped her head, closing her eyes tightly. It just wasn't making sense.

"Are you okay?" Shaun asked.

She noticed his look had changed. He seemed almost pleased by her obvious frustration. "I'm fine. It's just that I've been through a lot, you know?" she began, wondering if an attempt to play on his sympathies might work. "More than a few people have taken to my story, wanting to know more about me and it's hard to tell where their curiosity ends and obsession begins." Katie pushed up from her seat. "If you recall anything else about Edward, or know of anyone who was close to him, I'd really appreciate you letting me know. Edward's in a great deal of trouble and I guess I should be grateful that he's off the streets, but I'm not entirely convinced of his guilt. I'm not entirely convinced that he intended to harm me, either. But, the FBI's got him now and I guess I'll never know his true intentions." She began walking towards the door, hoping he would stop her. And he did.

"Katie." Shaun rose quickly. "Do they really think he's the Highway Hunter?"

Katie saw the curiosity now swimming in his eyes. "Did Edward ever mention anything to you about that case?"

Shaun immediately retreated. "Caught it on the news last week at the bar. That's all," Shaun replied.

"He's in a shitload of trouble, Shaun. They've got a strong case against him." She opened the door. "Thanks for your time. I won't get you into any trouble, I promise." Katie proceeded into the hallway and found herself back in the reception area.

The girl behind the desk had an anticipatory grin on her face. Katie replied with two thumbs up and a smile before leaving.

◆◆◆

When Katie returned to the station, Marshall was back in his office and she stopped in to see him. "So you got another case?"

"Yep. We're looking for a missing husband. Thirty-nine, white collar job with an investment firm. The wife doesn't seem to know much about what her husband does for work. She stays at home with their two young kids. He works late hours." Marshall pushed his fingers through his hair. "I don't know. I'm running background checks on them now. How about you? How'd you fare with Shaun Hudson?"

Katie cocked her head slightly.

"Gibbons told me." He raised a hand before she could speak. "It's okay. You don't have to account for every second of your day to me. You have a job to do and so do I. And frankly, I'm glad to see you're helping Gibbons out with this — and Scarborough."

"Hudson is hiding something, I just don't know what yet."

"What makes you think that?" Marshall asked.

"The kid was a nervous wreck, first of all. More than you'd expect him to be just for copying a set of files he shouldn't have. He started talking about how Shalot wanted him to go to those same 'parties' you learned of from those women."

Marshall shook his head. "So what's he hiding, then?"

"He asked if they thought Shalot was the Highway Hunter; asked if he really killed Lindsay Brown." Katie turned away. "I don't know. He seemed more than a little curious. He seemed — scared."

"Maybe we ought to find out a little bit more about him. Have you said anything to Gibbons yet?"

"No. Not yet. I just got back. But, you think it's worth looking into him further?"

"Why not? Scarborough and his team need all the help they can get. I don't know if it'll amount to anything, but better to be sure, rule it out, you know? I mean, the guy repaid Shalot with your personal information. I don't like him already."

♦♦♦

The haze that hung in the air mingled with the clouds as the sun fell behind the mountain. He'd never seen such a beautiful sunset before. The sky looked like an enormous water-colored painting. Maybe Phoenix wasn't so bad after all.

Nick turned from the stunning view, retreating back inside from the balcony of his hotel room where Georgia lay resting on the bed.

Agent Jameson was still at the sheriff's office, working in the lab with the local CSI team, still evaluating the crime scene.

The post-mortem revealed once again what Nick had already known, with one exception that could perhaps be the break they needed in this investigation. The exception was what Jameson had remained behind to work on. Getting a possible DNA hit in CODIS. They would again have to wait for confirmation.

It seemed the perpetrator may have gotten careless, leaving a trace amount of semen in the crease of the victim's inner thigh. From what they knew so far, none of the other victims had been sexually assaulted. This further confirmed what Nick had already seen coming, that the suspect or suspects, had become more unpredictable and began taking greater chances. This often happened when body counts were on the rise and a killer believed himself to be untouchable. Negligence would prevail.

Meanwhile, Nick was still coordinating with Kentucky, Colorado, and Virginia. The suspect in the surveillance video from Kentucky still hadn't been identified, only knowing for sure that he was male and about five feet five inches, slight build. What they knew for sure was that they were dealing with at least two distinct killers. Virginia had turned up evidence suggesting that their suspect was a male, medium to large build, based on the angles of the wounds on the victim and the depth of the incision in her chest.

Agent Myers further deduced, based on labs and forensics, that they were looking for Caucasian men in their mid to late twenties, also taking into consideration that the murders happened in rural, predominately white locations. With the exception of Lindsay Brown. She was still the odd one out.

16

AS IT TURNED out, Marc had been working on his own to identify the person who had anonymously shared so much about Edward Shalot. Katie remained awake at this early hour of the morning, a returned call having finally come from him late last night. She now sat at her computer, the lone glow casting unkind shadows on her face. Marshall would be up soon. She would tell him what she had discovered, what Marc had emailed to her, and they would need to inform Agent Scarborough.

Exhaustion only enhanced the sickening feeling that turned her stomach. It seemed she might have been wrong about Edward Shalot.

The sound of the bedroom door caught her attention, but Katie remained seated. She heard footfalls on the floor approaching from down the hall and cast her eyes away from the laptop, waiting for them to adjust to the dim, dusky light that was filtering through their apartment. Marshall stood in the doorway.

"Have you been up all night?" he asked.

"Marc sent me something. Something he got from his source," she replied.

Marshall cautiously approached, anticipating the bomb she was about to drop. "This same source who gave him the blog posts and surveillance photos? And did Marc happen to say who this person was?" He lowered himself carefully into the chair opposite the desk.

"You remember me telling you about Myers' profile of the suspects? How she believed it may have something to do with that religion called Discordianism?" Katie didn't wait for a reply.

"Anyway. I don't know how far she's gotten with that theory. I'm guessing she's still pursuing the idea, considering the ritualistic style of the murders, but Marc sent me this link to a website." She pressed a button on her laptop and turned the screen around so Marshall could see.

He began reading it.

As he read, Katie continued, "These people? They believe in the Chaos theory and the Law of Five. And a part of their beliefs is that in order to be close to their 'Lady of Discord,' they engage in what can only be described as orgies. The more the merrier kind of thing. The indiscriminate selection of multiple partners allows chaos to flourish."

"Christ." Marshall rubbed his face. "I haven't even had my morning coffee yet."

"Sorry." She continued. "From what I can tell, this religion, this Discordianism, doesn't seem to have any rules. Interpretation is left up to its followers. This particular faction seems to share the same sexual inclinations, the same interpretation of the religion."

"A little like our Edward Shalot," Marshall replied. "But that doesn't explain the murders. Unless." He paused for a moment. "Unless they needed to explore their theory of Chaos in more depth, to discover greater pleasures in the disorder. Maybe a few of these guys decided to take it a step further, but I thought you didn't believe Shalot killed Lindsay Brown, despite the evidence?"

Katie pressed her lips into a thin smile. "I don't. I think someone wants us to believe he did. Retribution, maybe. I don't know for what. But I'm convinced he's a part of this group. He sure as hell fits the bill. We need to let Agent Scarborough in on this. I have a feeling Agent Myers will be interested in our discovery."

"I think he'll also be interested in the fact that Marc Aguilar seems to be getting an awful lot of information from a source he claims is anonymous. Kate, you gotta get Marc to find out who this source is. This person seems to be the key to everything. If we can set up a meeting between the two, I doubt Scarborough would have any qualms about jumping in and arresting whoever it is Marc is talking to. We can't let it continue. Lives are at stake here."

◆◆◆

The speaker phone rang through to the other line as Marshall, Katie, and Detective Gibbons waited to speak with Agent Scarborough. Gibbons' people were still digging into Shaun Hudson, but so far, had nothing of any real significance.

They waited for the agent to pick up.

"Scarborough," he answered.

"This is Detective Gibbons. I'm here with Detective Avery and Katie Reid. Do you have a minute?"

"I do. Hello, Detective Avery, Katie."

Marshall nodded to Katie. "This is your find. Go ahead."

After the lengthy explanation into how she received the information from Marc, the website, and about the connection of the cultish religion to what they already knew of Edward Shalot, Scarborough remained silent.

"And when you talked with Shaun Hudson yesterday, he made mention of Shalot's interest in these sex parties?" Scarborough asked.

"He did. With little prompting, as a matter of fact. It was as if Hudson wanted to cast a dark cloud over Shalot. Reinforce the fact that he wanted us to believe Shaun had been used by him to get my files, and that Edward wasn't a quote, unquote, *normal guy*," Katie replied.

Marshall jumped in. "Gibbons and I were able to speak with a few of the women who had the unfortunate run-ins with Shalot. He asked them to join him in these parties as well. They expressed that he became angry when they turned him down, got physical with them too. They were too afraid to go to the authorities, so some took to the internet. With what we know now, I gotta think Shalot was recruiting for his little group of believers." Marshall looked to Gibbons for confirmation.

"I would have to agree," Gibbons began. "This could very well be the case."

"We've got Shalot in custody; we've got a DNA match. And from what I'm hearing, you all think he's a part of this cult that Myers initially based her theories on, and because of this information Katie received from Aguilar. So we are in agreement that he did, in fact, kill Brown?" Scarborough asked.

"I know that I'm probably the only one not convinced of Shalot's guilt as it relates to Brown. It just seems too convenient, too simple. I do, however, believe Shaun was lying about his involvement with Shalot, Agent Scarborough. He may be a part of this group as well," Katie said. "And I think we ought to press Marc Aguilar about this source. Whoever it is seems to be feeding him a lot of information; information that appears intent on convicting Shalot." This was the first time she would express the idea, but it had only just occurred to her. "We should consider the possibility that Hudson could very well be Marc's source. He's someone who knows a great deal about Shalot and about his extracurricular activities. And if he's involved in the same sort of thing, he may be looking for a way out. That would certainly explain why he might be the one sending Marc these details."

Scarborough's heavy sigh was amplified through the speaker. "We're still working on the Phoenix victim, but I think this is worth hopping on a plane and sifting through this information together. I'll bring the team with me. I know

Myers' already handed off some of her information to our guys in the BSU who specialize in cult activities. She might have more insight. It's what, nine a.m. now? I'll see if we can get on the next flight out of here. If so, it should put us back in San Diego by about eleven or twelve. We'll plan on seeing you all then." Scarborough ended the call.

The room fell quiet as the three appeared to be considering options for this new approach.

"First thing we need to do is get Marc down here. When I talked to him last night, before he emailed me the link, he mentioned that he'd been trying to arrange a meeting with his contact. If he can do that, we can put a wire on him or something. I don't know, but this source is the key," Katie said.

"If we get a name, we won't need to wire Aguilar. We'll arrest the son of a bitch for obstructing an investigation and if it turns out he's a part of this group, he'll go down for conspiracy to commit murder too," Gibbons replied.

"If Hudson is the source and he's knee-deep in this cult and looking for a way out, I don't get why he wouldn't just come to us anyway as soon as he discovered that Edward killed Lindsay Brown. We could have offered protection," Katie said.

"No point in speculating right now. Let's be sure we know who this source is first. Then we can deal with the aftermath," Gibbons started. "Avery, I know you're working on another investigation. Katie and I can handle Aguilar and we'll touch base when the feds get here."

◆◆◆

Marc agreed to meet with them at the same restaurant Katie had met him the other day. During her conversation with him, she thought he had grown nervous about the fact he hadn't gone to the police with the information his source had been feeding him. It turned out that it had been a bad call.

"I see him over there." Katie led the way to the table where Marc sat alone. "Marc. Thank you for meeting with us. This is Detective Dave Gibbons. He's working on the Brown investigation along with the FBI."

"Pleasure." Gibbons shook his hand. "Katie tells me you've been trying to get your source to reveal his identity. Any luck with that yet?" He wasted no time, as was his style. There was too much at stake and time was ticking away until the next victim.

"As I mentioned to Katie last night, he finds a way to contact me, not the other way around. He's never contacted me via email, so I have no way of tracking him down through an IP address. The guy calls the main line and gets transferred to my extension. If I don't answer, he doesn't leave a message. If I do answer, his words are brief, the call lasting probably less than a minute. I get my instructions on where to pick up whatever he's got for me and that's it." Marc looked to Katie.

She picked up on the fact that his look was intended to confirm she was still an ally. The idea that he was keeping this all to himself simply for the sake of a story went against everything she knew about him. "At the start of all this, Marc wasn't sure this source was genuine."

"That's right." Marc appeared reassured. "I get this call telling me that this Highway Hunter is coming to San Diego. I mean, do you have any idea how many crank calls we get at the station? Most of these people are just looking for their fifteen minutes. And that's when I first asked Katie to check in with her friend at the FBI."

Detective Gibbons seemed to consider Marc's words. "Look, I get that you were being cautious and we appreciate the fact that you went to Katie when you started getting this information and not straight to your producer. But that doesn't change the fact now that we have to find out who this person is."

"Katie's a good friend and the last thing I would want is to put her in danger." Marc raised a hand to get the attention of the waiter, then continued. "After I looked at that website this guy directed me to, I started to get really nervous. I know Edward Shalot's in custody, but I'm starting to believe that this person is involved in something very dangerous. Now, I don't know the details of your investigation, but I suspect the reason you're here is that you believe my contact is connected to the Highway Hunter killings and maybe Lindsay Brown was one of his victims."

"Marc, whoever he is, we're convinced, has close personal knowledge of Shalot and the people in his circle. I can't say much more than that right now. We need your help," Katie replied.

"Okay. So what do I have to do?"

"I'll need to get in touch with your station owners, let them know we need to trace the incoming calls, at least the ones that go to you. It's a start," Gibbons replied. "Have you noticed any patterns to his calls? Time of day?"

"Mostly later in the day. Last he made contact was yesterday afternoon."

"Let me make some calls and see if I can get a hold of the phone records too. I'll need you to give me a list of the date and times he's reached out to you. I can cross reference that information with the phone numbers. Who knows? He may be calling you from his own cell phone." Gibbons excused himself from the table.

"I'm sorry, Katie. This seems to have gotten out of hand very quickly. But you know I wouldn't intentionally put you in any danger. I didn't know Shalot was stalking you."

"It's not your fault, Marc. You came to me when you thought we had a situation. Shalot's still in holding with the FBI. He doesn't pose a danger to me now. To be honest, I'm more concerned about your source. I sure as hell don't want another victim to turn up before we find out who he is."

"No, neither do I. You don't mind?" Marc pointed to the French fries that the waitress had just set down. "I'm starving."

"Go right ahead."

Detective Gibbons returned to find Katie picking away at her meal while Marc had nearly finished his. "I've got my guys working on it now." He sat back down next to Katie. "Should have something by the end of the day. In the meantime, Marc, if you hear from him, call me right away. You understand?"

◆◆◆

The two had returned to the police station, but Scarborough's team hadn't yet arrived. She continued to research Hudson's background while Gibbons hustled to get the phone records from Channel 9 News.

Katie was all but convinced that he was the source. She'd discovered that more than a few of Shaun Hudson's "friends" on social media had interesting quotes and symbols that appeared to relate to the concept of the Law of Five and Discordianism. What proved even more interesting and helped to solidify the idea that Shalot was also a part of this group was the fact that some of these people were also connected to him. "Friends of friends," as it were.

But in none of this information did she find any suggestion of violence relating to these concepts or ideas. So where would the idea of killing, leaving symbols as proof that the believers of Chaos had done such horrific acts, have propagated in the minds of an unknown number of its followers? The answer must lie in the interpretation of those believers themselves.

If Agent Myers was correct and, right now, Katie had no reason to believe otherwise, what led to this violent interpretation? And what about Lindsay Brown? So far, no one had found anything that would suggest she was involved in this semi-faith faction.

The FBI had already pulled Brown's phone records. There were no threatening text messages, no voicemails from Shalot. Nothing that would indicate retribution on his part for her having filed the restraining order.

The sight of Marshall approaching in the distance caught Katie's eye. She noticed the time and hadn't realized so much had passed.

"Hey." He leaned against the edge of her desk, just inside the small cubicle. "You find anything interesting?"

Interesting would have been an understatement in this particular instance.

"You could say that," Katie replied. "What's going on with the Guzman case? Any closer to finding the husband?" She immediately regretted asking the question.

Marshall's face quickly masked in disappointment. "Turned over to Homicide. Mr. Guzman was found in the trunk of a car in Tijuana. Mexican authorities are working with the department. My part is finished."

"What happened to him?" Katie asked.

"Looks like a business deal gone bad. According to the wife, they'd been struggling financially for the past few years. Her husband had become increasingly private about his business dealings. Guess one of them didn't pan out."

"I'm sorry, Marshall." Katie rested her hand on top of his.

"Just another day in paradise." He shifted uncomfortably. "What have you found out about Hudson and his friends?"

She took the hint and offered no further words on the topic. Instead, she watched him compartmentalize the case, as he did with all of them, tucking them away neatly in his mind.

It was a skill she had begun to acquire recently, at least where her personal life was concerned. Filing away the events of the past. The loss of Sam, witnessing the death of Chief Wilson, and pushing back the most recent of news, the loss of her unborn child and perhaps the prospect of motherhood itself.

"From what I've been able to find online, most of his Facebook friends are college classmates or high school buddies. However, there are a handful that seem to have some commonality. Of those friends, most have liked pages relating to the religion or have liked events or gatherings of the faithful. I've written down the names of the people we should get background checks on. But, Scarborough may prefer his team handle that. He's got plenty of experts in that area and, by the sounds of it, they may already be looking into this information."

"I'm certainly no expert in cults and they've got the resources to dig a hell of a lot deeper than we do." Marshall retrieved the cell phone from his leather jacket. "He should be here soon."

◆◆◆

Agent Myers was the first to speak as the team sat around the conference table. On the wall-mounted monitor was an image of several people at a rally or gathering of some sort that Katie had discovered on a profile page of one of Hudson's friends. They were all facing a man standing on a podium. Behind him was a graphic chart. Symbols inside of symbols, pentagons and inside the pentagons were various other symbols relating to the religion. Once such pentagon contained the words "Law of Five."

"We need to know who this man is here." Myers moved the pointer to the man speaking at the podium. "I sent this to the BRIU, or Behavioral Research and Instruction Unit, for those of you not familiar with the many acronyms we at the FBI employ. They analyze these types of cults and discovered many websites that were tied to this particular group. From there, they determined that that this was held in San Francisco last year. It's too difficult to tell in this photograph if any of the audience members are Shalot or Hudson."

"Katie discovered a handful of Hudson's friends that appear to be involved as well, to what extent remains unclear," Marshall began.

"Based on what we know today, we believe there is going to be another victim. The inconsistencies regarding the death of Ms. Brown suggest she was never intended to be a part of this pattern. You all know that we have the man responsible for her death already in custody and now that we assume he is a member of this organization, we can use that to our advantage," Scarborough began. "He may know who this man in the picture is; in fact, he may be willing to tell us a whole lot more if he thinks it would be to his benefit. And we should make it appear as such. Detective Gibbons, we'd appreciate any help your people can give us in compiling background investigations on the list of people Katie gathered."

"Of course."

"In the meantime, Katie, as you've become very familiar with Shaun Hudson, I'd like you to come with me to see Shalot again."

◆◆◆

The lofty building, comprised of glass and metal loomed large as Katie and Nick approached its entrance marked with the FBI emblem.

Just as they were about to enter, Katie stopped.

Nick paused, his eyes narrowing. "What's wrong?"

"I feel like I shouldn't be here. I'm in over my head." She was reluctant to reveal this, fearing Nick would believe her to be weak. He'd always seemed to hold her in higher regard than she believed she deserved. "I'm an evidence tech. Why am I here?"

Nick turned squarely towards her, folding his arms. "You still don't see it, do you?"

She had no answer and waited for him to continue.

"You remember what I said to you that day? When we drove to the Davies' house to return their daughter's necklace?"

Katie lowered her gaze, because of course she had remembered. She also remembered what Mr. Davies had said to her that day. *"I know your heart is heavy,"* he whispered. *"But you need to live a good and happy life, Ms. Reid. It's the only way we win."* It was a moment that had changed her life.

"Yes. I remember." She turned her face up to meet his eyes again. "You said this was what I was supposed to do. That this is the stuff that makes me tick."

"Has that changed? Because I still see it in you. I left it alone. Didn't push you. After all you'd been through, it was the least I could do. But then you called me, remember?"

"I asked if you could help a friend."

"And I am. I'm helping a friend right now." Nick began walking towards the entrance again. "You have a connection with Shalot. I don't know why he latched onto you, but he did. We need to use that to our advantage." He pulled open the large glass door. "You coming?"

This wasn't about her, not really. This was about the victims who deserved justice. And if she had the ability, in some small way, to help find the person or people who killed these women, then she would need to do everything in her power to help, starting with facing a man who had been drawn to her in a manner that was frightening to consider.

She followed Nick inside. The lobby appeared more like a terrarium. Glass enclosure, plants climbing the walls in an attempt to reach the sun.

Nick signed her in as a visitor, handing her a badge. "Here; put this on."

They reached the security area where Katie was asked to remove her coat and empty her pockets. It was as if she was about to board a plane, but this was just part of the deal now. Every government building had a similar set up. It was a post-9/11 world.

They moved on after a thorough search and now approached the elevators. Nick stepped inside. Katie followed behind.

"When we get in there," Nick began, pressing the button to the fourth floor, "let me start. I don't want him to see you as a threat. You'll be the one to put him at ease, understand?"

She nodded.

The ride to the fourth floor took only a few seconds. The elevator doors parted and Katie stepped out first.

"Follow me." Nick took the lead down the long corridor.

Along the way, Katie felt the eyes of more than a few people land on her. Her reputation had indeed proceeded her. She began to wonder if there would ever be a time when people would see her as someone other than the Katie Reid from the papers and television. Although the public obsession with her had dwindled, her reputation among local law enforcement was still present.

Nick pressed a button leading to a secure area of the building. The door clicked open. "This is the place. Come on in."

Inside the room, she spotted Edward Shalot. He appeared drained of all energy, as if he hadn't eaten or slept the entire time he'd been there. But as she looked at him, his eyes revealed the slightest sparkle. A hint of a former life, or a former desire that had once again appeared, as if she was his salvation.

"Mr. Shalot," Nick began, "I understand you have been arraigned?" He didn't wait for a reply. "That means you'll be transferred out of here soon and into a nice cozy cell. I do hope you're paired with someone who doesn't mind that you killed a woman. They don't take kindly to rapists inside."

"I didn't rape her. I didn't kill Lindsay and you know it," Shalot replied, his eyes turning dark.

"We have evidence that suggests otherwise, Edward. But rather than drone on about that, I'm actually here to ask you about something else."

"And why would I answer any more of your questions? I don't see my attorney here, do you?"

"You are right about that, but this is regarding another matter, one that might see its way to helping you get out of this little predicament of yours. Now, if you'd like, I'll wait for your lawyer, but time really is of the essence here, Edward, and your cooperation would be greatly appreciated."

Edward shifted his eyes to Katie. "Why are you here?" His tone softened markedly.

"I'm here because I talked to Shaun Hudson and I thought you might be interested in what he had to say."

"You talked to him? He told you I had nothing to do with Lindsay's death, right?"

"He said you stole his password to the school's servers and got a hold of my records. That you used him to get to me." She cocked her head sympathetically. "Is that true, Edward?"

"Are you shitting me? That asshole handed over your files for a few bucks. I had to bail him out of some gambling debt." He pulled back, possibly realizing he'd said too much. "Look, I told you before. I just wanted to get to know you, Katie. That's all. I meant you no harm. You have to believe me." He leaned forward again. "And I didn't kill Lindsay."

"You keep saying that, Edward, but how do you explain your DNA they found on her?" This time, Nick jumped in.

Edward squeezed his eyes shut, turning his head back and forth. "I don't know. I swear to you, I don't frickin' know."

"What can you tell me about Discordianism?" Katie asked. She could see by his reaction that Edward hadn't expected this question ever to surface.

"I'm sorry; what?" His transparency was almost laughable.

"Discordianism," Nick stated slowly. "Is this a hobby of yours? Although from what the San Diego police discovered, it seemed as though you may have been actively recruiting new members? Is that right?" Nick paused only for a moment. "Or do you just like to scare women who don't want to participate in your freak show?"

Shalot was retreating. Katie had to get to him before he completely shut down. "How long have you been involved with this group, Edward? We have reason to believe someone who may also be a part of it could be responsible for the murders that have happened across the country in the past month. Maybe even Lindsay Brown's murder."

Edward seemed to perk up at this news.

"Look, I don't judge people's beliefs, but when those beliefs cause harm to others, that's not okay, Edward." She pulled out an envelope and laid its contents on the table. "Do you know this man?" It was the photograph of the man at the podium. "We'd like to talk to him."

Edward studied the picture.

Katie was about to speak, but Nick stopped her with a raised hand. She hadn't given him enough time to absorb the information. Shalot needed to think and Nick seemed to realize that.

"He's the leader. Well, not really the leader; there is no hierarchy. But he's the organizer of the events. The ones that are held here anyway." Edward cast pleading glances at both Katie and Agent Scarborough. "Look, I was only into this thing because it meant I got to have sex with a lot of women. And yeah, I tried to get a few of the women I knew involved. I didn't mean to lose my temper with them, but they were judging me. I could see it in their eyes. They looked at me like I was some kind of deviant."

"No one's claiming you're anything of the kind, Edward," Katie replied, working to calm him down. "Did you try to get Lindsay Brown involved too?"

"No. I knew right off the bat she wasn't the type. I just lost my temper with her because she was being a fucking tease. I hate that shit."

Nick looked away, appearing disgusted by the man's words. Katie caught sight of him and knew she had to continue before Nick lost his own temper with Edward.

"Who is he, Edward? If we can talk to him, he may know of others in the group who might have displayed a propensity for this type of violent behavior. It might be our only chance to find out the truth so you can get on with your life. Isn't that what you want?"

Edward was silent for much too long and Katie wondered if she'd blown her chance.

"His name is Branson. Lewis Branson." Edward appeared to regret his words, as if they would come back to haunt him. "He keeps a low profile. I don't know where he lives. I can tell you that I was there, at that rally. And so was Shaun Hudson."

It was only a matter of time before the next killing, assuming the "Law of Five" theory was in fact the catalyst to this gruesome set of murders across the United States.

Edward Shalot would remain in his holding cell until his next court appearance and then get transferred to a processing facility.

Katie watched as he was led out of the room, his eyes still pleading innocence. She began to wonder, if he knew more about this quasi-religion, then why wasn't he using this knowledge to help prove his innocence? The question remained, however, of the indisputable DNA evidence found on Lindsay's body. Edward Shalot had to know he would go away for life based on that alone.

◆◆◆

"So where are we headed now?" Katie asked from the passenger seat of Nick's rental car.

"I'm going to drop you off at the station. I'll need to head back here and put a call into Myers to get whatever we can on Branson and have her meet me here. We'll have to brief the ASAC. Agent Jameson is heading up this evening after he finishes in Phoenix. We're going to find out where this Lewis Branson lives and have a little chat with him."

Katie had seen that look on Agent Scarborough's face before. It was as if the fate of the next victim rested solely on his shoulders.

17

SHAUN HUDSON SHIFTED in the fifth-row seat of his lecture class on Pre-World War II European History. He would have preferred to stay home today, playing *Call of Duty* on his Xbox, but missing another class might get him kicked out. And if he got kicked out, he would lose his job at the Admin Building.

His mind was preoccupied with Edward Shalot. Shaun wondered how long it would take for the FBI and the San Diego Police Department to find out that he'd taken a payoff to hand over Katie Reid's file to Shalot, if they hadn't known already. It would only take the question to be presented to Shalot and he would rat out Shaun. Why wouldn't he? He was being held for murder and possibly could be connected to more than one. Why not take someone else down with him? This had all gotten out of hand and Shaun needed a way out.

He knew Edward's curiosity about Katie Reid verged on the obsessed. It seemed every time they hung out, he was always mentioning her in some capacity. He should have known then. But, he needed the money. He'd lost his ass in that poker game and Ty wanted to get paid. What choice did Shaun have?

Only now, sitting in the uncomfortable seat, he felt bound by guilt. Katie wasn't the type of woman to allow herself to get swept up in the likes of Edward Shalot. Even if she had been attracted to him, it would only take her finding out what they were into and she'd have been out the door in no time.

Still, it wasn't supposed to turn out this way. Lindsay Brown was dead, Edward was in some FBI holding cell, waiting to spend the rest of his life in prison for killing her and here Shaun was, listening to the professor speak of a time of conspiracies, spies, and the rise of a man who had once been an artist, but was about to become the most evil human being the world had ever known.

His cell phone vibrated in his pocket and he reached inside to silence the call. A few of his classmates cast disapproving looks in his direction. Most of his friends knew he was in class and so he was sure it was someone unknown to him.

At the end of the session, Shaun gathered his belongings and headed outside into the cool midday air. He retrieved his phone to find out the identity of the caller who'd interrupted his class. The ID said unknown, but there was a voicemail.

Shaun began down the concrete path towards his afternoon job in records, holding the phone to his ear to listen to the message. He closed his eyes as the message came, just as he expected it would.

The idea of leaving town now seemed very appealing, but they would most certainly find him. His gambling habit had gotten him into this and now he wished he'd never met Lewis Branson.

◆◆◆

Agent Myers stood outside the door where Scarborough was meeting with the ASAC. The man behind the desk, ASAC Newland, tossed a glance her way, signaling she had permission to enter.

"I'm sorry to interrupt," Myers began, "but we got a hit on Lewis Branson." She tossed a file on the desk, the contents of which spilled out in front of the men. "The man's been arrested for sexual assault and served time in Englewood, Colorado in 2006, served time in Roederer, outside Louisville, prior to that on a drugs charge in 2002, and has been living in Oceanside since 2013."

Scarborough looked to Myers. "Is it me, or does it seem like this guy lived near a few of our victims at one time or another?"

"Maybe he started up smaller groups of followers, moving on to begin other ones as he found his next home?" ASAC Newland replied.

"Our partners at San Diego PD came across this as well," Myers continued, flipping through the file and retrieving information on multiple websites. "These are essentially online communities for the followers to connect with one another. Although there seems to be no one in particular they reference as the leader, many of them defer to Lewis Branson for decisions on where to hold meetings and events. Branson does appear to be the de facto leader of the group."

Scarborough continued to study the information. "Let's get Detective Gibbons to take a trip up to Oceanside with us and catch up to Mr. Branson."

◆◆◆

The evidence collected at Lindsay Brown's home had all been catalogued. Katie turned in her report to CSI Sanderson. "Everything's in the system now," she said, handing him the printouts. "Here's the chain of custody as well."

"Thank you, Katie." Sanderson looked up from his computer monitor in the lab. "I understand you've been assisting the FBI on this matter as well?"

"Unfortunately, it turns out that I happened to have a class with the suspect. They thought I might be of use, that's all," Katie replied.

"Well, I'm sure your assistance was appreciated."

Katie smiled and started to leave.

"Will you be pursuing a position here in the lab when you finish your schooling? You know, there's a great deal of detective work involved here too," Sanderson told her.

"I haven't decided just yet." She turned to reply.

"If you do, I'd be more than happy to have you on the CSU. Just keep that in mind."

"I will, and thank you." Katie headed back towards her cubicle to log out and go home. It was approaching six o'clock already and, frankly, after seeing Shalot again, she thought a drink might be order.

"You heading out for class?" Detective Gibbons caught up with Katie in the hall.

"Not tonight."

"You know, Scarborough and his team found out where Lewis Branson lives. I'm riding up with them to Oceanside tomorrow morning. I guess the guy works at some warehouse, for a brewer, I think; not sure. Anyway, we're gonna have a word with him. They say he's served time and lived near where some of the victims had been found."

Katie felt as though she had done the best she could today and now it was likely that her time was up. Myers had been working with other agents to corroborate her findings, and now they would be able to talk to Branson in hopes he might give them some names. Shalot wouldn't be getting out at all by the looks of things and now the only piece of information they needed was Marc's source and Gibbons was all over that.

"Sounds like it should be an interesting conversation. Probably not coincidental that the guy lived near some of the same locations as the victims."

Gibbons continued beside her as they approached her cubicle. "Not really, no. They think that he may have started groups of followers in those areas."

"It's curious, though, that there's nothing I found in my research that would indicate a tendency for violence in any form from those who follow Discordianism. It doesn't seem to make sense."

"You're right." Gibbons leaned an arm over the top of her cube wall. "There's something else at play here. We're all hoping Branson can shed some light on it."

Katie shut down her computer and grabbed her things. "I'd better get going. Marshall and I are going to actually try to have dinner out tonight."

Gibbons stepped aside. "Must be difficult," he began. "My wife couldn't possibly handle knowing what I have to deal with on a daily basis."

Katie moved past him. "You might be surprised what she could handle. Good night and good luck tomorrow."

"Thanks." His voice traveled down the hall, reaching Katie before she turned the corner and disappeared.

Katie had her coat draped over her arm and stood in the doorway of Marshall's office. "Hey, you ready to get out of here? Thought we could pick a nice spot in the Gaslamp, have a quiet meal?"

Marshall turned away from his computer, looking at her slender frame that was partially obscured behind the coat she held in front of her. "You look a little tired; you still feel like going out?"

"I think both of us could use a break, don't you?" She ambled her way inside and sat down. "You still working on the Guzman case? I thought it was sent to Homicide?"

"It was. And, no I'm not working on it right now." Marshall rubbed the top of his head. That was his tell. Something was on his mind.

"What is it then?" she pressed on.

"I was looking into a few things. Shalot and Hudson. Both of these guys have clean records, well, except for Shalot's recent restraining order, but otherwise, they're squeaky clean. Both grew up in relatively normal families and middle-class neighborhoods."

"Okay." She wasn't quite seeing his path on this one and waited for him to continue.

"Look, I'm certainly no expert on the occult, but these types of things usually attract outsiders, you know? People who are maybe a little on the socially awkward side, maybe withdrawn. Bullied in school. People looking for acceptance. People looking to belong somewhere. Neither of these guys seem to fit that profile."

"Well," Katie started, "Edward doesn't exactly have a lot of friends."

"No. But he did back home, before he moved here last year. At least, from what I read in the fed's background investigation."

"He moved here last year? When and from where?"

Marshall clicked the mouse a couple of times, studying the computer screen. "Colorado. A place called Greenley, around mid-December last year."

His words sent an immediate chill down her spine. "Gibbons mentioned that he and Scarborough were going to talk to Branson tomorrow. He moved to Oceanside last year. From what I gathered, Myers discovered that Branson had lived in Colorado and served time in Englewood for an assault charge." Katie recalled the interview with Shalot earlier and began shaking her head. "Edward made it appear as though he knew of Branson only as the organizer of the meetings. I'm starting to believe he wasn't being completely honest as to the nature of their relationship. I just don't know why."

Marshall seemed to understand exactly what she was getting at. "I don't know if Myers made the connection yet or not, but I'd bet the farm that's where he met Branson."

Katie inhaled a deep breath. "So, how about we call out for some pizza? I have a feeling we'll be having dinner here tonight. Should probably ask Gibbons to join us too."

◆◆◆

Her hands were bound tightly around the pipe. Sweat dripped from her head, stinging her eyes as the drops continued down. Trisha had lost all track of time down here in the darkness. She didn't know how long she'd been here. Alone, afraid, Trisha thought for sure she would die in this place.

A small shaft of light emerged as the door opened. Trisha's eyes widened as she waited to see who was entering. It took her a moment to adjust to the figure that was approaching, but she suspected she already knew its identity.

"I see you haven't eaten anything, Trisha." The voice was that of a man's, gravelly and deep in tone.

She recognized it immediately. "Pretty hard to eat with my hands tied. Besides, I'm not hungry."

"You know, I'd have thought you'd be just a little bit more appreciative. After all, if it weren't for me, I doubt you'd still be here. You'd be like the others, tossed alongside some secluded highway, carved up and ready to be eaten by the animals."

Trisha would have preferred this to be over and so the thought of her lifeless body didn't seem so bad, considering the alternative.

"Well, as it turns out, you'll get a few days reprieve from the inevitable." The man hunched over and walked further inside the room until he was no longer cloaked in shadow.

Trisha took in his lanky frame and shoulder-length dark hair that he wore straight and parted down the middle, with a narrow face and a fading tan. Finally, his eyes came into view as he came closer. They were dark and void of all feeling, except lust.

Yes, Trisha would have preferred death to what awaited her in this moment. All she could do was detach her mind from what was about to happen to her and distance herself from her physical being.

She had once thought of Lewis Branson as a brilliant man. Had even at times desired to be with him when she would witness him address the masses. But all of that had changed when she said she was leaving the group, that it was time for her to move on, since she felt as though she had learned all she could.

Really, she had grown tired of the "shared sexual experiences." They were nothing more than meaningless encounters. The last one resulted in an unwanted pregnancy that she felt compelled to end. It was then she realized that there was more to her life than this place and these people who worshiped chaos. What did any of it mean? Nothing. Not to her. Not anymore.

But when she began speaking of her intent to leave, reasoning with some in the group that there must be more than this, well, Lewis Branson felt as though she'd betrayed him.

Trisha began to feel that maybe there was something to the rumors she'd heard over the past several weeks, that a new faction had emerged and Branson was taking a turn towards a darker, more extreme side to their beliefs.

Word had gotten out of her intent. That was last week, after the death of a woman in Colorado. She wasn't sure it was Branson, but if not him, then most certainly someone who was a part of this new idea he had been spreading. Turning the world back to chaos so that true order could once again be restored.

How this was to be accomplished through the murder of innocent people escaped Trisha. So now, she found herself here, tossed into what could only be described as a dungeon and inside that dungeon was a smaller room. That was where he was keeping her until she came back around to his way of thinking.

She had been down there before, in the dungeon, only in a much different capacity, as a willing participant. Now she was here not of her own free will, but at the will of Lewis and he was about to make her see the error of her ways. Again and again, he would make her see his point of view, as she once had.

Trisha closed her eyes, a tear falling as she thought of her parents, regretting having ever come into contact with Lewis Branson.

◆◆◆

Marshall grabbed the last slice of pizza and held it up. "Mind if I take it?"

"I'm stuffed. You go ahead," Katie replied.

The back of the station, where most of the offices were located, had grown quiet. Up front, of course, would still be busy with cops bringing in the riff raff, booking them, tossing drunks into the tank. All of the things that police officers were faced with on a daily basis.

But things were different in detective work. Lonely. Quiet. Even Gibbons had already left, claiming he needed to see his kids to sleep. Most of them worked ungodly hours and for not really much pay. They did all right, but they were still public servants, and were paid as such.

Marshall spotted an incoming email as he took a bite. "This is what I was waiting for. I asked Agent Jameson to send me some additional information on Shalot and Hudson; employment history and such." He downloaded the files, his eyes darting back and forth at the screen.

"Anything interesting?" Katie asked.

Marshall turned his monitor so that they could both see what Jameson had turned up. "According to Shalot's employment history, he worked at a place called Milgard Plastics in Greenley. No record of Shaun Hudson working there, though."

"Wait, hold on," Katie began. "What's this?" She pointed to a line item on the screen. "Whoa, am I reading this right? He was fired for sexual harassment?"

"Looks like it," Marshall replied. "This guy's a real piece of work."

"What I want to know is why the hell he moved here in the first place," Katie said. "It had to have something to do with Branson."

"Or you. How did he end up in a graduate class? *Your* graduate class? This is a middle class kid with no high level skills. He worked on the line at a plastics company." Marshall continued to review the files, pulling up Shalot's school records. "If you look at what Jameson found, he never lived in Connecticut and, by the looks of this, never attended the University of Connecticut as it states on his UCSD records. It's been fabricated, Kate. Someone made up his credentials."

"Who has the ability to do that?" Katie asked, already knowing the answer. "I wonder if someone who worked in Records could create a false transcript." She didn't like what was coming to the surface, that it seemed Shalot had been placed deliberately in one of her classes. "Marshall, I think Edward Shalot *is* here because of me and I think Branson helped him to get here, indirectly, at least. The guy picks up and leaves a year ago? Right around the time we were all over the news. Then he ends up in one of my classes?"

"Shit. There's more to this than we know and my guess is that Scarborough and his team aren't looking too hard into anything as it relates to Shalot right now. They've already got him in custody and are dealing with too many other victims. They're going to be focusing in on Lewis Branson." Marshall looked at the time on his phone. "I think we got enough to bring Hudson in. I'll call Scarborough and give him a heads up."

"What about Lewis Branson? If we bring Shaun Hudson here, and they all know this guy, word could get back to him, and he might just take off if he sees the need. Right now, we don't know if he's a suspect," Katie said.

"Then we'll have to make the timing work. They're all going to Oceanside to talk with Branson in the morning. We'll bring Shaun in at the same time."

♦♦♦

The key lodged for a moment inside the lock, as it often did when the air was particularly damp as it was today, but Marshall persisted until finally the dead bolt retreated. He held the door open for Katie. She dragged herself inside the dark apartment, running her hand along the wall until she found the switch.

"We've got to get some rest. There's not much more we can do tonight." Marshall removed his coat and tossed it over the back of the couch.

"So much for a quiet dinner out," Katie started. She knew what they were facing, but didn't want to think about it any longer. She had been a target yet again and, by some miracle, someone made sure Shalot took the fall for Lindsay Brown, but neither knew for sure if Katie was truly safe. There could be others.

The two climbed into their bed and Marshall turned on his side to face her. "I'm so sorry."

Katie placed her hand over his cheek. "For what?"

"For letting this happen again. I thought we were through with this sort of thing. I thought you were out of danger. And now here we are again, wondering who might want to harm you."

"Marshall, you can't control the actions of others. My story was out there for all to see." She paused for a moment because, of course, this had gotten to her as well. Just when she believed they could live a normal life, away from the morbid interests that had fallen on her, this discovery was frightening and brought back memories she would have preferred to keep buried. "Shalot's in custody. Shaun Hudson is some scared kid who may be involved in this cult, but I don't believe for one minute he is anything more threatening than a pawn in someone's game. And you're here. I always feel safe with you beside me." She leaned in to kiss his lips.

"What do you think about Montana?" Marshall started. "Seems like a nice, quiet place."

Katie parted her lips into a smile. "Sounds good to me."

18

DETECTIVE GIBBONS APPEARED stunned by the news as he listened to Marshall and Katie fill him in on what they had discovered after he left late last night. "Scarborough's gonna be here in ten minutes. It should take us about an hour to get to Branson's place of employment. Have you heard anything from his team as it relates to Shalot?"

Katie pushed back a few loose strands of hair from her face, tucking them behind her ear. It was her own tell that Marshall knew all too well. A nervous habit that meant she was about to put on the front, disguising her true fears. She knew better than to let anyone else see what it was really doing to her. "They know he never attended U-Conn, confirmed it with the university already. In fact, he never finished a four-year college at all. Shalot moved to Colorado five years ago. He had to have hooked up with Branson around that time. Probably met through one of the community websites, which essentially served as recruiting grounds for Branson."

"But these murders committed by the Highway Hunter, do they think Branson did it?" Gibbons asked.

"No idea," Marshall replied. "My guess is your little visit with him later this morning should shed some light on that question."

"Right. I heard that Jameson had stayed in Phoenix a while longer because they thought they'd had a DNA match in their database. I think they're still waiting on it, but if that's true, this could all start coming together very quickly." Gibbons swallowed the last of his coffee and tossed the paper cup into the trash can.

"Agent Scarborough is letting us borrow Jameson today actually, while you and Myers go with him to Oceanside," Katie said.

"Morning." Scarborough appeared in the doorway of Marshall's office. "I see we're all getting an early start today."

Katie looked to Agent Scarborough and couldn't help but smile. It seemed that no matter the situation, there was a common thread among the people in this room. They weren't cops on patrol who were perhaps faced with more imminent threats every time they pulled someone over for a simple traffic violation. But they still dealt with murderers, abusers, and people who were the embodiment of evil itself. And yet, they came in to work every day as if they were tasked only with crunching numbers or making sales. How they separated their lives from the nefarious minds of those with whom they came in contact remained a mystery. "No rest for the wicked," Katie replied.

"You ready to go, detective?" Scarborough rested a hand on Gibbons' shoulder. "Agent Myers is waiting. We'd better get a move on." He looked to Katie. "Jameson is heading your way now. He knows the drill. Get what you can on Hudson and let's bring him in. I'll touch base with you after we've had a talk with Branson."

◆◆◆

The I-5 was still seeing the effects of the morning rush hour traffic. Nick continued northbound at a much slower pace than he would have preferred. Gibbons, who had obviously become accustomed to the snail's pace of California commutes, seemed unaffected.

"I don't know how you people put up with this." Nick cast a disapproving glance to Gibbons through the rear view mirror. "I thought traffic in Virginia was bad."

"You work at Quantico?" Gibbons asked.

"Mostly. There and D.C. I live in Woodbridge, which is pretty much in the middle, although it doesn't seem like I'm home often enough."

"So you married? Got kids?" Gibbons continued, clearly making an effort to pass the time.

"Nope. Neither," Scarborough replied, shifting a quick glance to Myers, who was in the passenger seat.

Gibbons seemed to pick up on the exchange and didn't inquire further. "Me? I got a wife and two boys. Ten and Twelve. They're a handful."

"I'll bet," Myers replied.

Nick wasn't particularly good at the small talk. Not that he didn't like Detective Gibbons. He seemed all right. It was just that he preferred not to get too close to people. The more he knew about them and vice versa, the more potential danger there could be. He wasn't a paranoid kind of guy; it was just reality. "I think that's it up ahead." Nick pointed to a large commercial complex.

"You think this guy is going to talk to us?" Gibbons asked.

"I'm sure he already knows we've got Shalot in custody and when he finds out about Hudson, I think he'll be concerned about his two lemmings, or rather what they might say." Nick pulled into the parking lot in his silver rental sedan and killed the engine. He turned back to Gibbons, who had one foot out the door. "I think our best approach is to make him aware that we are only interested in Shalot and Hudson. That he's not the one we're after. My guess is that he'll be reluctant to say much in front of his employer. If he's willing, let's try to get him outside." Nick opened the driver's side door and stepped into the chilly morning air.

Myers stepped out, placing her conservative black-heeled shoe onto the asphalt. As she emerged from the car, she smoothed back her red hair, which she wore in her typical bun, appearing a little apprehensive.

Nick knew this was outside her wheelhouse. She didn't often interview suspects or persons of interest, as Lewis Branson had been designated at this point in time. Analysis, psychoanalysis, social analysis; these were her specialties. But Jameson, who was well versed in this sort of thing, was needed back at the precinct. So he would have to rely on Gibbons, a homicide cop who was a little rough around the edges, but who could clearly handle himself.

There was a growing concern Nick had for Katie after learning that Shalot worked very hard to get close to her. Up until this point, he hadn't realized just to what lengths the man had gone to be near her. As far as he was concerned, Shalot wasn't a threat anymore and, he hadn't put much thought into anything other than finding the killers who they were sure would take another life and soon.

Marshall, however, had seen it differently. His concern was that there could be someone else, maybe even Branson himself who was looking to get at her. Nick had no basis to argue against him, even if he believed Marshall was just being himself where Katie was concerned.

Nick had witnessed that sort of behavior before, the type displayed so prominently in Shalot. Others who had grown obsessed with a victim, particularly one whose case had reached the level of attention Katie's had. The media was so good at creating back stories, true or false. They could make one seem like a saint or a sinner with just a few well-placed words, photos, and video footage. He watched as they all had put Katie on a pedestal last year, admiring her for her strength and resolve to capture the man who had killed young children and tried to end her life as well. She deserved the praise. He knew that better than most, but the attention risked exposing her to people like Shalot.

The three arrived at the front desk of the office and it could not have been more obvious that they were cops.

"Can you tell me if Mr. Lewis Branson is working today?" Nick asked.

The burly-looking man flipped through a binder that lay open on his desk. "Looks like he just came in." He looked up at Nick. "And you are?"

Nick retrieved his badge. "I just need to ask Mr. Branson a few questions." He turned and extended his hand towards Gibbons and Myers. "They're with me as well. We won't be long."

The man's eyes narrowed. Nick thought he might have had reason to be concerned that the federal authorities were at his door, but he only turned away, heading into a back office. It was presumably the office of the gentleman who operated the place.

"Can I help you?"

This was the guy in charge. White-collared shirt, blue tie, navy dress pants. "I'm here to speak with Mr. Branson in connection with an ongoing investigation in San Diego. I, along with Special Agent Myers and Detective Gibbons with San Diego Police, would like to have a quick word with him. Is he available?"

The boss grabbed a radio from the front desk. "Can you send Lewis up here, please? There're some people that want to talk to him."

The radio cracked a moment later. "He's on his way."

"Please, have a seat. He'll be right up." The boss turned back towards his office, but not before casting a curious look at the federal agents.

Lewis Branson emerged from the back of the building, wiping his hands with a paper towel.

Nick thought he looked different from the picture. Less confident. Thinner. Not even remotely like a leader, but maybe that was the point. According to Myers' research, they didn't believe in leaders.

"Mr. Lewis Branson?" Nick asked.

Myers and Gibbons rose from their seats.

"I'm FBI Special Agent Scarborough. This is Special Agent Myers and this is Detective Gibbons with San Diego Police."

"You'll forgive me for not greeting you properly. I've been working on a forklift this morning and, as you can see, grease isn't easily removed." Branson turned up his blackened palms. "What's this about?"

"Mr. Branson." Nick looked around at the growing number of workers who happened to be in the area. "Would you mind stepping outside with us for a moment? This is a somewhat delicate matter that I'm sure you'd prefer to keep to yourself."

Branson's mouth thinned until his lips turned white. "Of course."

Nick led the way through the front door. A small concrete-formed table with adjoining benches was just a few feet away. As the group sat down, Nick wasted no more time.

"Mr. Branson, are you acquainted with an Edward Shalot or Shaun Hudson? Both live in San Diego."

Nick watched the man carefully, reading his shifting expression. He was convinced that Branson knew the men, simply by the way his eyes widened almost imperceptibly. It was the look of recognition.

"I think I've heard the names, but I can't recall from where." Branson's brow furrowed as though in deep thought on the matter. "Why? Did something happen to them?"

"No. They're fine," Nick replied. He didn't like that Branson made no mention of the fact that Shalot's name had been in the news. "What do you know about Discordianism, Mr. Branson?"

"I'm sorry?" He paused. "Discordianism?" All color had drained from Branson's face. "I'm afraid I'm not familiar with that term."

"It's a religion, of sorts. One that seems to have attracted the men I asked you about." Nick was about to go against his own advice, retrieving the file that contained a picture of

Branson at the rally. "You sure you're not familiar with it?" He slid the photo in front of Branson.

Myers tossed a glance to Gibbons, and then shifted it to Scarborough. But Nick pressed on, ignoring her obvious attempt to get him to reel it in.

"Mr. Branson," Myers quickly interrupted, "you're not in any trouble here. We simply want to know if you are acquainted with these gentlemen. One of them is currently in custody in relation to a murder investigation. Perhaps you've heard it on the news? A young woman by the name of Lindsay Brown was attacked and killed in her home last week. It appears as though Mr. Shalot was the last one to see her alive." Myers caught sight of Nick's disapproving stare. "We would like to know if you are also a part of this group in which he often participated, we thought you could give us some insight that might help our investigation."

Detective Gibbons wasn't about to step on the toes of these apparently dueling federal agents and so he decided on another approach. "Mr. Branson, do you come down to San Diego often? Would you be able to provide information as to your whereabouts last Thursday night?"

"I'm sorry; am I being charged with something?"

"Not at all, sir. We're just ruling people out at this point. There are a lot of people involved in this investigation, Mr. Branson. It really is in your best interest to cooperate fully. If you don't answer our questions, we'll have no choice but to request that you come down to my station and make a statement. Now, I'd prefer it if we could avoid that and just get to the heart of the matter right now." Gibbons eyed the windows lining the front of the building. Several people had positioned themselves in a manner as to get a better look at the happenings outside.

It seemed Branson noticed this as well. He quickly turned back. "Okay. Look. I know them." He held his hands up preemptively. "I'm sorry I was hesitant before, but I'm sure you can understand how intimidating this is. "Edward Shalot was a part of our small group, yes. But he was always standoffish, never really assimilating to the lifestyle."

"Lifestyle?" Scarborough asked.

"Yes. It's a long and complicated story, but Discordianism follows a theory of chaos and with that comes a lifestyle that most people wouldn't understand. But as I said, Shalot wasn't like the rest of us."

"Do you believe he was predisposed to violence?" Myers asked.

"Maybe. I don't know. I didn't get to know him very well. Some of the women in our group, well, they didn't care for him much. Got a little too rough. That's not really our thing."

"Mr. Branson, I'm not going to lie to you; we believe there may be people in your organization that might have something to do with the Highway Hunter. I trust you've heard the name?" Nick didn't wait for a reply. "We are confident one of them is Edward Shalot. What we want to know from you is that if you believe anyone else in your group might lean towards the same tendencies as Shalot. Do you understand my question?"

"Yes." Branson appeared to harden his stance. "You think I'm involved with people who are killers. Does that sum it up?" At this, he was becoming defensive. "We're not freaks and murderers, you know. We just choose to live differently than the rest of you do."

"I'm not suggesting..." Nick started.

"Yes, you are. Look, I don't believe any of my members are capable of murder. Edward Shalot is different and I've been working to put distance between us because, frankly, the man is obviously insane. Hell, maybe Shaun Hudson is involved. I don't know. It's clear you've got reason to suspect that he is. But Agent Scarborough, I can assure you, we do not condone violence and certainly not murder. I can't explain how Shalot could possibly interpret our faith in such a manner. It's not what I preach and not what any of my followers believe."

Nick continued to study Branson's features, searching for meaning behind his words. "Okay. Well, thank you for your time, Mr. Branson. That's all we've got for now. But if we have any further questions, can we count on your help?" Nick asked.

"Of course. Anything you need. I have to get back to work now." Branson pushed up from the table and headed back inside the building.

Once Branson had disappeared, they returned to the car.

"He's trying to throw Shalot under the bus. He was nervous, I'll tell you that much." Nick turned on the ignition.

"I thought you weren't going to go on the attack?" Myers asked.

"Didn't you see the look in his eyes? He was lying. I had to make him aware that I knew he was lying." Nick's voice elevated just slightly to make his point. "Dammit. I feel like we're going in circles here. What do we need to bring this guy in? He's behind this. Has to be. I'm sure he and Shalot met in Colorado long before any of this started."

"Even if we can prove that, we're no closer to finding out who the others involved are. Jameson is still waiting on a positive match from the sample in Phoenix. If that comes back and we've got a name, we'll be able to determine if that person is a part of Branson's group too. In my opinion, that would be enough to bring Branson in, voluntarily or not," Myers said.

"Don't go working yourselves up too much just yet. This isn't over. I say we drive to the guy's house and check it out." Gibbons slouched down in the back seat.

"We can't do that. We don't have a warrant," Nick replied.

"Who said anything about a warrant? I'm just saying we ought to check out his neighborhood. The kind of place he lives in. You know, just have a look around. And if it so happens that the place is unlocked, then so much the better."

Nick eyed Gibbons through the rear view again. Only this time, a half-cocked smile crossed his face.

19

THE CALL HAD come when Agent Scarborough arrived in Oceanside and now it was time for Marshall and Agent Jameson to catch up to Shaun Hudson.

"The kid should be getting out of his first class of the morning. Should we head over to the campus and pick him up?" Marshall said.

"Sounds good. You want me to track down Ms. Reid?" Jameson asked.

"No. I think you and I should handle this. I'm not sure she needs to be there. The guy might get a little aggressive and she doesn't need to be around that."

Jameson shrugged his shoulders. "Okay. You ready to go?"

Marshall grabbed his keys, leading the way towards the front of the station.

The doors of his car were unlocked remotely and Marshall tossed his coat into the backseat, sliding behind the wheel. Jameson entered the front passenger side.

"Nice car."

"Thanks. Just a little beefed up from the standard department-issued Ford, but I like it."

"So, you were the one who worked with Scarborough to find the man who kidnapped Katie?" Jameson asked without hesitation.

"Yep. That's me. Scarborough's a hell of an agent. You're lucky to be working with him."

Jameson gripped the handle above the passenger door window. "He is. I don't think the guy actually sleeps, though. He's probably one of the most dedicated agents that I've had the pleasure of working with."

"I hear you may get a break on the case in Phoenix?" Marshall pulled into the south parking lot of the campus.

"It might be another day or two, I don't know, but yeah, we got a sample that didn't match the victim and they're running it through CODIS and we're praying for a hit."

"Let's hope you get it before the next victim." Marshall looked at Hudson's class schedule. "According to this, he should be in building C104. I say we wait for him to come out."

Jameson nodded, opening the passenger door. "I could get used to this weather." He placed the sunglasses on his face. "If I was at home right now, I'd be scraping ice off my windshield and raking up a pile of leaves from my driveway."

"Where's home?" Marshall asked, closing the driver's side door.

"Alexandria." Jameson straightened his tie, smoothing it over his shirt. "There's building C over there."

The two made their way to the building and stood outside. It would be another twenty minutes before Hudson was due to finish. Marshall retrieved his cell phone and began scrolling through his emails. So far, nothing from Katie. She'd been left out of the loop with regards to Hudson and Lewis Branson. It wouldn't sit well with her and it was only a matter of time before he would hear about it. But there were times when her involvement might lead to situations he'd rather not put her in. This was one of those times.

Gibbons had let her go off on her own to talk with Hudson the other day. Marshall wasn't happy about that and felt that Gibbons had put her at risk. Katie wasn't a trained officer. If something had gone wrong, if Hudson had turned violent, she would have had zero protection. Was he the only one who understood that fact?

Jameson glanced at the time. "Kid should be coming out now."

They stood watch outside the double doors, waiting for Hudson. There was another exit on the opposite side, but they took their best guess assuming that Hudson would head out this way towards his next class, kitty-corner to the building they were at now.

Hudson emerged through the doors and didn't spot them at first. Marshall quickly approached.

"Shaun Hudson?" He already had his badge out.

Hudson was clearly startled by the unexpected presence of a cop. His face turned a sickly pale and he looked as though he might faint at any moment.

"I'm Detective Marshall Avery with San Diego Police and this is FBI Special Agent Dwight Jameson."

Jameson pulled his badge. "We would like to question you about your relationship with Edward Shalot, the man in custody for the murder of Lindsay Brown." Jameson stepped towards the kid.

"Okay, okay. You don't need to put cuffs on me. I'll go with you and answer anything you need." Shaun noticed a growing number of students hanging nearby.

"You're not under arrest, Mr. Hudson. Not yet. This way, please." Marshall placed a hand on his shoulder and pointed him in the direction of the parking lot.

◆◆◆

"Look, I'm telling you, I don't know anything about Shalot other than what you already know." Hudson leaned against Marshall's car.

"You work in Student Records, is that right?" Marshall asked.

"Yes."

"We know you gave Shalot the files of another student, but what we really need to know is who instructed you to falsify his transcripts so that he could attend this school?"

In that moment, a call came in on Marshall's cell. He retrieved the phone and noticed it was Katie. "I gotta take this." He stepped away from the car while Jameson continued with Hudson.

"Hey, I'm sorry I didn't tell you I was heading to see Hudson with Agent Jameson."

But before he could continue, she stopped him.

"You're with Shaun Hudson now? Oh my God. Detective Gibbons just forwarded me an email from the officer working on the phone records from the news station. Said he was in the middle of talking to Branson and asked me to look into his findings."

"Go on."

"It's Shaun Hudson, Marshall. Just like we thought. He's the one who's been passing along the information, trying to point us to Shalot."

"Son of a bitch." Marshall looked over his shoulder. "He's the goddamn source? Shit." He rubbed his head, thinking of how he was going to handle this.

"Marshall?"

"Yeah. I'm here. He works to get Shalot into the school and now he's handing over everything he can to convict him? I gotta go sort through this. Agent Jameson's talking to him now. I need to get back over there. I'll call you later." Marshall ended the call and walked back towards them. "I hear you like to gamble, Shaun."

Hudson looked at him. "Sometimes, yeah. Doesn't everyone?"

"No. Not everyone." Marshall looked to Jameson, trying to convey that he was onto something. "You owe anyone money right now?"

"No. Look, I don't know what you heard about me, but I told Agent Jameson that I didn't make up any transcripts to get Edward Shalot into this school. I mean, shit, I don't have that kind of authority to get into those systems."

"Well, that doesn't matter much right now, but I did just get some very interesting information. Why don't you tell me about your relationship with that reporter from Channel 9 – what's his name? Marc Aguilar?"

At this, Shaun Hudson lost all color and couldn't swallow the lump that had risen in his throat.

"Come on, Shaun. I know you were working to put the blame on Shalot for the death of Lindsay Brown, feeding Aguilar all sorts of dirty secrets about him, but what I don't know is why, or who directed you to do it," Marshall continued.

"We know you and Shalot are involved in some group led by a guy named Lewis Branson," Jameson said.

Hudson's eyes momentarily widened at the mention of Branson. "It's just some stupid game. That's all it is. No one takes the shit seriously. We get our rocks off once in a while and laugh and joke around. The whole thing is based on some great cosmic joke."

"Tell that to the victims of the, what do you call it, Law of Five?" Marshall moved in close. "Enough of the lies, kid. You and I both know you gave Shalot a false background. Made it look like he graduated from Connecticut. Then decided it was okay to hand over the personal records of a student to him. A student who also happens to work for the San Diego Police. A student who happens to be my fucking girlfriend." Marshall grabbed the neck of Hudson's t-shirt. "Now tell me who instructed you to set him up? Was it Branson? Did you owe him money and he said you'd be even so long as you hand over some useful information to that reporter?"

"Hey! Avery, back the fuck up. What the hell is wrong with you, man?"

"Someone directed this guy to create a false identity for Shalot." Marshall tugged on his jacket, realizing he had lost his temper. "I want to know who. Is Lewis Branson after Katie Reid?"

"You better talk, man. I can only do so much," Jameson warned.

Hudson straightened his shirt, his hands still trembling. "I started visiting this online chat room. I was just curious; experimenting, you know? I'm a history major and, at the time, we were studying the founder of the Illuminati.

"Anyway, I was just playing around on the internet and came across this off-shoot of the Illuminati's 'New World Order,' called Discordianism. I thought it was kind of cool; the whole chaos and theory of how everything occurs in fives and shit. So I found this chat room where the members hung out. I got to know some of them.

"About a year or so ago, I went to one of their meetings. It was more like a rally. That's where I first met Shalot and Lewis Branson. He was kind of like the leader, only there really is no leader. It's complicated."

Marshall was ready to punch the kid, but continued to wait for him to reveal something that might actually be of use.

"I was just hired on at the school Admin office and was getting ready to start my second year. I was blown away by the things Branson was talking about. The order of chaos and the Greek goddess Eris. The whole Law of Fives, where everything is related to five. It'll blow your mind."

This time, it was Agent Jameson who appeared to be losing his patience. "Look, you better start telling us something that has to do with why you made up those records and started handing stuff off to that reporter. Did Branson pay you to do it? Give you a little seed money for poker?"

"Branson knew I liked to gamble. He also knew that I was having some recent financial troubles as a result. I like to play poker with the guys once in a while and sometimes the cards go against me." Hudson looked to the men, who appeared to be at the end of their rope. "I knew of Edward Shalot from the rally and Branson asked that I help him get into this school a while back. I didn't ask why. I just took the money. He offered me five grand to enter fake transcripts into the school's system. I mean, I didn't know the guy had a thing for that chick who had been all over the news last year."

Jameson cast a look to Marshall, as if ensuring he wasn't about to lunge at the kid.

"I just took the money and did what I was told. Then, just before Lindsay Brown died, Branson asked me to help him out on some other stuff and said he would make it worth my while. Like making sure you all found out that Shalot wasn't a stand-up guy. That he liked to hurt women." Hudson shook his head. "Look, am I going to jail for this?"

"Did you two hang out with other people who followed Branson?" Marshall asked.

"Sometimes. Yeah. But it's not like it was my whole life or something. Shalot was more into it than I was. He would try to drag me to swingers clubs, strip clubs, whatever, to try and find women who were interested in the lifestyle. But me? Look, I'm not gonna lie. The parties they threw were pretty freakin' awesome. But, it was just a side thing for me. That's all. Shalot took personal offense to anyone who wasn't into it."

"Offense enough that he might kill for it?" Marshall asked.

Hudson cast his eyes upwards towards the men hovering over him. "I guess."

◆◆◆

Agent Scarborough pulled up to Lewis Branson's home that he was renting from a retired couple who now lived in Florida, according to Myers' information.

"This is it." Nick cut the engine. "Let's have a look around."

They stepped out of the car, approaching the front of the house in a casual, non-threatening manner, although no one appeared to be out and about that might take any notice. It was midday on a Wednesday and this was clearly a working-class area. Most would likely be at work right about now.

Nick cupped his hands over the front window and leaned in. "Doesn't look like anyone's home."

"No car in the driveway either," Myers said. "I'm assuming he lives alone."

Detective Gibbons was the first to try the front door. "Locked." Without waiting for further direction, he took to moving around the side of the house towards the gate. He stood on his tip toes to peer over it and spotted a padlock on the other side. No way in there either.

As he stepped back, Gibbons landed on a large stone, causing his ankle to twist. "Son of a bitch!" He knelt down to rub the pain away. That was when he noticed the narrow window covered in what looked like black fabric. The outside of the window was covered in filth and partially obscured by the dirt and grass from the side yard. "Hey!" he shouted.

Nick and Agent Myers appeared from the front of the home; both jogged to meet him.

"You all right?" Myers asked.

"Yeah. I'm fine. Just twisted my ankle." He pointed to the window. "This place has a basement."

Nick squatted down to get a better look. "It's blacked out." He reached out and pushed on it, but the window didn't budge. He looked back to Gibbons and knew what he had to do next.

Nick got on both knees, ignoring the dirt and grass that would stain his otherwise perfectly pressed black pants. Using both hands, he pulled on the window frame. It was an old style aluminum frame that had a crank on the inside to open it and it had clearly been neglected over the years. The frame shifted inside the concrete that surrounded it. Nick turned to Gibbons and smiled. "The owner should really get this fixed." He pulled on it a little more, careful not to shatter the glass, and the frame slowly edged out of its opening.

Myers lowered a hand and helped Gibbons back to his feet. "Don't think that I'm even remotely small enough to slip through that space."

"Come on. You can squeeze through that, no problem," Gibbons said jokingly.

"No one's going in. I just want to get a look inside." Nick bent down further, leaning his head in as far as it would go, which wasn't far. The window opening wasn't more than eight inches tall, at best. The house had been built before current laws dictated that basements have a window well with a ladder for emergency escape. This window probably did nothing more than allow the basement to flood after a good rain on occasion.

"Holy shit." Nick pulled his head out. "We need to call for backup now!"

"What? What is it?" Myers asked.

"Screw backup. Knock the damn door down!" Gibbons said. "What the hell's in there?" He hobbled back to the front entrance, Scarborough and Myers following behind.

"What are you doing?" Myers asked. "I'm gonna call Oceanside PD now."

"Just hold up." Gibbons turned to Nick. "What exactly did you see in there? A dead body?"

"No. The place is covered in red paint. Go have a look for yourself." Nick turned to Myers. "That symbol is all over the walls."

"What symbol?" Gibbons asked.

"The V that's been carved on all the victims' bodies. Same one that was carved into Lindsay Brown."

"Jesus!" Gibbons picked up a planter that had been placed on the porch and tossed it through the front window.

"What the hell are you doing?" Meyers said. "We need to let the local authorities know we're here."

Gibbons looked around. "Oh, I'm sure one of the neighbors will call after hearing that." He pulled his sleeve over his hand and cleared the glass in order to step over the frame. Once inside, he opened the front door. "Let's go have a look inside that basement."

"You're bat-shit crazy, you know that?" Myers walked through the door.

"Maybe. But this is a hell of a lot faster than waiting for PD to get here. You both said yourselves that we were running out of time before another murder happens. Maybe we just prevented that."

The basement door in the kitchen was bolted shut. "Someone doesn't want anyone down there," Scarborough said. "Or they don't want anyone down there to get out."

In that moment, a faint, but noticeable scream drifted from beyond the door.

"Did you hear that?" Scarborough used the butt of his gun to break the lock and unlatch the bolt. He led the way down the dark staircase.

Myers found the switch, but Nick had already reached the bottom. The room illuminated in an instant.

"What the fuck?" Gibbons hopped down the steps on one leg as the room revealed itself to him.

The walls were covered with symbols. Pentagons with images and more symbols inside them. They had seen these before. And the V was everywhere, spray painted in blood-red.

"The photograph of Branson at the rally; the background looked almost the same," Myers said.

"Hello? Is there anyone in here?" Nick yelled. It looked as though there was just the one room, but where had the voice come from?

There it was again.

"Over here." Myers ran to the wall on the right side. "There has to be an opening here somewhere."

Scarborough and Gibbons joined her.

The voice continued. It belonged to a woman, one who was clearly terrified.

"Nick, over here," Myers said. "This door — she's inside."

The small door where Myers stood could only house something along the lines of a sump pump system or maybe a small storage area.

"It's locked." Myers turned the handle. "This is the FBI. Are you okay?" she shouted through the door.

"Get me out of here!" the woman yelled.

Nick again worked to break the lock. This one proved easier than the door at the top of the stairs. He proceeded to open the door with caution, unsure of what he would find behind it.

Inside was a woman, her hands bound to a pipe that disappeared into the concrete floor.

"You're okay. I'm with the FBI. You're going to be fine." Nick moved in towards her and examined the cuffs. "Gibbons, call for backup. Tell them to bring bolt cutters."

20

THE CONFIRMATION THAT Shaun Hudson had been Aguilar's source was enough for them to arrest him. He'd withheld information pertinent to an investigation. They placed him in the back of Marshall's car and headed to the station. Neither had believed Hudson's assertion that he hadn't known Shalot killed Lindsay Brown. It would be priority to question Hudson further so that he might implicate Branson or others in the Highway Hunter killings and Marshall and Jameson were confident the kid had that information.

Upon their arrival, the two hadn't yet known that the others were in Branson's home, trying to free a woman he'd held captive.

Katie waited for Marshall outside the interrogation room where they had just left Hudson. "They found a woman in Branson's home. She was in bad shape, Marshall."

"Scarborough called you?"

"Gibbons did," she replied. "This woman they found had a lot of information to share about Lewis Branson. He went on to tell me that Branson had wanted Edward Shalot out of the way. According to what this woman said, Shalot had become too volatile and couldn't be counted on any longer. That his obsession with me had gotten out of control and he risked exposing Branson."

Marshall gently took Katie by the arm and led her out of the hallway. "Let's go to my office. Jameson can handle this."

Marshall closed the door to his office as Katie took a seat.

"Why didn't you tell me you were already going after Hudson this morning? I would've liked to have been there with you." She began.

"Because I needed to be sure you weren't around if things went south. We had originally gone to see him based on what you and I had discovered last night, but when you called about the phone records, it was enough to arrest him. Look, Kate, you're not a trained officer. There are some things that I have to handle on my own. I'm sure that's not what you want to hear, but it's the reality of the situation. I can't always be worried about your safety."

"Then stop worrying about it." She quickly lowered her tone, realizing her frustration had taken over. "I'm sorry. It's just that this directly impacts me and you know it. You're right. I don't carry a gun, but damn it, since when are we not a team?"

Marshall fell into his chair. "We are a team, Kate. But there are still people out there who, given your very public story, have a morbid interest in you. Shalot is one of those people. He and Hudson are involved in some bizarre shit that honestly scares the hell out of me." He paused for a moment to regain control of the conversation. "So what do we know about this woman they found?"

"She was handcuffed to a sump pump pipe in his basement. You remember that photograph posted online with Branson speaking at a gathering?"

Marshall nodded.

"The basement was covered in those same symbols. And, the V. Lots of them. From what that woman stated, she was trying to leave him, but he wouldn't let her. She'd heard that Branson had encouraged a few of the members to show the world that chaos would reign. That it was necessary to restore order. My guess is that Shalot was one of them."

"For God's sake." Marshall shook his head. "But Gibbons also mentioned that Branson wanted Shalot out of the way?"

"According to the woman, Branson was grooming him. He wanted him to be 'second in command,' so to speak."

"Okay, Shalot's in custody and people are still dying. So, there are others out there 'restoring order'?" Marshall asked.

"It got back to Branson that Shalot thought he could go it alone. That he was building his own following. Only Shalot had taken it a step further than Branson intended, insisting that his followers leave their mark and make themselves known as the 'Brotherhood of the Five.' These were only rumblings she had come across, but all of it scared her enough that she wanted to leave.

"I don't blame her." Marshall leaned in, his face masked in anger. "Are they after you?"

"No," Katie said. "Not that Gibbons mentioned."

Marshall leaned back in his chair and turned towards the window, peering out in silence. "That doesn't explain why Shalot's been insisting to you that he's innocent. We've got his damn DNA on the victim. What did he hope to gain by this?"

"I don't know yet. But, I think Branson wanted to put a stop to him. He seemed to know that Shalot had gone way off the rails and risked exposing all of them. We'll know more when they get back from Oceanside, but I think that was why he used Shaun Hudson to feed information to Marc. The authorities discovering that woman locked up in his basement probably wasn't part of the plan, though."

"Did she believe Lewis Branson would kill her?" Marshall asked. "Son of a bitch sounds just as crazy as Shalot."

"Gibbons said she was pretty shaken up. Branson did a number on her." Katie witnessed the shift in Marshall's demeanor. It wasn't fear and it wasn't anger. It was rage she saw behind his eyes.

◆◆◆

Agent Jameson was standing outside the interrogation room when Marshall approached. "Have you spoken to Hudson? Is his attorney here yet?"

"I think they're bringing him down now. He just arrived. Did you hear what they found in Oceanside?"

"I did. We're getting close now, we have to be." Marshall leaned against the wall, folding his arms. "I'm sure they're already on their way to arrest Branson."

Katie caught up to them in the hall and soon spotted a young man wearing a suit rounding the corner. "That must be him."

Marshall now stood at attention, waiting for the suit to introduce himself.

The young attorney, Katie believed, couldn't have been more than twenty-four, maybe twenty-five, although he looked about fifteen. She would be turning thirty in just a few months, but felt much older.

"I'm Jackson Parrish. I'll be representing Mr. Hudson. I understand you would like to interview him?" the lawyer said.

Marshall shook his hand. "Yes. I'm Detective Avery. I'm working with FBI Agent Jameson on this investigation. This is Katie Reid. She will be accompanying us in the interview."

"Nice to meet you all. Shall we go in?" Parrish asked.

Jameson held the door open. Inside, Shaun Hudson, even with his husky build, looked small and frail, like a frightened boy.

"Mr. Hudson, I'm Jackson Parrish, your court-appointed attorney. I'll be representing you. This is Detective Avery, Agent Jameson and Katie Reid. They'd like to ask you a few questions."

"I know who they are." Hudson's intonation suggested he might be reluctant to cooperate.

"I see. Well, shall we get started?" Parrish retrieved the digital recorder from his briefcase and placed it on the table.

"This is all being recorded anyway, Mr. Parrish." Marshall pointed to the cameras mounted on the walls.

"Of course. I just prefer to have my own records." Parrish gestured to Marshall. "Please, begin."

Katie kept quiet for the moment, letting Jameson and Marshall take the lead. Marshall began to speak.

"Shaun, you and I met earlier today. Is that correct?"

He nodded.

"Mr. Hudson," Parrish began, "you'll need to speak so we can have it for the record."

"Yes. I met Detective Avery earlier today, outside of my class."

"Thank you." Marshall continued. "The FBI will be taking Lewis Branson into custody in a short while. He apparently kidnapped and was holding a woman against her will. Do you know Mr. Branson?" Marshall needed verbal confirmation although he already knew the answer.

This appeared to be news to Hudson as his voice trembled in response. "Who—who is she?"

"That doesn't matter right now," Jameson started. "Do you know Lewis Branson?"

Hudson looked to his attorney, ensuring it was okay to answer. "Yes. I know him."

"And you know Edward Shalot?"

"Yes. You know that already," Hudson replied.

"Shaun, who instructed you to create false transcripts for Edward Shalot so that he might attend UCSD?" Agent Jameson continued.

"I'm sorry." Parrish held up his hand and turned to his client. "You don't have to answer that, Shaun."

"I suggest you advise your client to help in any way that he can. He's in a great deal of trouble and the FBI might find their way to working out a deal if he answers our questions," Jameson said.

Hudson didn't wait for his lawyer, opting instead to heed the advice of the agent. "Lewis Branson offered me a substantial amount of money to create Edward Shalot's false records. Look, I told you before; I wasn't into this thing like these guys. I just needed the money. I fucked up, okay? But that doesn't make me a killer."

"You're not here because you're suspected of killing anyone, Shaun." Marshall looked on with an artificial concern. "Do you know why Branson wanted Shalot here? Why he asked that you forge those records?"

"No."

Marshall paused for a moment and caught sight of Katie. She appeared aloof and disconnected.

He turned back to Hudson. "Did you know Lindsay Brown?"

Shaun looked again to the lawyer, who didn't object to the question. "Yes."

"How did you two meet?"

"Through her roommate. She's a part of the community."

This wasn't the answer Marshall had expected. His pulse began to quicken. "The roommate? Lindsay Brown's roommate?"

Katie seemed to perk up at this revelation. No one had talked to the roommate since Lindsay was found dead. There had been no evidence that suggested she was anything more than a roommate who happened to be out of town that night. At least, that was what she told the authorities.

"Was the roommate the one who introduced Edward to Lindsay as well?" Katie asked.

"Her name is Laura Kempt." Shaun began rubbing his palms together. His knee hit the bottom of the table in a nervous twitch.

Marshall picked up on the shift. He watched as Shaun's chest began to rise and fall quickly. "Shaun, did Laura know Shalot before he met Lindsay Brown?"

"Yes, I—I think so, yes. He did."

Marshall slammed the table. "Dammit!" He pushed himself up from the chair and began pacing the room. "So,

Laura made the introduction to Lindsay, why? In hopes Shalot might recruit her as well? But, when she wasn't interested, Shalot lost his temper, as he was known for, and threatened her." He began to rub his fingers through his hair again.

Katie knew he was trying to put the pieces together, but she thought she might have already done it. "Shaun, we know that Branson felt Shalot was getting out of control and that he feared Shalot would turn his own followers against him. Do you know who's in the Brotherhood of the Five?"

Marshall stopped pacing and focused his attention on Katie.

"I didn't kill Lindsay. Edward didn't kill Lindsay." Hudson paused, seeming to realize he had no choice but to reveal the truth. "Laura did. She loved Edward, but he didn't feel the same. Edward Shalot loved you and she couldn't stand that. Branson used that to his advantage."

Parrish dropped his head into his hands, sighing heavily. He looked to Marshall. "You have any more questions?"

"If you knew this, Shaun, why the hell didn't you come forward?" Jameson appeared on the verge of losing control. If they'd known, they might have been able to prevent the death of the woman in Phoenix; possibly, but now it would remain an unrealized opportunity.

"I don't know. I was afraid. Lewis twisted Laura around, making her believe Edward would never love her, and she would have to resort to desperate measures to change that. Then he called me just days before she died. It was as if he knew what would happen, what Laura would do. That's when he offered me more money to start leaving tips about Edward. I needed the cash." Shaun Hudson appeared to crumble under the weight of his cowardice.

"If Laura Kempt killed Lindsay, she would've had to have known about the Highway Hunter killings; the carving, the dandelions. Who told her, Shaun? And what do you know about these murders?" Katie asked.

"I don't know anything. I promise you. I don't know who's behind those horrible murders that have been all over the news. I guess I thought it could be Edward; I—I'd heard rumors from other members. Look, I only did what I was paid to do. I'm sorry. I don't know anything more than that." Shaun lowered his head.

They all seemed to pick up on the fact that this kid was in way over his head, but they needed more from him.

"I can only assume that Laura slept with Shalot at least once, which was enough to obtain and plant DNA on Lindsay's body. And since she had just filed a restraining order, at Laura's behest, Shalot was the obvious suspect. DNA would confirm that," Marshall said. "But that doesn't answer the question as to how she knew of the other killings. She had to be one of Edward's followers, considering she was in love with him."

"I think Branson probably wanted Edward dead, but Laura couldn't do it, so she did the next best thing—she framed him," Jameson began. "Shaun, do you know who Edward's followers are? This Brotherhood of the Five? If you do, you have to tell us. We believe there's going to be another murder. Shaun, we need you to do the right thing here."

Katie looked to the lawyer. "Mr. Parrish. We need those names. There is another life at stake." Perhaps pleading to the lawyer would help. Maybe he could convince Shaun that it would only help him to cooperate.

"I'd like to speak with my client alone for a moment."

"Of course." Katie rose from her chair.

Jameson held the door, closing it behind him when they'd filed out. "It's as if he was playing double agent or something. Doing what Shalot wanted while working to help Branson too."

"When is Scarborough due back? Have you heard from him?" Marshall asked.

"Don't know, but I'll find out. He may get the answers we need from Branson himself. I'm tired of screwing around with this guy. The problem is, the fifth murder could happen today, tomorrow, three days from now. We just don't know, but we need to put a stop to it."

Agent Scarborough, along with Detective Gibbons and Agent Myers, appeared at the end of the hall.

"We just booked Branson into federal custody. We've got him on kidnapping for now. What did you find out with Hudson?" Scarborough said.

They moved to the conference room and Agent Jameson filled the team in on what they had discovered about Hudson, Shalot, and the roommate, Laura Kempt.

That was enough for Scarborough. "Son of a bitch. Branson won't talk without a lawyer. I won't get any names from him, assuming he knows who the Five are. It's gotta be this kid and it's gotta be now."

They returned to the interrogation room, where Hudson was ready to talk.

"My client wishes to make a deal prior to speaking on the matter any further." Parrish pushed a sheet of paper towards Agent Scarborough.

Nick read the document, handing it to Marshall and Detective Gibbons to confirm. Although, ultimately, this was a federal investigation and any deals would have to be agreed upon by the feds. Nick was simply giving the San Diego police a chance to review it.

"Agreed," Nick replied. "Now, you need to tell me who is in Shalot's group and where we can find them. There is at least one life at stake."

"I don't know where they live; I'm not even sure they're responsible for any of those Highway Hunter murders, I mean, I would've come forward if I thought..."

"The names, Shaun." Jameson appeared to have grown impatient with the kid's back peddling.

Hudson looked to his lawyer and nodded his head. Parrish tore a piece of paper from his notebook and handed it to Agent Scarborough.

"We need to run a search on these names." Scarborough looked to his team. "We know where Laura Kempt is staying. We'll pick her up first. As soon as we have a location on the others, call it in. Get units out there as quickly as possible."

"Gibbons and I can track down Kempt," Marshall said. "Give Jameson a chance to find the others."

"Good." Nick turned to leave without another word.

◆◆◆

The agents mobilized quickly. Scarborough called in to the local departments where the suspects were thought to live. All were near where the victims had been found. It seemed their little network was bigger than they thought. Shalot recruited far and wide.

Jameson and Myers had returned to the conference room and Katie decided to join them, feeling a little obsolete at this point.

It was as if the entire department was just set on fire. Captain Hearn was on the phone with the ASAC in the FBI field office, coordinating efforts and working to effectively shut down any and all websites where the followers made contact with one another. Junior detectives working under Gibbons were taking Hudson's statement and working on the terms of the deal the FBI had struck with him.

Katie wasn't about to sit idly by. This involved her whether Marshall wanted to believe it or not. Shalot was the mastermind behind all of it and he ultimately wanted her.

"What can I do to help?" she asked Agent Myers.

"We're entering the names into NGI now. We're hoping to get hits on them. If these are our suspects in connection with the other four murders, setting aside what we already know of Lindsay Brown, then any DNA, hair samples, or any identifying factors that would have been entered by local authorities would give us a hit in CODIS. We'll cross-reference the two and hopefully come up with a match."

Katie leaned over Jameson just enough so that she could get a glimpse of the program. "I'm familiar with CODIS. That's the DNA database, right?"

Myers nodded.

"I'm not familiar with NGI, though."

"It's the Next Generation Identification program; the replacement for the fingerprint system we used to use called IAFIS."

Katie knew she was in over her head when it came to FBI acronyms, but she was starting to get the gist.

"NGI is an identification program using advanced biometric identifiers. Whereas we used to rely mainly on fingerprints, photos, identifying marks, this system goes a step further. A lot further, actually. Facial recognition, iris data, even palm prints." Myers couldn't help but smile. "This is definitely next generation stuff, right here."

Katie liked Agent Myers. Admired her, even. "So, Agent Jameson inputs the names into the system, searches for any records, arrests, prints. That sort of thing?"

"Exactly."

"We got a hit!" Jameson turned the screen towards Agent Myers. "Hayden Jennings, twenty-four, currently lives in Roanoke." He looked up at Myers. "Not far from our first victim."

"The guy's got quite a record. Assault, sexual assault, larceny. What else do we know about him?" she asked Jameson.

"I'll pinpoint an address so we can call out the local authorities and get him into custody. I'm still working on the others. No hits yet, but it can take a while to search."

Agent Myers stepped back a few feet and Katie followed. "So, I hear you been through a pretty rough ordeal." Myers said.

Katie raised the corners of her mouth just slightly, hesitant at Myers' question.

"I'm sorry," Myers began. "Not my business. It's just that Agent Scarborough thinks very highly of you. He said you held your own when the shit hit the fan, so to speak."

"Agent Scarborough was there when I needed him. Stood by me every step of the way, without making me feel like a victim. He's a good man. Tough, but good."

"He is." Myers grinned.

Katie picked up on her tenor. It was one of admiration, certainly, but also one of a woman who seemed to be in love with the person of whom she was speaking. "Are you married, Agent Myers? Got any kids?"

"No husband, no kids. Guess you could say I'm married to the job. You know, that old cliché?"

"Sounds like you might have quite a bit in common with Agent Scarborough."

Jameson raised a hand. "Got it. I got the address of Hayden Jennings."

"Let Scarborough know now. I'll put out an ATL." Myers rushed to her seat and opened her laptop.

That was a term with which Katie was familiar. Most people called it an APB, or All-Points Bulletin. But in the recent past, she'd heard it called ATL or Attempt to Locate. It would take years to learn and understand the vernacular her own agency used, let alone that of the FBI.

Katie left the conference room in search of Marshall. She wanted to tell him what they had found. But when she arrived at his office, it was empty.

A uniformed officer walked past her.

"Hey, have you seen Detective Avery around?"

"I think he left with Detective Gibbons a few minutes ago. They were in Captain Hearn's office earlier. I heard them talking, but I think they left after that."

"Okay. Thanks."

Katie headed back to the conference room where Agent Scarborough returned and was now in a huddle with Jameson and Myers. Suddenly, she felt even more out of place than before.

"Katie." Scarborough caught sight of her and waved her over. "I know Avery and Gibbons are tracking down Laura Kempt. I'd like you to come with me to talk to Shalot again." Nick turned to Myers for confirmation, then began. "We just got word that a woman has gone missing in Sparks, Nevada. It seems Branson is looking for a way out of this jam and let us in on the details. One of Shalot's followers is responsible, but he insists he doesn't know who or where, only heard that it was going down. Shalot must know something as to the woman's location and we need him to talk before we lose someone else." He paused for a moment. "This won't be easy, but Shalot will be a hell of a lot more talkative if you're there. He wants to win you over, impress you."

Katie squeezed her eyes shut, not wanting to believe that someone would kill to impress her.

"I know," Nick continued. "It's pretty screwed up, but I think he'll want to prove to you that he's the savior of this next victim. That her fate rests in his hands; a God complex. Will you come?"

"Of course."

"Good. I've been in contact with the sheriff in Sparks to let them know what they're dealing with. They're doing everything they can on their end. The rest is up to us." Nick stepped out of the huddle. "Jameson, follow up with Roanoke on that address. Call the field office, let them know too." He led Katie to the door. "Myers, continue to coordinate with the local authorities where our victims were found. Make sure they've entered everything they've got into the database. We're going to need all the help we can get to identify the suspects unless we can get to Shalot fast."

◆◆◆

Katie felt a sense of déjà vu on the ride with Agent Scarborough. It seemed impossible to consider that she was in this situation, although it was nothing like before, when Hendrickson was after her. This time, she'd have to play up to the man who was obsessed with her. She would be in the position of power, not tied up to some chair, waiting to get the crap beat out of her, or worse. Unfortunately, that fate was placed upon another innocent victim. She would have to get Shalot to talk if they stood a chance at all of saving this woman.

"Hudson knew the names of Shalot's followers, but nothing more. I thought maybe Branson would have more information, but he said Shalot was acting on his own." Nick said.

"For God's sake." Katie turned to the passenger window, watching the buildings of downtown move past, almost in slow motion. Traffic was heavy, as usual, further adding to the sense of urgency they each felt in that moment. "Do you think this will ever end?"

"I'm sorry?" Nick briefly glanced in her direction.

"Do you think I'll ever stop being the girl who got away? The girl who brought down a murderer?"

"Eventually." He seemed to consider his next words carefully. "The world we live in today connects all of us in ways we've never experienced before. Fame or notoriety is so easily obtained now. One only need to post a video of anything onto the internet, good or bad, and it can make them famous overnight. The impact of that influences people whose ideas of right and wrong are blurred, or completely distorted. We can't filter them out either.

"Your case received national attention. That doesn't fade quickly and neither do the people who want to know you." Nick took a deep breath. "It will pass eventually, Katie, and you'll go on to live a normal life. I truly believe that. Not everyone turns out to be an Edward Shalot."

He pulled into the garage of the FBI field office. "They know we're coming and should have already prepped Shalot and his attorney."

"How much longer can you keep him in holding?" Katie asked.

"His next court appearance is scheduled in three days. He'll then be transferred to a federal processing facility while he waits for trial. We've got hard DNA evidence on him, Katie. It won't take long to get a conviction and no judge in the world would set bail on this case."

"Even if he didn't do it? I mean, it's not like he's going to admit to instructing any of his followers to commit murder. If we're lucky we'll get the name of the one in Sparks, but how are you going to keep him here?"

"We got the word of a kid looking out for himself, telling us it was Laura Kempt who killed Lindsay. Hard to dispute the physical evidence we've already got. We'll have to see what Avery and Gibbons find when they locate her." Nick opened the car door. "Come on. Let's get this over with and see if we can save someone's life."

21

DETECTIVE GIBBONS ROLLED up to the apartment complex where Laura Kempt was said to be staying until the house she shared with Lindsay Brown was no longer a crime scene.

"Let's see if this chick's still here." He stepped out of his black Chevy.

Marshall followed, pulling on the jacket he'd tossed in the back seat.

They climbed the flight of stairs, the metal railing clattering in their wake. The complex was old and hadn't been well cared for. Kempt had told the police she was staying with a cousin and, to their knowledge, she hadn't known they'd taken Hudson in for questioning. Nor had she known that Branson had a woman tied up in his basement.

Marshall tapped his knuckles against the hollow front door that was painted green, although the color was faded and the paint peeled around the frame. A momentary shift of the cream curtains caught his eye, but when he turned, the fabric was released and swung back into its place. "Someone's here."

"San Diego Police. Open the door please," Gibbons said, looking to Marshall.

The handle turned slowly and the door opened on hinges in need of oil. "Can I help you?" The woman behind the door held it open only a few inches, but it was not Laura.

"We're here to speak with Laura Kempt. Is she available?" Marshall asked.

The woman's eyes darted between Gibbons and Marshall. For a moment, Marshall thought she might slam the door in his face. Instead, the woman stepped back, opening the door further.

"Yes. Please come in."

Marshall nodded to Gibbons as both stepped through the doorway.

"I'll go and get her," the woman said.

When the woman disappeared beyond the corridor, Marshall laid his hand over his .40 caliber Glock. "I've got a bad feeling about this."

"Yeah. Something's not right." Detective Gibbons released the flap from his holstered gun, ready to draw.

The small apartment was in disarray. Dishes piled in the sink, Chinese takeout boxes opened and scattered throughout, and it was in desperate need of a vacuum.

Marshall heard the faint sound of whispering voices traveling down the narrow hallway. He raised a finger to his lips and then pointed in the direction of the noise. A nod to Gibbons and they began moving slowly towards the back room, guns still holstered, but at the ready.

"Is everything all right?" Marshall asked, only steps from the room in which the women were speaking. "Laura Kempt? We're with the police and we'd like to talk to you." He turned the handle of the door. The voices silenced immediately. Marshall looked back to Gibbons as if ensuring he was prepared for whatever they might find behind the door.

It took a moment to register, but as soon as he saw the knife in her hands, Marshall knew what was about to happen. "Laura. Stop. Put the knife down."

Laura Kempt was sitting on the edge of the bed. The knife, with a three-inch serrated blade that would likely be used to skin an animal, rested against her wrist, the pressure turning her skin white beneath it.

"Don't come any closer." Her pallid face glistened with perspiration.

The woman, her cousin, clutched the bedpost at the end. "Please, Laura. They're here to help you."

A brief glance was exchanged between Marshall and Detective Gibbons, who was standing next to him. It seemed to have occurred to both of them that the knife looked remarkably similar to the one the ME believed was used on Lindsay Brown. Short blade, serrated, leaving the skin torn and jagged.

"Laura, put the knife down so we can talk. I'm sure you're frightened right now, but we are here to help." Gibbons had been a negotiator with the SWAT team prior to moving to Homicide. Different scenario, but generally included the same principles: ensuring the suspect that the intention was to help, not harm; get them to let their guard down just long enough to move in and retake control of the situation.

But so far, Laura appeared unmoved. Her cousin was still shaking as she gripped the post.

"You think I don't know why you're here? You think I don't know who you are, Detective Avery?" Laura pressed harder on the knife, forcing a drop of blood to spill from her wrist.

"We need to find out what you know about Edward Shalot and Lewis Branson. That's why we're here." This time, it was Gibbons who replied. He saw Marshall flinch at the fact that she knew who he was. It had caught them both off guard, but Gibbons held firm.

Laura's mouth upturned into the slightest knowing grin. "He was in love with Katie Reid. Well, what he thought was love. If you ask me, he was obsessed with her. And it was threatening to ruin everything."

"Obsessed?" Marshall scoffed at the irony. "You're the one threatening to end your life because of Shalot. You're the one who planted his DNA on Lindsay's body."

"Ms. Kempt. You need to come with us now," Gibbons said, shooting a concerned look to Marshall. He clearly wasn't helping to calm the woman.

"What about the others? You know where they are? Shalot's followers?" Marshall persisted. His tone turned deep, heavy with anger. He was losing control and he could feel it in his bones.

"Why should I help you, Detective Avery? You can't help me. No one can." Laura pulled the knife away from her wrist and jammed it into her thigh. Screaming, her face writhed in agony. She had hit her femoral artery. Blood spilled over her leg like oil spewing from the ground.

Her cousin screamed in horror, covering her mouth as she watched Laura crumple to the floor.

Detective Gibbons rushed to her side, laying her down and pressing against the wound, working to slow the blood loss, but he couldn't dislodge the knife. "Call for help!" he shouted to Marshall.

Marshall pulled out his cell and called 911, identifying himself. "We need an ambulance at 475 Holston Avenue, apartment 2221. Suspect down." He moved towards Gibbons. "We need to get that knife to forensics."

"Jesus, Avery! Help me out here." Gibbons' hands were covered in blood. "Get me a fucking towel or something!"

He was numb, detached, but he did as Gibbons asked. "Where are the towels?"

The cousin pointed to a cabinet in the hall.

Marshall returned with a handful of dingy linens, but it was clear Laura was bleeding out. He handed one of them to Gibbons and moved behind the dying woman to elevate her head, placing another towel beneath for support. He leaned in. "What does he want with Katie?"

Laura Kempt was drained of color, but she managed to look up at Marshall. "He wants to take her from you." Her eyes began to flutter. She was losing consciousness.

A few moments later, the sound of sirens wailed in the distance. The cousin was huddled in a corner, weeping. Marshall watched as Gibbons worked to save the life of this woman. A woman who had killed out of jealousy. And Marshall was left to deal with the aftermath: the knowledge of what Shalot and his followers were capable of doing and, if given the chance, might also do to Katie.

Shalot was still in custody, but with the knife in Laura's possession and her admission of guilt, how long would it be before he would have to be released? They would need something more than the words of Lewis Branson and Shaun Hudson to keep him.

◆◆◆

The viewing room at the FBI field office was much more sophisticated than the one at the station. Monitors were lined up on the desk. There must have been at least half a dozen, each displaying every possible angle of the room. The two-way mirror was large and allowed for unobstructed viewing.

Katie could see Edward Shalot on the other side of the mirror, shackled to the floor, hands cuffed to the table. It seemed the FBI was taking greater precautions now that they knew what they were dealing with. A man who was holding the strings, leading a handful of people under the façade of a religion whose intent was to restore order through chaos. He had convinced them that Branson wasn't a true believer, convinced them to kill for their beliefs.

She knew why Scarborough wanted her there. He had hoped that Shalot would reveal the location of the missing woman to win Katie over. She shuddered at the thought and folded her arms as if protecting herself from the cold.

"You ready?" Nick placed a hand on her shoulder and walked out into the hallway.

She nodded and followed him. A few steps away was the door to the interrogation room where Shalot waited.

"His lawyer is being brought up now." It seemed Nick could feel her anxiety. "You can do this, Katie. I know you can."

Her mouth tightened into a thin, unconvincing smile when a man approached. It wasn't Nathan Bender, Shalot's previous attorney. She looked to Scarborough, ready to ask the question, but Nick preempted her.

"Shalot was assigned a federal public defender. His previous lawyer was assigned by the state," Scarborough said.

"Mr. Trainor," Nick extended a greeting. "Thank you for coming down. I assume you've had time to get acquainted with your new client?"

"Yes. Thank you, Agent Scarborough" he returned the greeting.

"I'd like to introduce you to Ms. Katie Reid. She works for San Diego police and has been an integral part of this investigation."

"I am familiar with Ms. Reid. I understand she is an acquaintance of my client. But I'm not quite sure why she needs to be here, especially in light of the news."

"I'm afraid that's not up to you, Mr. Trainor," Nick replied. *What did he mean, in light of the news?* "Let's get started. We don't have time to mess around."

Katie's expression quickly shifted from delight at Scarborough's tough position regarding her necessity to fear at the sight of Shalot when she walked into the room. His face was changed. It no longer seemed to profess innocence, but rather seemed to display an arrogance she hadn't seen in him before.

His eyes were glued to her as she moved to the table, taking a seat across from him. Something was wrong, but she didn't know what it was. Her gaze turned to Scarborough. He had picked up on it too. It seemed the only people who knew what was happening were Shalot and Trainor.

The agent guarding the door proceeded to close it as Trainor was the last to enter and take his seat next to his client.

"It seems there has been a recent development that has come to my attention," Trainor began.

Katie's heart sank. This was it. Something had happened and neither of them had known what it was. She looked to Scarborough.

"I'm afraid I'm not sure what you are referring to, Mr. Trainor. Would you care to elaborate?" Nick asked. His cell phone vibrated against his waist. On retrieving it, he noticed the call was coming in from Marshall. "If you'll excuse me, I need to take this." He had known Marshall and Detective Gibbons were tracking down Kempt and assumed they must have found her.

"Yes. Of course," Trainor replied.

It was the phone call Laura made the moment she heard the police were at her door. A call she'd made to the FBI office where Shalot was being held. It seemed Laura had been keeping tabs on Shalot, as per Branson's request. She knew he'd been transferred to their custody. She only needed to listen to the news for that information. And what Laura had relayed to them just before stabbing herself had quickly made its way through the field office and to Shalot's attorney.

Scarborough had been in such a hurry to question Shalot, he brushed past everyone in the office to reach him. And as he now stood outside, prepared to answer Marshall's call, ASAC Newland waited.

Katie didn't want to be left in the room alone with these men. There were people in the viewing room – she was safe – but somehow, that didn't seem to matter. Shalot cast his eyes on her, devouring her features. Trainor could have cared less as he scrolled through his cell phone, taking no notice of his client. But she had been here before. Now was her opportunity to be the one in control. She wasn't the one in shackles.

"How did you come to know about me?" Katie leaned in, pressing her weight against her forearms. She looked directly into his eyes, mirroring no fear in her own.

Shalot cocked his head and raised an eyebrow. "I saw you once." He turned his gaze to her short, brunette hair. "Your hair used to be long. I liked it better that way. Did he make you cut it short?"

Katie slammed her fist against the table, nearly cracking the half-inch thick acrylic that rested on top of the hardwood. "Where did you see me?"

Trainor suddenly perked up. "I think you'd better wait for the big boys to get back, little lady. You have no right asking my client anything."

"Your face looked so beautiful, but I could see how much pain you were in. How much he had made you suffer."

Katie began to rise and turned from Shalot, peering into the two-way mirror.

"You were being interviewed by a reporter shortly after you returned to San Diego. After you'd killed him — the man who took you, I mean. Well, I know *you* didn't actually kill him. Your cop boyfriend came to the rescue, didn't he? And then there was our friendly neighborhood FBI Agent Scarborough." Shalot lowered his face towards his cuffed hands and scratched at the tip of his nose. "Funny how you and that agent have crossed each other's paths once again."

Before she could reply, Scarborough returned. He brushed past Katie without a glance and immediately approached Shalot. "Where's that woman being held? The Sparks woman? Where the fuck is she?"

"Whoa, whoa, whoa." Trainor stood up, thrusting his arm between the two men. "You better check yourself, agent. Now I see where Ms. Reid gets it from."

"Your client has ordered the deaths of four women and now a fifth has gone missing. You better see to it that he starts to cooperate. We may no longer have proof that he killed Lindsay Brown, but if you don't think Lewis Branson will sing like a fucking bird, you're sadly mistaken." Nick turned to the man in shackles. "He knows all about your little group, doesn't he, Shalot?"

Katie didn't know who that call had been from, but someone must have found something to prove Shalot wasn't the killer. Her legs were heavy, and the sensation that had just passed through her was something between vindication and terror at the fact that her assumption had been correct. Shalot may not have killed Lindsay, but he was the ringleader of a naïve and easily submissive group of people who hung onto his every word, willing to kill in the name of him and his beliefs.

But where the body could be weak, the mind could be strong, and so she forced herself nearer to him. Nearer to a man who wanted her for himself. "Tell me where she is, Edward. Tell me and you can have me."

Nick whipped his head around as she said those words.

"How can I have you? You think I'm stupid enough to believe you would ever choose me?"

"Okay, I think we're done here," Trainor said.

"You found calm in the chaos. Acceptance. No pressures to conform to a puritanical society. That's why you followed Branson to begin with. You didn't like the rejection from women who you thought were trash. The group didn't reject you though, did they? Not at first. Not until you started laying claim to Branson's role as leader. Taking the message of the law of fives to its most literal meaning and bending it to suit your needs. The five cycles of humanity." Katie softened her stance, her shoulders dropping, her face revealing concern. "I wouldn't have rejected you. I understand that you thought you were doing the right thing. Showing the rest of society just how wrong they were and how they knew nothing of the true meaning of life."

Trainor snapped his case shut. "If you'll show us out, Agent Scarborough."

Katie retreated, but did not break her stare. Edward believed her; she could see it in his eyes. *Just wait.*

Nick walked around the table, removing the cuffs from the table and the floor.

Shalot laced his fingers as he continued to hold Katie's gaze.

Tell me, goddammit.

"Let's go; we're done here," Nick said, taking her arm.

22

THE PARAMEDIC SEARCHED for a pulse, but there was no pulse left. He raised his head to Gibbons, who stood only feet away, as he watched the man do his job. The look on his face was enough. Laura Kempt was gone.

Her cousin was moved to the other room where she sat wrapped in a blanket, clearly suffering from shock. After some questioning, it became clear that she had known nothing of Laura's activities, nothing of the cult to which she belonged.

Marshall remained in the small dining area adjacent to the kitchen while several officers began collecting evidence and preparing the scene for the medical examiner's office. They would remove the body.

They would be forced to let Shalot go. He didn't kill Lindsay. The possible murder weapon still protruding from the leg of the now deceased Laura Kempt.

According to the call he had just made to Scarborough, all they had at the moment was a list of names and one other address. It would take too much time to find out where the fifth victim was being held and if she was still alive.

The best Marshal could hope for now was for them to tack a surveillance team on Shalot until they caught the remaining followers. Scarborough might be able to convince a judge to hang on to Shalot a while longer under suspicion of conspiracy to commit murder, but they needed one of the Brotherhood to offer up real evidence against Shalot. Until that happened, Shalot could very well be set free in a matter of hours and Marshall couldn't accept that.

Shalot's apartment building was about a twenty-minute drive from his current location. Marshall's cell phone rang several times. At least two of the calls were from Katie, but there was no time. He had to do this before Shalot was set free, if it came to that, and he didn't know when it would be, but it would be soon. It was the only way to keep her safe. She would only try to stop him.

♦♦♦

Marshall climbed to the second-floor apartment. It was approaching midday on Friday and he expected most of the occupants of the building to be away. He cast a look left, then right. No one seemed to be around. He wrapped his fist with his jacket and punched a hole through the front glass window. The window remained intact and he was able to pull the sliding single pane open. Again, he turned to check his surroundings. The noise from the break echoed, but still no one emerged. He stepped inside.

Dust floated in the shafts of light that occupied the apartment. The blinds had been drawn, but the afternoon sun found its way inside, leaving a dusky glow in its wake. If Shalot was to be set free, even if only for a short time until the Feds could build a case against him, Marshall knew Katie wouldn't be safe.

He didn't know what he was looking for that they hadn't already found when he and Gibbons were there the other day and the FBI had already done a sweep too.

He meandered in the gloom, finally finding some light as he flipped the switch near the kitchen. The living area lit up. It looked no different than before. Had he expected it to? Shalot had been in holding for the better part of a week. No one had been here since then.

Marshall figured he had a couple of hours in which to work. Once all the paperwork was through the system, he assumed Shalot would come here first. Where else could he go?

The laptop was gone. A few items appeared to be laid in a haphazard matter. The FBI had done their job, by all accounts.

He moved towards the bedroom and stood at the threshold. A full-sized mattress lay on the floor. A sheet and blanket were crumpled and rested on it. The pillow had formed to the shape of Shalot's head.

Marshall walked in, now standing inches from the mattress. He surveyed the room. An old oak dresser in need of repair sat in front of the bedroom window. A flat-panel TV rested on top of a shoddy-looking stand and there was the small desk where they found Katie's files.

The closet ran along the east wall. Marshall approached it, pulling the bi-fold doors open. To his surprise, Shalot's clothes were meticulously placed in order of type and color. For a man who believed in chaos, this struck him as peculiar.

He inserted his hands between the articles and began pushing them aside, peering behind them, again looking for something he wasn't sure of yet. Marshall moved down the line until he reached the jackets that hung at the far end of the closet; they were difficult to reach.

But when Marshall began shifting them, pushing the hangers closer together, he noticed something unusual. "What the hell?" He pressed the clothes as far as he could to expose what appeared to be a safe inside the wall. A small one to be sure, but it was a safe. The Feds appeared to have missed it, and he had too the first time, but here it was and he needed to know what it contained.

A keypad served as the locking mechanism and Marshall hadn't a clue as to how to get inside. But he was sure he would find something worthwhile and so he began to hunt for any tools Shalot might have.

On the balcony beyond the living room, he'd spotted a door. *Storage room.* The heavy sliding glass door leading to the balcony resisted, but Marshall was able to push it open enough to slip out.

The handle was locked, much as he expected, but this was a simple privacy lock. The kind one would find on a bathroom or bedroom door. A large rock rested against the outer wall of the balcony. It must have been used to prop open the storage room when it was in use. He reached for the rock that was about the size of his hand and held it on top of the doorknob. Retrieving is gun, Marshall began to use the butt of the handle as a hammer against the stone. A few hard hits and the knob broke, dropping to the ground. He placed his gun back into its holster and pushed the other side of the knob free, leaving only the latch to push back and the door would swing open freely.

The storage room appeared to be no larger than about a six by eight space. The inside contained several shelves mounted to the walls, each displaying various cans of paint, most of them having been opened. Brooms and a mop rested against the back wall and a shop vac sat on the concrete floor. But he could find nothing else that might be of use. "Damn it."

Marshall returned to the living room, leaving the storage room door ajar. The idea that he might lose his badge over this mattered little to him now and so leaving evidence behind of his visit was of no consequence. Besides, he thought Captain Hearn would understand. He knew what Katie had been through. Maybe that would be enough to get him to turn a blind eye to this quest to find something that would put Shalot away before he ever got a chance to be set free.

He'd spent too long now in search of a tool with which to open the safe. With no other way to get inside it, Marshall would need help. The only person he trusted to keep this quiet was Agent Scarborough. Detective Gibbons was a good man and a great detective, but Marshall saw how he looked at him earlier today as he stood frozen, watching Laura Kempt bleed out. There was a slim chance Gibbons might turn on him; slim, but he just couldn't risk it.

He removed his cell phone from his inner coat pocket and made the call. The line rang for too long and just as Marshall was about to end the call, the agent picked up. "Scarborough, it's Avery. I found a safe in Shalot's apartment, in a closet. I need your help to get inside. I know there's something there that will give us what we need to put the bastard away before you release him."

"Oh Christ, Avery. Are you there now?" Scarborough asked.

"Yeah."

"We turned him loose thirty minutes ago. Get the hell out of there, Avery."

"Goddammit! You couldn't find a way to keep him? Laura Kempt just killed herself because of Shalot. Shit. What about Branson? What about Hudson?"

"She admitted to killing Lindsay Brown; you said so yourself. Detective Gibbons bagged the knife and had your lab compare it to the ME's report. It's a match, Avery.

"As much as I didn't want to let that son of a bitch go, I got nothing else. I need more than Branson and Hudson saying that he's put together some sort of brotherhood that's going around killing people. I need proof of it!"

Marshall wanted to hang up right then and there, but he knew Scarborough was right, which made his presence here, in Shalot's apartment, even more critical.

"The guy's been in custody for almost a week under charges that he killed Lindsay Brown," Nick continued. "Now we find out that he didn't. After this, my boss is going to want more than hearsay because the media's going to tear us a new one for this. Shalot will make sure of that. Look, we're already tracking down one of his followers. Hudson gave us Hayden Jennings' name and we got a match in the system. We're already working to locate him in Virginia. Once we do that, we'll get what we need from him to put Shalot away for good.

Avery, we're putting a team together. They'll keep tabs on him from here, but you need to get out of there."

The sound of a key turning in a lock grabbed Marshall's attention. "Shit. He's here." He didn't wait for Nick to reply, only dropped his phone back into his pocket and placed a hand on his holster, unsnapping it and ready to pull it on whoever was about to open that door. He could hear his heart pounding in his ears. It was the second time today he'd been faced with drawing down on someone. Not since Hendrickson had he been confronted with that choice.

He recalled the broken glass on the ground beneath the front window of the apartment. It would be easy to spot and would alert anyone outside that someone had forced his way in. Marshall had left the sliding pane open too so he could get back out. His eyes were fixed on the door, then the window, then the door again. Someone was waiting out there and he knew who it was. He suspected Shalot knew who was inside as well.

Finally, a push on the front door, slowly, cautiously. "Detective Avery, you have no right to be here. I could have your badge for this. I saw your car in the parking lot, but I didn't know you had it in you to break into someone's home," Shalot said. "I'm unarmed, detective, and I'm coming in now."

This son of a bitch was behind all of it. Everyone knew it and yet here he was, a free man. He'd been tracking Katie down for a year and Marshall couldn't bear the thought of him sitting near her in class, thinking about how he could have, at any time, followed her out into the parking lot and taken her. He could have taken her the way Hendrickson had. The man was crazy; believing in some crazy damn cult, demanding that his followers kill innocent people to prove what? Loyalty to him over Branson? Or was it just his own brand of control because he had none in other areas of his life? Whatever the reason, he indirectly perpetrated those brutal murders under the guise of a perverted belief that chaos was the rule of law.

Marshall's hairline began to drip with sweat. The hand that rested on his gun felt clammy. He waited for Shalot to come inside, but had not drawn his gun. Not yet. Not unless the man gave him a reason.

Shalot's foot appeared in the opening, his leg, then his body, but he continued to hold the door in front of him. "I'm unarmed, detective."

"Put your hands up, then," Marshall replied, his nerves fully on edge. Was he prepared to do it? Was he prepared to kill someone? If it meant keeping her safe, then there was no question in his mind.

Shalot finally emerged from behind the door, his hands held firmly above his head. "See? All okay here, Detective Avery. Everything's fine. The FBI let me go. I told you I didn't kill Lindsay Brown."

"You might not have, but you sure as hell ordered the deaths of other innocent people. Your followers? Is that what you call them? What's in the goddamn safe, Shalot?"

A smile that seemed to teeter along the lines of being amused and pissed off appeared on Shalot's face. "The FBI couldn't even find that. You are very good, detective, but as you can see, I am now a free man and you have no right to be in my home. You might want to consider leaving before I decide to press charges. What would Kate think?"

Marshall was the only person that called her Kate. A memory flashed before him as he reflected on the moment he and Scarborough stepped down the stairs into that basement where Hendrickson had her, holding a knife to her throat. Threatening her as this man would surely do, given the chance.

Rage began to build inside him now. The idea that Shalot presumed to know Kate. Presumed to call her Kate. Marshall would not see her hurt again. She'd been through too much, more than anyone should ever have to suffer. He knew Shalot would be a constant presence if the FBI couldn't press charges. He would never go away, much like Hendrickson hadn't until they finally put a stop to him. They would always be looking over their shoulders.

Shalot stepped inside, moving just a few feet closer to Marshall, as if testing him. "You're not going to shoot an unarmed man. You're a cop. Cops don't do that." He moved a little closer now. "I'd like to sit down on my couch and rest for a while, if you don't mind. The past several days have been quite an ordeal. I believe you can show yourself out."

"Tell me what's in the safe and I'll leave."

"Nothing but my passport, a watch my father gave me, and a few bucks."

"You're lying," Marshall said.

"Not that it's any of your fucking business, though, is it?" Shalot had grown flushed with color, appearing aggravated. "I'm innocent, okay? I didn't do shit to that Brown girl."

"Shaun Hudson says differently. He says you wanted to bring Lindsay into your sick little group. But then, she wasn't that type of girl, was she? I bet you didn't count on Laura Kempt. She wasn't very happy that you spurned her affections. Instead, working to take a woman who had already been taken by another. Branson saw that and turned her against you. They put a great big shining spotlight on you, didn't they? Making Lindsay appear as though she'd been killed like the others."

Marshall took a few steps forward and noticed Shallot stiffen with alarm. "Hudson says you needed to prove your power over Branson, demanding that your loyal followers kill innocent women, carving their bodies with a 'V,' putting flowers in their hands, showing the world that there would be more coming, that the Law of Five demanded it. Then you had them tossed on the side of the road where the animals could gnaw away at their flesh."

"It's a five, you fucking idiot, not a 'V'! You know, the Roman numeral?" There was no question of the look of regret on Shalot's face now. He'd revealed too much.

Marshall knew he had him, but still needed something concrete. "Open the safe. Now."

Shalot stood still for a moment longer.

"Now!"

He flinched at the raised voice and began to move towards his bedroom, Marshall following closely behind, his hand still on his gun.

They reached the closet. "I told you, there's nothing in there." Shalot's back was turned to Marshall as he spoke, facing the opened closet. He shifted the clothes aside.

"Do it."

Marshall stood less than a foot behind the man, watching as he pressed the numbers on the keypad. The sound of his gun withdrawing from its holster caused Shalot to stop cold.

"Keep going."

Shalot did as he was told. The safe door clicked and swung open automatically.

Marshall took a step back, raising the gun from his hip, and waited for Shalot to move aside. Instead, Shalot thrust his forearm and struck him square in the face. In a burst of searing pain, Marshall's eyes exploded with stars and he rocked back.

As he struggled to regain balance and clear his vision, a blow struck his gut. Shalot was attempting to take the gun as Marshall doubled over in pain.

The comprehension of what was happening knocked Marshall almost as hard as Shalot had. The man wanted his gun.

The two fell to the floor, wrestling for control of it. Marshall belted him in the jaw. He reeled back, but quickly recovered. Shalot worked to pry Marshall's hand from the butt of the gun, but Marshall held firm.

He knew what would happen if Shalot took it. His thoughts turned to Katie. "You won't hurt her. I swear to God, I'll see you dead before I let that happen!"

They thrashed around on the floor, limbs entangled, but Marshall still had the gun. Shalot's hands clasped over his, scratching and clawing away, trying to get a grip. There was only one thing Marshall could do now.

He released the safety and tried to gain a foothold on Shalot, giving him room to point the barrel and shoot, but Shalot was strong and in a better position.

The gun turned, Shalot the one gaining control. Marshall fought with every modicum of strength he had. He needed to put this man down. Much longer and he'd lose his strength. The barrel began to turn back to Shalot.

A crash sounded from the front room, startling both the men. The gun fired.

"FBI!" Scarborough heard the gunshot and ran towards the noise. Jameson was with him and followed.

Shalot scrambled to get up and was covered in blood.

Marshall lay still and placed a hand on his stomach. He raised his palm and saw that it was shrouded in blood, his blood. He'd been hit.

Shalot stood on shaky legs, trying to make it to the door.

Marshall spotted his gun a few inches away and listened as the agents rushed nearer. "Kate." He turned towards the gun, his face twisting with pain, but he couldn't make a sound. His fingers reached the tip of the gun, enough to get a hold on it. It was all he could do to raise it, but he pointed the gun at Shalot's head and fired.

The bullet struck him in the back of the neck, immediately severing his spine. Shalot fell to the ground, landing face first.

The agents, with weapons drawn, emerged from the hall.

Scarborough held his gun firmly, pointing it at Shalot, unsure of what exactly was happening. He looked at the men, both covered in blood, both lying on the ground. "Avery! Christ's sakes." Scarborough rushed to his side.

Jameson quickly tended to Shalot, checking for a pulse. "He's dead."

"We need to get Avery to the hospital, now!" Nick pressed on the wound in Marshall's stomach. "It's all right, man. Hang in there. Help's coming."

"The safe." Marshall's tone was weak, barely audible. "Check the safe." His eyes peered beyond Nick's, towards the closet where the door to the safe remained open.

Nick looked back. "Jameson. Bring me a towel and then check that safe." He continued to apply pressure to Marshall's stomach, but the blood kept coming.

Agent Jameson returned with a towel and stepped over the body of Edward Shalot. Blood pooled at his head and Jameson was careful not to step in it. He handed the towel to Scarborough and moved to the safe.

Nick pressed the towel against the wound and it quickly soaked with blood. "What the hell's in there?" he asked Jameson.

A look of dread masked his face as he turned back to Scarborough. "Pictures." He held photographs loosely in his hands. "It's the victims. Four of them."

They looked as though they'd been taken by cell phone, grainy and slightly blurred, perhaps having been captured by shaky hands. The photos showed each victim on display, posed. Jameson knelt down to Scarborough to allow him a better look.

"Goddamn it. You should have told me you were coming here, Marshall," Scarborough said.

"I had to find a way to keep him behind bars. He was after her." The weakness in his voice prevailed with each word.

"Katie." Nick shook his head and turned to Jameson. "Where the hell is that damn ambulance?"

Marshall knew Scarborough was pissed that he'd risked coming here. "I had to protect her."

The sound of sirens brought relief to all of them.

"Have you found the missing woman in Nevada?" Marshall asked.

"No. Not yet," Nick replied.

Marshall's eyelids began to lower, threatening to close.

"Keep your eyes open, man; come on." Nick tapped Marshall's cheek lightly to rouse him. "Help's almost here. Just hang in there."

Jameson waited at the door. Several footsteps sounded on the metal staircase as the EMTs made their way to the apartment. Nick had also radioed for backup after Marshall's call, discovering that he was in Shalot's apartment. Detective Gibbons arrived behind the ambulance.

"He's in there." Jameson pointed to the back bedroom where Shalot's body lay over the threshold and into the hall.

"Goddammit! What the hell happened here?" Gibbons demanded but did not wait for a reply, instead moving in the direction of the bloody scene. He locked eyes with Scarborough, although he seemed to offer no assurances as to the state of his downed colleague.

The paramedic quickly attended to Marshall, pushing Scarborough away. "His pulse is weak; he's lost a lot of blood," the man called to his partner at the doorway. "We need to get him out of here now."

The EMTs did what they could to stave off further blood loss, but Marshall was in dire shape. They loaded him into the ambulance and headed for the hospital just ten minutes away.

Scarborough followed behind, insisting Jameson and Gibbons wait for the CSU and secure the scene. Now, he had to tell Katie. He took a breath and prepared for the difficult phone call. "Katie? I need you to meet me at SD Medical Center. It's Marshall." He wasted no time in getting to the point.

"What? What's happening? What's wrong with him?" Her voice cracked with panic and confusion.

"Just get down there, Katie. I'll explain later." Nick knew she would need to leave fast and talking on the phone, asking questions, would only delay her. This was bad. He knew it was bad. Shalot might be dead, but they still hadn't tracked down the whereabouts of the final victim and Nick couldn't let another one die. Nor could he lose Marshall Avery.

He quickly placed a call to Agent Myers. "Shalot's dead. Do we have anything more from Branson?" he said, squeezing the steering wheel until his knuckles turned white. Everything seemed to be falling apart and he was losing control. Marshall went off on his own and got himself shot, killing the one man who was pulling the strings. Now they had another woman missing. Number five. And they needed to find her. Pressure was coming at him from all angles. His ASAC, the media, and police departments hounding him for information when he had virtually nothing. He prayed that Richmond police had at least located Hayden Jennings. Maybe he would know where the next murder would be.

Nick slammed the wheel. The call to Myers was coming through weak; he didn't have much of a signal along this narrow stretch of road that had been cut through the hill. He couldn't hear her.

"Say again? I think I'm losing you, Georgia."

"Sherriff's office said they're doing all they can, but can't find the woman."

"We gotta find her, damn it."

"They're doing everything they can, Nick. They'll find her. Where are you?"

"Pulling into the medical center. Marshall Avery's been shot. He killed Shalot. The dumb bastard went off on his own."

"Oh God. I'm sorry, Nick. Is he gonna be okay?"

"I don't know. I don't know. I gotta go now. Katie's probably here and I need to tell her what happened. You call me when we find that woman!"

"Will do."

Nick ended the call and cut the engine. On his approach to the emergency entrance, he spotted Katie just inside and she wasn't alone. Captain Hearn and half a dozen officers waited in the lobby. When a cop went down, everyone rallied.

He stepped through the sliding glass doors and caught her attention.

Katie ran towards him. "What happened, Nick? Please, tell me. They said he's in surgery for a gunshot wound. I need to know. Please." Her breaths were shallow and her forehead, once smooth, now lined with concern for the love of her life.

Nick took hold of her arms in a gentle but firm manner. "Katie. You need to calm down. I'm sure they're doing everything they can for Marshall."

She yanked her arms from him. "Don't you treat me like a goddamn child. That's Marshall in there. Tell me what happened!"

Heads began to turn in response to her raised voice. Captain Hearn was now making his way over.

Nick saw the look in Hearn's eyes, demanding an explanation. "Marshall went to Shalot's house to find anything we might have missed that would prove he instructed his followers to kill those victims. He didn't know Shalot had been released." He paused, working to find the right words. "I don't know exactly what happened, Katie. Except that there was a struggle. Shalot reached for Marshall's gun and, somehow, during the altercation, pulled the trigger and hit Marshall in the stomach."

Captain Hearn turned away, rubbing his head in the same manner that Marshall always did when he was trying to process information. He said nothing, only shaking his head. His eyes shut tightly.

Tears fell from Katie's face in a thick stream, running down her now pallid cheeks. Her heart was breaking right in front of him. "Marshall took him down, Katie. He took Shalot down because he wanted to protect you. Don't give up on him now. Not when he needs you the most."

Katie buried her head inside Nick's embrace. "I can't lose him. I can't. I've lost too much. Please don't take him from me."

Her words were not meant for Nick, but seemingly for God himself.

"Captain Hearn, can you find someone who knows what the hell is going on?" Nick asked, still comforting Katie. He would do so until she was ready to let go.

Agonizing minutes had passed before Hearn returned with a doctor. "Katie? Dr. Patel would like to speak to you."

She finally raised her head. Her hair was damp with tears and clung to her face. She tried to brush the strands away as she returned her weight to her own two feet.

Nick still held on, making sure she was steady.

"Yes?"

"I'm Dr. Patel. Marshall Avery is your boyfriend?"

"Yes," she whispered.

"I'm so sorry, but he lost just too much blood. I'm afraid we did everything we could to help him."

The doctor's words echoed in her ears. Her head grew light and her body faltered. *Not again. Please God, not again.*

"Oh, Katie. I'm so sorry." Captain Hearn tried to rest his hand on her shoulder.

She pulled away. "No. No. He's not dead. Tell me he's not dead!" Her knees buckled and she started to fall.

Nick quickly reached out for her. "I got you, Katie. It's all right."

"I'm so sorry," Dr. Patel repeated his distant apology.

"Thank you, doctor." Nick continued to support her. "Can you get her some water or something?" he asked Hearn. "Come sit down, Katie." He had to virtually carry her to the lobby chairs.

"I can't breathe." Katie gasped for air, her eyes flooded with tears, clouding her vision. "Oh God. I can't do this again. Please, help me." Her breaths grew shorter and faster. Her cries sounded as though she was standing squarely in front of death itself, begging it for mercy.

Her pain spread to everyone, gripping them as it had her. The other officers, Captain Hearn; it was too much for them to witness. Most turned away, trying to hide their own emotions.

"Calm down, now." Nick smoothed her hair. "Shhhh." His own voice had wavered. "You have to slow your breathing, Katie. Slow down. I don't want you to pass out."

"He can't leave me. I'll be left with no one." She sat up, reaching for a tissue on the table and began wiping her face. It was red and swollen and full of grief. "I have to see him. I need to see him. Please, Nick."

He had known the condition Marshall was in. He knew it was a bad idea to let her see him that way. "I—I'm not sure that's a good idea, Katie. They need to take care of him first, okay? You'll be able to see him soon."

Nick's cell phone rang. He wrangled his hand from behind Katie and felt for his phone in his front pocket. It was Myers and he prayed for some good news.

◆◆◆

The officers swarmed the building, a small house tucked away in the hills on the edge of town. It appeared to be abandoned, but a car was parked beneath a makeshift overhang fastened to the side of it.

"This is the police; open the door," Officer Nealy shouted. He was the man leading the charge. "Go around the side; check the other exits," he said to one of his men.

"We're coming in." Nealy pushed hard against the door, but it would not budge.

Squad cars lined the front of the property, lights flashing. The paved road was narrow and only a few houses occupied either side. It was one of a few older neighborhoods, sparsely populated as people took to moving closer to town and hopefully jobs. It seemed that it wasn't the only abandoned house either. Several were boarded up, a result of a continuing failing economy.

"Step aside, sir. We got this." Two officers with a battering ram pushed through the door with ease.

The house reeked of rotting food. The advanced state of disrepair suggested the dwelling was barely inhabitable at all. Gold shag carpeting, grossly stained and worn out in several areas. Dark wood paneling on the walls and heavily curtained windows that allowed for little light to enter. But what was on the walls brought great concern and possible assurance that this had been the right place. Spray painted Vs marked the panels in a dark red paint, meant to look like blood.

A sound emanated from one of the rooms. Officer Nealy raised his hand to quiet the others. "Sparks Police. If anyone's here, come out with your hands where I can see them."

A young man in a dingy white tank top and baggy jeans appeared from beyond the dining area near the kitchen, his hands held above his head. "Don't shoot."

"Down on the ground! Down on the ground!" the officer shouted.

As the man lowered himself to the floor, officers hurried to restrain him. His arms were pulled back and placed in cuffs.

"Where is she?" Nealy demanded.

The man looked down the hall and Nealy immediately stepped in that direction, aiming his gun along the way, another officer following closely behind.

Nealy lowered his weapon at sight of the horrific scene. The man behind him turned away, sickened and almost gagging. He rushed to the woman, the plastic lined floor crumpling under his feet.

She lay on the small bed, her arms hanging over the edge and covered in streams of blood. Officer Nealy had never before seen anything like this and worked hard to contain his own reflexes. He placed two fingers at her neck and checked for a pulse.

◆◆◆

"Scarborough here."

"They found the woman, Nick. I'm sorry." Myers hesitated. "They didn't get to her in time."

Nick looked down at Katie, still huddled in a ball next to him, dabbing her eyes. "For Christ's sake." He felt as though he had been beaten. Marshall was gone and now so was the woman. Number five.

"They got Hayden Jennings, though, and he's talking," Myers continued. "Richmond police say he's spilling everything he's got."

"They're all dead now. What the hell does it matter?" Nick replied.

Katie turned her eyes to him. He immediately regretted the comment.

"Because we got the kid in Virginia and Sparks is holding this new suspect and he might know about others involved too. This thing isn't over, Nick. We both know that."

"Just—just give me a few minutes, okay. I gotta sort through this here at the hospital."

"Is Detective Avery all right?" Myers asked.

Nick didn't want to answer the question; not in front of Katie. "I'll call you later. Just talk to Richmond, talk to the Sparks Police, and find out what you can. See if you can brief the Las Vegas field office too. We need some goddam help here." He ended the call.

Captain Hearn offered Katie a cup of water. She reluctantly took hold and managed a small sip, placing it onto the side table. "What's going on?" he asked Nick.

"They found the woman. We were too late. They caught the suspect, though, so now we've got two of them. Myers is working to find the others. That's all I got. Hell, I don't even know if this thing is over yet."

Hearn looked to Katie and Nick could see the question forming on his face. He wanted to know what to do about her. She couldn't be alone. Not right now, but Nick still had a case to solve. There were others out there following Shalot's lead. He didn't know what the hell to do next.

"I'll keep her with me. We've got a spare room." Hearn said.

"I'm not leaving without seeing Marshall," Katie said.

"I know, but I need to take care of some things. The captain's going to take you to his home, okay?" Nick replied.

"You know, you haven't been to the house since we converted Sydney's room. She left for college this year, remember?" the captain said.

Katie didn't reply.

Nick motioned Hearn away from her for a moment. "Look, don't let her see him until they've got him cleaned up. She doesn't need to remember him that way. I gotta see Myers, but I'll be in touch."

Hearn shook his head. "I'll take care of her. She's one of mine, remember?"

Nick patted Hearn on the back and walked towards Katie again. "I'll be back soon. Captain's gonna see to it that you get to say goodbye." He gently pressed his lips against the top of her head.

23

THE CLOCK IN the waiting room ticked far too loudly, further amplifying the headache that had worked its way from the base of her neck to the top of her forehead. Three hours had passed and Katie still had not been allowed to see him. Thirst and hunger settled in, neither mattering a single bit to her right now. She'd rejected the offer of a mild sedative, instead ensuring that she felt the pain, not wanting to numb it away.

Saying the words still seemed impossible. Admitting that he was gone; unbearable. This was not her life. What had she done to deserve this? Losing those who meant everything to her.

Katie placed a hand on her stomach, recalling that a part of him had lived in her, if only for a few short weeks. She'd regretted the relief she felt when it was over. As if it had been too much; the thought of motherhood, the thought of bringing to life a part of Marshall.

It wasn't her fault and her head knew that, but her heart didn't agree. Now she had nothing of him. Material things, yes. An empty apartment that he owned, full of his things. That wasn't nearly enough. She wanted him back. He came into her life at a time when she needed him. What was she supposed to do now?

"Katie?" Captain Hearn approached her from the front desk. "They said you could see him now." He helped her unsteady legs find their ground.

She leaned on him for support as he led her to say goodbye.

Marshall wasn't in the morgue, lying on a cold steel slab. Instead he was in a private room, covered from head to toe with a white sheet. The room was dimly lit, the lowering sun casting a grey light through the thin curtains. Captain Hearn turned on a switch and a florescent light in the ceiling above his body illuminated. The ugly glow threw shadows against the undulations of his sheeted frame. Katie turned to the captain.

"I'll be right outside," he said, closing the door until it rested just against the casing as he stepped out.

Katie was weak, shattered from the pain, but she moved towards him, unsure if she could pull back the sheet from his face. The tears flowed freely once again, her heart aching at the sight, the kind of ache that felt like her heart might just stop beating.

She rested her hand on his covered arm. He felt cold through the sheet. The reality started to bear down on her now. He was here, but it wasn't him. Not anymore. The last time she looked upon a dead body it was her closest friend. Only, he had been there with her. Helped her through it. She was alone now.

Katie took hold of the sheet and gently, slowly pulled it down to his neck. His eyes were closed; his face was an unsettling shade of ashen and purple. His hair looked as it always had, as it had when she said goodbye to him this morning before work. She leaned in closer, resting her flushed cheek against his cold face, turning it wet with her tears. Her quivering lips touched his. They were cold too. Their last kiss, she recalled, had been warm and soft, his lips moving in sync with hers. Now he was gone.

◆◆◆

"Are you sure you don't want to stay with us tonight?" Captain Hearn asked for the third time as he drove Katie back home.

"Thank you, but I think I prefer to be home. I'll feel closer to him there."

"Okay, but we should stop to get you some food. You haven't eaten all day."

"Please, captain. I just want to go home." Her eyes suggested that while she appreciated his help, he needed to leave her be.

Hearn continued to drive downtown to the apartment she and Marshall shared. The hour was approaching eleven and the streets were quieter than usual. He pulled into the parking garage and helped Katie upstairs.

She began searching for her keys and was overtaken once again in a wave of emotion. The waves came without warning and, once they hit, she couldn't control them. Katie raised a hand to shield her eyes.

"Here, hand me your bag. I'll find them." He searched through the small purse until he found the keys. He held up one that looked as though it was a key to a home. "Is this it?"

She glanced to him for just a moment, nodding her head.

The blast of cool air inside felt like a shock to her system, but her body had been overheated all afternoon. She stepped inside the dark apartment and flipped the switch next to the door. The dining room light turned on.

"Let me help you get settled," Captain Hearn said.

"Thank you, sir, but I'll be okay." She knew he didn't want to leave her in this state. He'd been a mentor and very much a father figure to her and she loved him for it, but no one could make this better. Not him, not Nick Scarborough; not anyone. Instead, she reached around his plump mid-section and hugged him.

"He was a good man, Katie. Know that," Hearn said.

"I do. I know. Thank you." She pulled away and managed a meager smile. "Goodnight, sir."

"Goodnight, Katie."

She was alone for the first time since Nick called her earlier today. She still hadn't understood why Marshall had gone to Shalot's home. Why would he have done that? Unless he knew something. That was the thing about Marshall. Once he got a hunch, no one could convince him otherwise. And that was especially true if he thought it would protect her.

She dropped to the sofa, curling her legs beneath her, and peered out the window onto the city lights. "I'll never forgive you for this." The words were not directed to Marshall. They were directed to a God who she believed had abandoned her.

Katie rested her head on a pillow tucked in the corner of the sofa. The smell reminded her of him. Everything in there was a reminder.

◆◆◆

Sleep could not take hold and now she watched the sun rise in the morning sky. Wave after wave of heartache and grief consumed her through the night, mind and body. Even the knock on the door didn't break the grip that the pain held on her heart.

The sound came again. This time, she shifted her head slowly towards the door, for a moment believing it was Marshall and that he'd just misplaced his keys.

"Katie? It's me, Nick."

Her eyes blinked. It was not Marshall. He was never coming home again. She rose from the couch, her legs aching from having been in the same position most of the night. Pulling the door open, she then walked back to the sofa.

Nick didn't look much better than Katie. "How you doin'? Have you eaten anything?"

Katie shook her head.

He walked to the couch and sat down next to her. "We did it, Katie. We know everyone who was involved. Hayden Jennings, the man who killed the woman in Virginia, told us where to find the others. The local authorities, the Feds; we're all out rounding up the remaining suspects. According to Jennings, Shalot and Branson were each vying for position and Shalot had grown more and more extreme, recruiting others in the process. It's over now, Katie."

None of this meant anything to her. Not anymore. His words rolled off of her with ease. Shalot was dead. Another person Marshall had to protect her from, only this time it had cost him his life. That was all that mattered. She turned to Nick. "You think I care about any of this?"

Nick lowered his head. He seemed to think this news would help. "Marshall took out the worst of them. He got Shalot. That should matter to you."

"You would've caught Jennings anyway and he would have told you what you needed to get Shalot. Marshall died for nothing because he thought Shalot would go free and come after me. Don't you see that?" She turned away. "I can't do this, Nick. I don't want to be around anyone right now."

"I don't believe he died for nothing. I believe Marshall did what he thought he had to do to protect you."

"Maybe you should tell that to his mother and brother?" Katie knew it was the grief talking, but she didn't care and was directing her anger towards Nick.

"I'm sorry to have bothered you. I'll leave you in peace." Nick moved towards the door. "Please let me know if I can help with arrangements." The click of the latch sounded as he walked out.

Katie lifted herself off of the sofa and shuffled down the hall to their bedroom. She stood in the doorway, staring at the bed that they had shared. It didn't seem long, in the grand scheme of things, not nearly long enough. She'd been with Spencer much longer. But Marshall was different. He'd unlocked something inside her that she didn't know existed.

He'd forever changed her path in life. She felt lost now as she scanned the empty room. His side of the bed still tousled from the restless night he'd had. The last night she'd shared with him.

Katie sat on his side of the bed, lifting his pillow to her face. It smelled like him, his cologne and hair gel. A corner of her mouth raised as she recalled his morning styling routine.

Placing the pillow back down, Katie pulled out the top drawer of his nightstand. Inside was a Tom Clancy book. He wasn't much of a reader, but he did enjoy it when time allowed. She pushed it to the side; some lose change was beneath it. Further back was the remote for the TV, but it was the box in the far back corner of the drawer that caught her attention.

She wrapped her thumb and forefinger around it and retrieved the box. Her brow creased as she worked to figure out what it was. The top raised with ease, and inside was a smaller box. There was no guessing as to the contents it held. It was navy blue velvet and shaped in a most familiar manner.

Her heart dropped to her stomach as she raised the lid. Inside was a ring. Square cut diamond, gold band. It looked very old; vintage, they called it nowadays. Beautifully ornate. She slipped it on her ring finger. The fit was perfect.

It was nearing their one-year anniversary. Not from the day they met, but from the day they moved in together. "He was going to propose."

The wave of grief that came this time felt like a tsunami.

24

THE SOUND OF her cell phone vibrating on the nightstand penetrated the sleep that had finally caught up with her. Light had not yet found its way into her bedroom and as she turned towards the sound, the digital clock confirmed that it was an hour that was barely considered morning. Five a.m. A full day had passed and she had hardly moved from that spot.

The caller ID gave her pause as to whether to answer. Condolences were not something she could bear to hear right now, considering she'd found peace in her dreams. That peace was gone now.

"Hello."

"I'm so sorry to hear about Marshall. Is there anything I can do for you, Katie?"

"Why are you calling so early, Marc?" Acknowledging his comment would only bring more tears.

"I—I wanted to tell you that we're running the story this morning. The Feds confirmed only hours ago that the Highway Hunter was—well, you already know. National news has picked it up, but I wanted to say that I would be anchoring it on the six a.m. news. Katie, I just can't believe what happened and I can't tell you how sorry I am."

Katie remained silent. What was there to say? It was a national story, she knew that. Marshall would be called a hero. She knew that too. But no one would know that he died because he needed to protect her—again. Neither Nick nor Captain Hearn would let word get out that Marshall was at

Shalot's for any reason other than because he found evidence missed the first time around. They would not say he broke in. They would not say he felt Shalot would come after Katie. They would not say that San Diego Police Department veteran Detective Marshall Avery died because of Katie Reid.

"Thank you, Marc. And thank you for telling me. It's okay. I'll be okay. I need to go now. Goodbye." She turned to her side, the side where she would normally find Marshall sleeping.

It was only a matter of time before Nick would call, or show up at her door. He would shield her from the press, not letting it be known that she had been involved in the case. That Edward Shalot had developed an obsession with her and that was why he was here in San Diego. None of that would ever come to light.

The darkness still surrounded her and now it had found its way inside her once again. But the worst had yet to pass. Captain Hearn would have already called Marshall's mother and brother. She still hadn't met either one of them. His brother, Kyle, four years his junior, had moved back to Chicago where he lived with his wife and two girls. His mother, Vivian, had moved in with her sister in Florida two years ago. Both were retired and living in St. Petersburg.

There was still so much to Marshall that she had yet to uncover. He rarely spoke of his family and she didn't even know why.

Katie took a deep breath and pulled herself out of the bed. There were things that needed to be done. She had to find the strength to do them.

◆◆◆

Her arrival at the station set off an outpouring of sympathies, making it difficult for Katie to keep it together. She found her way into the captain's office as quickly as possible.

"Katie? You didn't have to come in today." He moved towards her for an embrace.

She couldn't let him hold her; it would bring too much to the surface and so she pulled away quickly. "I need to collect his things, captain—from his office. He's got so many books and things. I just need to bring them home."

"Katie, sit down—please." Hearn moved back to sit behind his desk. "I informed Marshall's mother late yesterday. She's coming in today. I've already made arrangements to pick her up from the airport. I told her you were resting at home and that I would ensure you were made aware of her arrival. I hadn't realized you two had never met."

"No. Not yet." She twisted the ring on her finger that was intended as an engagement present.

"Well, Marshall was a very guarded man, Katie. You know that perhaps better than I." Hearn took pause. "Listen, I'm working on the press release this morning. Marshall will receive the Category I Protocol."

This was law enforcement's funeral protocol for full, military-style honors reserved for those killed in the line of duty. It was a major public event that would draw thousands to pay their respects.

"This is in accordance with his mother's wishes as well," Hearn continued.

"Of course." Katie wasn't his next of kin, not officially, and so they would defer to his mother on these matters.

"There's one other thing. Agent Scarborough is busy briefing the local authorities in the other jurisdictions where the victims were found. He's got his hands full at the moment, but asked that I ensure your name is kept out of the media as much as possible, which I agree is the right course of action. But I want you to be prepared. There will be the inevitable connection with Marshall to your case last year. All of that will come to light once again. There's only so much I can do to squelch that, I'm afraid."

It seemed there was no escaping her past. Katie would forever be labeled "the girl who got away." Now, greater attention would be thrust on her again. Her boyfriend, the man who killed her abductor, was gunned down in the line of duty. There was no doubt the book offers would come flooding in once again. The thought of reliving everything, dealing with this loss, the attention; it was too much for her. It was too much for anyone.

"Agent Scarborough did mention he would be returning here for the service, along with his team. But I suspect you'll hear from him sooner than that. He holds you with great regard, Katie."

"Thank you, sir. If it's all right with you, I'd like to pack up Marshall's things now." Katie stood up and turned towards the door. "When is his mother scheduled to arrive?"

Hearn glanced at his watch. "She should be here in a couple of hours."

"Okay." Katie disappeared behind the door.

◆◆◆

She waited with Captain Hearn at the airport and tried to think of what to say to Vivian. The woman had lost her son and it seemed impossible for her to imagine what that must be like. But then, she had lost a child; a child that would never have come to be, but a child nonetheless. It was only now that the full impact of that loss was coming to surface. Along with so much pain she had already suffered and was continuing to suffer, this was one more thing.

Stop. Katie reminded herself that this wasn't about her, not right now. This was about Marshall's mother. Her thoughts turned to her own mother, whom she hadn't yet told. It had hardly been a day yet and so many things still needed to be done. She would need her parents now and was grateful to still have them. They were all she had left in this world.

A woman who appeared to be lost in the distance caught Katie's eye. She'd seen pictures of Vivian, of course, even if those pictures were somewhat dated. She still recognized the small woman who had begun her approach.

"That's her." Katie raised a hand and stepped towards the woman. She had managed to catch her attention.

The captain followed closely behind. "Mrs. Avery." He reached for her small suitcase. "Let me get that for you. I'm Captain Hearn."

She smiled at the captain, but quickly turned her gaze to Katie. "Kate." She moved in for an embrace. "How are you, sweetheart? I'm so sorry we have to meet like this." Vivian's lips quivered, but only for a moment as she seemed to quickly regain composure.

"I'm okay, Mrs. Avery. I'm glad to meet you." Katie held on to the woman who was a few inches shorter and a little full around the middle. Still, she was very beautiful; her hair, short, tapered at the neck, fully grey, no attempt to conceal it. Her face was heavily lined, those lines only enhancing her caring eyes. Katie noticed the pink tint and mild swelling still visible in them from hours of shedding tears.

"Let's get you two back to the car. I'll drop you at home." Captain Hearn ushered the grieving women out of the terminal.

◆◆◆

"I'll stop by in a few hours to see if either of you need anything." Captain Hearn stepped towards the door of Katie and Marshall's apartment.

"Thank you, sir," Katie replied.

"You know, I haven't been here since he first bought this place." Vivian wandered around from room to room. "Of course, that was well before you came into his life."

"When he lived here with his fiancée."

"Yes. But I knew that would never last. Marshall was never the type to walk away, even if it was the best thing for him. Eventually, she did and then he met you." Vivian moved to the dining chair where Katie was now sitting. "You were the best thing to ever happen to him; you know that, right? He always said that to me."

Katie hadn't known how often Marshall had conversed with his mother. She was ashamed not to have known.

"I suspect you had no idea that he and I often spoke of you. Marshall was a very private man, even with those whom he loved the most. My dear, you were everything to him. I'd never heard him speak of a woman the way he spoke of you. That was how I knew you were the one for him. It took him a while, but he finally found you."

Katie could feel her eyes begin to sting. She could not let herself break down in front of Vivian. She could not make this about her. Vivian had already lost a husband and now a son. She deserved strength.

"I loved him very much, Mrs. Avery." Katie raised her hand to wipe the tear that threatened to spill.

"Oh." Vivian leaned in and took hold of Katie's hand. "I hadn't realized he had already proposed. He said he was waiting for your anniversary in a few weeks." She eyed the ring and ran her index finger over the diamond. "I never took this off, not for several years after Marshall's father died. I just couldn't bring myself to do it."

She leaned back and smiled. "I offered to give it to him when he wanted to get engaged the first time, but he insisted that I keep it, that Dad had given it to me. But when he mentioned he was going to ask you to marry him last month, he asked if he could have it."

Katie had no idea of any of this. How could she have not known? "I want him back so much." There was no point in trying to keep it inside. The emotions were too strong.

"I know you do, dear." Vivian grasped Katie's hands inside hers. "So do I."

25

THE STATION WAS quiet, except for a skeleton staff holding the place down. Most of the employees – officers, technicians, and administrative support – were still working their way home from the service.

Marshall's brother and his family had returned to their hotel with Vivian and her sister, Marshall's aunt. They would stay another night, then return home to Chicago and Vivian to Florida. Her own parents had come down, but she'd asked them to wait for her at the apartment after the service. She needed to be alone, if only for a short while.

It was over now. So many people had turned out to honor him. Katie couldn't help but show a hint of a smile on a face that hadn't done so in more than a week. She was proud, so proud of him, and he was loved by everyone in this department.

She sat alone in his office. His personal effects were now gone. In fact, as she looked around, it didn't feel like his office anymore.

"Hey." Gibbons leaned into the doorway. "Can I come in?"

"Of course."

"I didn't expect to see you in here. Thought you'd be home by now," Gibbons said.

"I guess I'm not ready to let this office go just yet. I know the captain's gonna put someone in here next week."

Gibbons dropped into the chair across from her. "How you holding up?"

She managed a shrug of her shoulders.

"Yeah," Gibbons replied. "Nice of Agent Scarborough and his team to come, though. I haven't seen him in a while. Did they already take off?"

"No. He said he was going to stop by the apartment and bring me dinner tonight. I think he's heading out tomorrow, though. Still cleaning up from the case, I hear."

"You know, Avery was right about Shalot. From what Scarborough told me, he had recruited several people. They were already lining up their next five victims. Jennings, one of 'the five,' gave the Feds everything they needed. Branson's going down and so is Hudson."

Katie turned away.

"I'm sorry." Gibbons seemed to pick up on the fact that this wasn't the time. "You don't need this right now. I was just..."

"It's okay. Really. There was nothing Marshall wouldn't do to protect me or anyone else, for that matter. It was his job."

Gibbons nodded, his lips pressed tightly together. "You planning on finishing up your schooling?"

He hadn't intended to make her uncomfortable, she knew that, but she really wasn't ready to talk about any of this stuff. Not now, hours after she had buried her fiancé.

Katie twisted the ring again. It was becoming habit now. "I haven't thought about it much, but I don't think so. I'm not really sure what I'm going to do now." It was the first time she'd actually admitted as much. What was she going to do now? Without Marshall by her side, without him guiding her, teaching her, loving her. She hated herself for ever wanting him to stop protecting her so much.

"Well, I know he'd be damn proud if you decided to swear in. Work towards detective."

"I don't know. I just don't know what I'm going to do." Katie felt the familiar chills that came whenever her emotions were about to get the best of her. She took a deep breath.

"I'm sorry, Katie. I got no business. It's just... Well, maybe we can talk another time. I'll let you be."

She watched him leave, a final turn to smile at her, and he was gone.

◆◆◆

Katie pushed around the food on her plate as she sat down for dinner with her parents back at the apartment.

"I wish you'd try to eat just a little, honey. I can see how thin you've gotten. Please. You need your strength," Deborah pleaded with her daughter.

She picked up a forkful and placed it in her mouth.

"Thank you."

After managing a few more bites, Katie excused herself and landed on the couch, curled up in her usual position. She turned on the television, almost immediately regretting the action.

"Slain veteran officer of the San Diego Police Department, Detective Marshall Avery, was laid to rest today after a full honors service where nearly ten thousand people, including officers from several other California police departments, fire departments, and civilians attended."

A helicopter had flown over the streets during the service, where people lined up to watch the procession. A few close-up shots showed officers saluting as the cars passed by. A brief shot of Captain Hearn at a podium near the burial site appeared. Fortunately, the cameras didn't catch her, or if they did, didn't show her. They did, however, show Vivian accepting the American flag. Katie closed her eyes.

"Detective Avery was gunned down in an altercation with a suspect in the Highway Hunter investigation who we now know was the ring leader of the cult and directed the murders of five

innocent woman. Their calling card, a roman numeral five carved into their victims' chests.

Detective Avery leaves behind his mother, brother, two nieces and his girlfriend, Katie Reid, whom you'll recall was involved in the child abduction case that captured our attention just last year."

Katie pressed the off button on the remote, tossing it next to her.

"I thought they weren't supposed to mention you by name?" John asked. "Goddam media."

"It's okay, Dad. It's not like everyone didn't already know that we were together. I guess I was just hoping they'd let it go this time."

"Yeah, well, sons of bitches don't need to keep rehashing old news." John set his plate down in the kitchen and walked towards Katie. "Do you need anything right now?"

"No, Dad. I'm fine, thank you."

A knock on the door sounded.

John jumped to attention. "That better not be some damned reporter wanting to ask you questions." He stepped purposefully towards the door, peering through the peep hole. "Oh."

"Who is it?" Katie asked.

"It's that FBI Agent Scarborough. You expecting him?"

"Yeah. I forgot he was stopping by. He was gonna bring dinner. It's okay to let him in."

John opened the front door where Nick stood with two plastic bags hanging from his hands.

"Mr. Reid. It's good to see you again. I've come to see Katie and bring her some dinner." Nick cast a glance around the side of John's stout figure. "Oh, I see you've already eaten."

"I'm sorry, Nick. I forgot that you were stopping by. My mother made dinner for us. But, please come in." Katie walked to the breakfast bar, leaning against it. Her mother was right. She'd grown weak and felt very lightheaded from the quick rise to her feet.

"Well, I'm sure this will keep until tomorrow." Nick set the plastic bags on the table. "It's Chinese. I hope you like Chinese."

"I'll just put this in the fridge," Deborah said. "Nice to see you, Agent Scarborough."

"Please. It's Nick."

"Come sit down," Katie said, leading him to the sofa. "You hungry? Wanna eat some of that Chinese you brought?"

"No, no. I'm fine." Nick hiked up his dress pants and lowered himself down.

"You know," Deborah began, "I think your father and I will go and walk off this dinner. It's a lovely evening. We're not used to it being so warm this close to Thanksgiving."

Katie turned to her mother, grateful for the suggestion. "You should take your sweater anyway, Mom. It still might be a little chilly."

Katie and Nick waited for her parents to leave. She had only spoken to him briefly since everything happened. If she was being honest with herself, she'd admit it was because she had held some anger towards him. It was unfair and he didn't deserve it, but she felt it just the same.

The door closed and Katie returned her attention to Nick. "They said my name."

"What's that?"

"On the news. The anchorwoman said my name. They were talking about the funeral and just happened to bring up last year."

"Dammit."

"It's okay. I guess it doesn't really matter. I've been ignoring their calls all week. I'll just keep ignoring them. I've talked to Marc a couple of times, but not once did he ask me about what really happened."

"Listen, Katie. I—I don't know really what to say here. I feel responsible for what happened. If we'd just—"

"Don't. It's not your fault. Marshall did what he thought he had to do. End of story." Katie surprised herself with her ability to hold firm. "I'm just glad you took 'em down. All of them. And I'm glad Shalot's dead." She started to feel the stinging in her eyes again, but pressed on. "So when are you and your team heading back to Virginia?"

"Tomorrow." Nick rested his elbows on his knees and began rubbing his hands together. "Are your parents staying with you for a while?"

"I'm actually going home with them. Taking some time off. The holidays are coming and Captain Hearn thought it'd be a good idea."

"He's right. You know, Katie, you've been through more than your fair share."

That was an understatement. "Yeah. I guess you could say that."

An awkward silence fell between them. What was there left to say? He'd done his job and now he would move on to the next case. As far as she was concerned, her life was as up in the air as it ever was. She couldn't stay in this apartment, that much she knew. It was just too painful. Too many reminders. Vivian had broached the subject in a roundabout manner, but didn't say it outright. Katie knew she wanted to keep some of her son's things.

She began twisting at the ring again.

Nick watched the absentminded gesture, noticing the ring for the first time. "Is that—new?"

Katie hadn't realized she'd been spinning it again. "Yeah. I guess you could say that. I found it in Marshall's nightstand a few days ago in a blue velvet box. Guess he was planning on us getting engaged. Imagine that. It's the ring his dad had given his mother."

Nick's shoulders dropped, his face turned down at what should have been wonderful news. "He was going to ask you to marry him?"

"Yes." Katie drew in a deep breath. "Vivian said I could keep it, if I wanted to. Said Marshall would have wanted it that way."

"Of course. It's very beautiful," Nick replied.

"Did you know his dad was murdered back in Chicago when he was a kid?"

"No. I didn't," he whispered.

"Stabbed on the L. Never caught 'em." Katie looked Nick straight in the eyes. "That's why he became a cop."

Nick reached for Katie and pulled her in close. She began to weep and he stroked her hair to comfort the woman who had lost so much.

◆◆◆

The New Year had arrived and Katie prepared to go back home to San Diego. The suitcase lay open on her bed in the room her parents kept for her whenever she came home. The rain still came down as she pulled the curtain back to reveal the great oak trees in front of her family's home. December had already soaked them through and it seemed January wouldn't fare much better. She was almost glad to get back to the nice weather she'd left behind.

Katie had been allowed peace and privacy up here and wondered if that would last once she got home. The story, of course, had died down. They always did. Nick sent her a few emails since she'd been away, checking up on her. Only occasionally did she actually sit down and check her emails. A few trickled in from Marc Aguilar. One or two from Marshall's brother, but that was about it.

Deborah had taken to washing and folding all of Katie's clothes, placing them neatly on the bed, ready to simply set inside the suitcase. It felt good to have her parents by her side. After the long-time strained relations, she needed them now more than ever.

Katie was not looking forward to walking back into the apartment though. Marshall's apartment. She'd asked the super to check in on it once in a while to air it out, but it had been empty for almost two months.

Marshall's will named her to take ownership, but she could not remain there. Instead, on her return, she would put it up for sale, find someplace else to live. A place that held no memories of her past, but the packing remained to be completed. That would be the worst part; putting his things in boxes. Most of it would be donated. She would keep a few things and take some to Vivian. That would be her next task, one she wasn't quite prepared for.

◆◆◆

Katie knocked on the door of the small home where Vivian Avery lived with her sister. The flight into Tampa had been long and the cab ride to St. Petersburg even longer, it seemed. But she was here now, holding a box of Marshall's belongs she would give to his mother.

The door opened and although Katie couldn't see through the thick mesh screen door, she knew it was Vivian on the other side.

"Hello, dear." Vivian pushed open the screen. "Please come in." Stepping aside, she waited for Katie to enter, watching her drag a suitcase behind her and holding a box against her chest. "How was your flight?"

"It was fine, thank you." Katie continued through the foyer, waiting for further instruction.

"Here; let me take that from you." Vivian took hold of the box and placed it on the table against the wall of the entryway. "Come and sit down. Can I get you a coffee, tea?"

"Just some water, please. Thank you." Katie sat down on the light blue sofa, sinking a little in its oversized cushions.

Vivian returned, handing the glass of water to Katie and taking a seat in the large side chair.

"I'm sorry it's taken so long for me to bring you his things. It's just, well, it's been hard."

"Of course it has. It's been very hard." Vivian reached for Katie's knee, patting it for a moment. "Have you returned to work?"

"Yes. I got home about three weeks ago and went back to work shortly after that. I guess that was late January." Her sense of time was all but lost. Each day rolled into the next without much distinction. Each was consumed with grief, guilt, and anger. It was now early February and Katie felt like she'd lost him only yesterday. But that was the thing about losing someone. Time seemed to stand still while everyone else continued on with their lives as if nothing had happened. It made her angry how people could just go on like that. Didn't they know that he was gone? Didn't they care?

Captain Hearn did. She knew that. Since she got back, he'd been trailing her around like a shadow. Not letting her go to any homicide scenes. Instead, she was collecting evidence from things like store robberies and the occasional home invasion.

She'd quit her graduate work and went home every day by herself to an empty apartment, not quite ready to put it up for sale. It didn't matter that the money she would make off of it would set her up pretty well. Marshall had bought it before the boom and bust the first decade of the new millennium saw. It would be enough for her to buy a house, if that was what she wanted.

"Oh." Katie retrieved the box at the entry and returned, handing it to Vivian. "These are some things I thought you'd want, like we talked about?"

"Thank you, dear. You know, you could have just mailed them to me. You didn't have to come all this way to deliver it."

"Yes, I did. I would never risk his things getting lost. I had to be sure you got it."

Marshall had kept very little from his childhood. In fact, Katie suspected if any of those things still existed, they existed here with his mother. Instead, she brought photos. Mostly of him, but some of the both of them together. The posthumous metal that the Mayor had bestowed on him. Katie felt she should have that too, and a few other trinkets she thought Vivian would want.

It appeared as though Vivian wasn't ready to open the box. Katie didn't insist. Instead, the two spent the afternoon together, shopping, walking along the pier, enjoying a time that would probably be their last. Katie would have loved having this woman for a mother-in-law.

And, as they enjoyed one another's company, Katie could see Marshall in his mother's eyes. That mix of hazel and green, always shifting with the moods. She was grateful Vivian still had a son who had given her grandchildren. At least she would never be alone.

26

SPRING WAS MOVING in quickly, not that the weather ever shifted with the seasons much in San Diego. But the flower fields in Carlsbad had already opened up, marking the beginning of the season.

Katie stood in the middle of the living room, the tiled floors exposed in the now empty space. The furniture was sold or given away and the keys were due to be turned over to the new owner in just a few hours. She had found another place to live and the moving truck was due there later. The landlady offered to open it up for them since Katie couldn't make it there in time. Instead, she would arrive to a place already filled with boxes and brand new furniture.

She began her final pass through, walking down the hall, double checking the bathroom, moving to the office; it was empty too. And, finally, she stopped inside the bedroom. Her mind called forth a time when she rested comfortably in his arms. A time when he tackled her and tossed her onto the bed, pinning her down with kisses. She could see it as if it was happening right at this very moment. As if he was right there with her.

Katie closed her eyes, trying to savor the memory, but it vanished too quickly and, upon opening them again, the four grey walls reminded her that he was gone. Katie turned away.

The only thing left to do was turn off the light switch that illuminated the hanging fixture where the dining table used to be. Katie turned it off. A final look around and she closed the door, standing on the landing and locking up the apartment for the last time.

♦♦♦

"I'm on my way there now. Will you be there?" Katie asked, calling from the car. "Great. See you soon."

She pulled up into the single-car driveway, stopping just beyond the garage door. This was it. Her new home. The hedges were neatly trimmed and it appeared to have a fresh coat of paint on the outside. The landlady mentioned she would spruce it up a bit before Katie moved in. The soft yellow color reminded her of Sam's house and the thought made her smile.

An elderly woman sat in the Adirondack chair on the front porch. A man, whom Katie assumed was the son, sat next to her. He was the first to stand on Katie's approach.

"Ms. Reid?" he said, walking towards her with a pleasant smile.

"Yes. I'm Kate. Hello." She shook his hand.

"Nice to meet you. I'm Ron Mitchell and, of course, you know my mother." Ron moved up the steps towards his mother.

"Nice to see you again, Mrs. Mitchell. Thank you for letting the movers in. I can't tell you how much I appreciate that."

"That's quite all right. I'm sure you've had a time getting down here, so it was no problem at all. Here are the keys. All the utilities are on, of course." Mrs. Mitchell took her son's arm as he helped her down the steps of the porch. "Oh, and I hope you don't mind, but I picked up some basics for you at the store. Milk and bread and such. Now, you holler if you need anything. Ron will take care of anything that needs fixin'. Glad to have you here, Ms. Reid."

"Please, call me Kate. Thank you both for everything. Have a good night."

Ron walked his mother to the car and opened the passenger door for her.

"That girl's had a rough go of it. I hope she'll be all right on her own." Mrs. Mitchell said in a hushed tone so Katie wouldn't overhear.

"She'll be fine, Mom. She's a grown woman."

◆◆◆

It had been a tough night, but Katie got through it. New places were always difficult to get used to. Not to mention the new bed and furniture. Nothing was the same, except for the pictures she dug out of one of the boxes, setting them on the fireplace mantle last night. Katie needed him to be with her and he was. She knew that, could feel it too. It was the only familiar thing in the whole place.

Her pants were pressed, and the blouse she'd chosen still smelled of her former residence. But she was ready for work. A quick glance at the hour and she quickly realized now was the time to go if she didn't want to get caught up in traffic. The meeting was scheduled for nine a.m.

The garage door opened. It sounded a little creaky. She would be sure to pick up some WD-40 on the way home and take care of that tonight. As she backed out of the drive, her cell phone rang.

"Hello?"

"You still planning on being here by nine o'clock?"

"Yep. That's the plan. I'm actually leaving the house right now. I'll see you soon." Katie dropped the phone in the center console and continued to reverse onto the street. It was the first time she'd seen the house in the morning light. The sun was almost over the roofline behind it and cast a beautiful orange glow against the green of the hickory and mulberry trees that towered over the home. It looked peaceful, safe.

In the months since Marshall's passing, Katie had grown to discover that it was possible to feel safe on her own. She'd always needed him for that. She hadn't realized it at the time of course, but she had. He knew that and took on the burden of ensuring her safety. It had cost him his life.

Even before Marshall, she'd needed Spencer in much the same way. Katie had never lived on her own. In college, she had Sam as a roommate. Then she and Spencer moved in together. Then it was Marshall. They'd practically been inseparable since Hendrickson. Now she was alone and was beginning, just beginning to think that it was okay.

♦♦♦

After searching for nearly ten minutes, Katie finally found a parking spot. She checked the time on her phone and had five minutes left before the meeting. The unfamiliar traffic conditions had been worse than she'd expected. That seemed to always be the case, though, when one was in a hurry.

Stepping out of the driver's side door, Katie walked to the other side to retrieve her carrier bag. This was an important meeting and she was more than a little nervous now that she had actually arrived.

The weather was cooler than she'd expected as well and she wished she had thought to bring a sweater. Never mind now. The glass doors parted automatically on her approach and she stepped inside to a slightly warmer environment, although her skin still felt chilled, but that was probably just nerves.

"Good morning. I have a nine o'clock meeting." The clock above the lobby desk showed 9:05. It must have been fast. "Looks like I'm a little late."

"No problem, Kate. I'll let them know you're here," the gentleman behind the desk replied as he picked up the phone. "Kate Reid is here to see you." He set the receiver back down. "He'll be right up. Why don't you have a seat?"

She nodded her head and walked towards the seating area, picking up a magazine, not caring which one. The pages flipped by with her not really taking any notice, just needing something to do with her hands.

Several minutes seemed to pass by at a snail's pace. The longer she waited, the more nervous she became. The clock on the wall now showed 9:15. The tapping of her heel on the floor echoed and she caught herself, stopping immediately.

"Kate! You're looking well."

She stood up and dropped the magazine back onto the table. "Thank you. I actually managed a decent night's rest."

"I'm so sorry to have kept you waiting."

"That's fine. I know how busy you are Nick, I mean, Agent Scarborough."

"Well, shall we get going?" Nick walked next to her and opened his arms wide. "Welcome to Quantico."

THE END

ABOUT THE AUTHOR

Robin Mahle lives with her husband and two children in Arizona. Having always been a lover of books, Robin attributes her creativity to the wonderful overseas adventures she has shared with her husband of 17 years. Traveling throughout Europe and having lived in England opened her mind and with that came a steady stream of story ideas inspired by her author-idols in the mystery/suspense genre.

If you enjoyed Ms. Mahle's work, please share your experience by leaving a review on Amazon.

OTHER WORKS

All the Shiny Things – A Kate Reid Novel (Book 1)
Gone Unnoticed – A Kate Reid Novel (Book 3)
Blackwaters- A Kate Reid Novel (Book 4)
Endangered - A Kate Reid Novel (Book 5)
The Pretty Ones – A Kate Reid Novel (Book 6)
The Kate Reid Series Box Set (Books 1-3)
Inherent Clarity
Landslide
Beyond the Clearing
Primal Deception - A Lacy Merrick Thriller (Book 1)
Shadow Rising – A Lacy Merrick Thriller (Book 2) – **coming Spring 2017.**

Sign up to receive **Robin's Newsletter so you can stay up to date on her new releases, events, contests and even exclusive new material! Visit: robinmahle.com

Made in the USA
Lexington, KY
24 March 2017